DROP DEAD GORGEOUS

A Novel

LINDA HOWARD

THORNDIKE
WINDSOR
PARAGON

LIBRARY OF CONGRESS CATALOGING-IN-PUBLICATION DATA

Howard, Linda, 1950–
    Drop dead gorgeous / by Linda Howard.
        p. cm.
    ISBN-13: 978-0-7862-9006-2 (hardcover : alk. paper)
    ISBN-10: 0-7862-9006-4 (hardcover : alk. paper)
    1. Weddings — Planning — Fiction. 2. Attempted murder — Fiction. 3.
Large type books. I. Title.
    PS3558.O88217D76 2007
    813'.54—dc22

                                                                    2006034759

BRITISH LIBRARY CATALOGUING-IN-PUBLICATION DATA AVAILABLE

Published in 2006 in arrangement with Random House, Inc.
Published in the U.K. in 2007 by arrangement with Piatkus Books Ltd.

U.K. Hardcover: 978 1 405 61692 8 (Windsor Large Print)
U.K. Softcover: 978 1 405 61693 5 (Paragon Large Print)

Printed in the United States of America on permanent paper
10 9 8 7 6 5 4 3 2 1

DROP DEAD GORGEOUS

CHAPTER ONE

My name is Blair Mallory, and I'm trying to get married, but the Fates are NOT cooperating . . . I hate the Fates, don't you? Whoever the dumb bitches are.

I sat at my dining table and stared at the calendar, checking open dates against the multitude of schedules spread across the table: my schedule, Wyatt's schedule, Mom's and Dad's schedules, my sisters' schedules, Wyatt's mother's schedule, Wyatt's sister's schedule, Wyatt's sister's kids' and husbands' schedules . . . it was never going to end. There was no good open date for everyone until the day after Christmas, which was *so* not going to be my wedding day. My anniversaries would forever suck, if we got married the day after Christmas, because Wyatt would already have given me all the good stuff he could think of. No way. I don't sabotage myself.

"You're huffing and puffing," Wyatt observed without looking up from the report he was reading. I assumed it was some sort of police report, since he's a lieutenant on the local force, but I didn't ask; I'd wait until he was out of the room to read it, just to see if it was about anyone I knew. You'd be amazed what some people will do, people you'd never in a million years think would get up to such hijinks; my eyes had certainly been opened since I'd been dating Wyatt — well, since I'd been reading his reports, which, come to think of it, actually preceded our dating, this time around, anyway. There are benefits to dating a cop, especially one who is fairly high up on the food chain. My gossip cup runneth over.

"You'd be huffing and puffing, too, if you were trying to deal with all these schedules instead of sitting over there reading."

"I'm working," he retorted, confirming that he was indeed reading some sort of report; I just hoped it was juicy, and that he'd leave it unattended while he went to the bathroom or something. "And you wouldn't have any problems with schedules if you'd do what I suggested."

What he'd suggested was getting married in Gatlinburg, at some tacky wedding chapel and without all my stuff around me. I could deal with the wedding chapel, but having tried to pack for a special event before, I've learned a hard lesson: you always forget something. I didn't want to spend my wedding day rushing around trying to find a replacement for what I'd forgotten.

"Or we can get married at the courthouse here," he pointed out.

The man doesn't have a romantic bone in his body, which is actually okay, because I'm not much of a romantic either, and too much mushiness would get on my nerves. On the other hand, I do know How Things Are Done, and I wanted pictures to prove it to our children.

And that's another thing that was stressing me out. My thirty-first birthday had come and gone, putting me that much closer to amniocentesis. Whatever children I was going to have, I wanted to have them before hitting the age where any obstetrician with an ounce of self-preservation and a healthy fear of lawsuits would automatically order the amnio. I don't want to have a long needle stuck in my belly. What if it hits the baby in the eye, or something? What if that long sucker goes all the way through and punctures my spinal column? You know in *Peter Pan*, where the crocodile has swallowed a clock and you can tell the croc is getting

9

closer because the ticking gets louder? My biological clock was ticking like that damn crocodile. Or maybe it was an alligator. Doesn't matter. Instead of "*tick tock*" it was saying "*Amnio*" (the entire word wouldn't fit the rhythm of tick-tock) and I was having nightmares about it.

I had to get married, fast, so I could throw away my birth control pills.

And Wyatt just sat there reading his damn report while I was stressed almost to the point of screaming. He wasn't even trying to cheer me up by telling me what was in the report so I'd have a better idea if I needed to read it later to get all the details — not that he ever did. He was a positive hog when it came to police business, keeping it all to himself.

"I'm beginning to think it's never going to happen, we're never going to get married," I said glumly, tossing my pen onto the table.

Without moving from his sprawled, re- laxed position, he gave me a pointed look. "If it's too much for you, I'll handle the details," he said. If there was a faint sharpness to his tone it was because he was becoming impa- tient with what seemed like an endless pa- rade of delays and obstructions. He wanted to marry me; he didn't like the inconven- ience of sleeping over at my condo — not to mention that he saw no reason why I should still be living there, instead of with him — and he was ready for me to get on with all the girly stuff, which was how he regarded the details of the wedding, so he could get on with all the manly stuff. "You'll be Blair Bloodsworth before the week is out."

"Since it's Wednesday already, that's —" I stopped, my brain literally frozen as his words sank in. No. *No!* I couldn't have over-looked something that glaring, that in-your-face. It simply wasn't possible, unless I'd been so crazed by lust I wasn't thinking straight. As excuses go, that works for me. Deciding how my oversight had happened, however, didn't make it go away. I grabbed the pen and scribbled down the offending words, then wrote them again just to make certain my synapses hadn't short-circuited. No such luck.

"Oh, no!" I stared in horror at what I'd written, which of course really got Wyatt's at-tention, which of course was what I'd in-tended. Not that I plan these little episodes, but when the opportunity presents itself — I gave him a tragic look and pronounced, "I can't marry you."

Wyatt Bloodsworth, police lieutenant, alpha male, all-around tough guy and the man I adored, bent down and slowly beat his head against the table. "Why me?" he groaned. *Thunk.* "Was it something I did in a past life?" *Thunk.* "How long do I have to pay?" *Thunk.*

You'd think he'd ask why I couldn't marry him, but no, he had to act like a smart-ass. Actually, I think he was trying to out-drama me, on the theory that the best way to fight fire was with fire. I couldn't decide which I resented more, the idea that he thought I was a drama queen, or that he thought he could out-drama me. The man doesn't exist who can — never mind. Some roads I just shouldn't go down.

I crossed my arms under my breasts and glared at him. It isn't my fault that crossing my arms lifted my breasts and pushed them together, nor is it my fault that Wyatt is a breast man — and an ass man, and a leg man, and any other woman-part you want to name — so therefore it isn't my fault that when he lifted his head to bang it again his gaze sort of snagged on my cleavage and he forgot what he'd been about to say. I had just taken a shower and was wearing only a robe and underpants, so it was also reasonable that the robe had done what robes do, which is sort of come untied, which meant I was also not at fault that more than just cleavage was showing.

I'm always amazed at what a flash of nipple will do to a normally clear-thinking man — praise the Lord.

I also never fail to give thanks for that reality of life. Praise the Lord again.

But Wyatt's made of stronger stuff than the average man, as he never fails to point out to me, usually while making the case that he was taking pity on said average man by marrying me himself, thereby taking me off the market. Somehow he's got the idea that I'm always trying to get the upper hand in our relationship, which shows you just how smart he is. Damn, I hate it when he's right.

He eyed my nipple, his face taking on that ruthless, focused look men get when they want to have sex and are pretty sure they're going to get it. Then his gaze narrowed and he switched it back up to my face.

First, let me say that Wyatt's gaze can be intense. His eyes are this sort of pale green, which can be piercing. He's also a cop, as I believe I've mentioned a time or three, so when he levels that hard cop look at you, you can feel sort of pinned. But I, too, am made of some stern stuff, and I gave him back as good as I got. A split second later I glanced down at myself as if I had no idea what he'd been staring at, and jerked the robe back in place before resuming my glare.

"You did that on purpose," he accused.

"It's a *robe*," I pointed out. I love stating the obvious, especially to Wyatt. It drives him nuts. "I've never seen a robe that stays tied."

"So you don't deny it."

I don't know where he got the idea that if I don't answer a question directly, I'm admitting to whatever charge he's made. In this case, however, I felt perfectly justified in issuing a straight denial, because the whole nipple thing had been coincidence, and any woman worth her salt seizes her opportunities as they arise. "I deny it," I said, a hint of challenge in my tone. "I'm trying to have a serious conversation, and all you can think about is sex."

So of course he then had to prove I was wrong, and he tossed the report on the table. "Okay, so let's have this serious conversation."

"I've already started it. The ball's in your court."

From the way his eyes narrowed I could tell he had to mentally backtrack, but he was sharp; it took him only a couple of seconds. "Okay, why can't you marry me? But before you get started, let me point out that we *are* getting married, and I'm giving you another week to get the date nailed down or we're

14

doing it my way if I have to kidnap you and haul your ass to Las Vegas."

"Las Vegas?" I sputtered. *"Las Vegas?* No way. Britney put Las Vegas at the top of the tacky list when she got married there. I spit on the concept of a Vegas wedding."

He looked as if he wanted to bang his head again. "Who the hell are you talking about? Britney who?"

"Never mind, Mr. Clueless. Just put Las Vegas permanently out of your mind as a wedding spot."

"I don't care if we get married standing in the middle of the highway," he said impatiently.

"I want to get married in your mother's *garden,* but now that's a moot point because I can't marry you. Period."

"Let's backtrack and try this again. Why not?"

"Because my name would be *Blair Bloodsworth!"* I wailed. "You said it yourself!" How could he be so oblivious?

"Well . . . yeah," he said, looking puzzled.

He didn't get it. He really didn't get it. "I can't do it. It's just too cutesy. You might as well call me Buffy." Yeah, I know I didn't *have* to take his name, but when you start negotiations you always start high, right, to give yourself some wiggle room? I was opening negotiations. Not that he needed to know that.

His frustration peaked, and he roared, *"Who the hell is Buffy?* Why are you talking about these people?"

Now I wanted to beat *my* head against the table. Did he never read a magazine? Watch anything besides ball games and news channels on television? It was scary to realize we lived in two different cultures, and that except for football games, which I love, we'd never be able to watch television together, never be able to spend a comfortable, companionable night together in front of the romantic glow of the tube. I'd be forced to kill him, and no woman on the jury would vote to convict me, either.

In a flash I saw how our lives together would have to be: I'd have to have my own television, which meant I'd have to have my own television-watching room . . . which meant Wyatt's house would have to be remodeled, or at least reconfigured. I cheered up immensely at this thought, because I'd been wondering how to break the news to him. I really like his house, or at least the basic layout of it, but the decoration is strictly man-alone, which means it's barely habitable. I needed to put my stamp on it.

"You don't know who Buffy is?" I whispered, my eyes big with horror. Play it for all it's worth.

He all but whimpered. "*Please.* Just tell me why you've decided you can't marry me."

A rush of well-being filled me. There's just something satisfying about hearing a grown man whimper. And if Wyatt didn't actually make the sound, he came pretty damn close, and that was good enough for me, because, believe me, he's *not* the whimpering type.

"Because *Blair Bloodsworth* is too cutesy to be bearable!" Oh, God, I was beset by B-words. "People would hear that name and think, okay, she has to be a blond nitwit, one of those people who snaps gum and twirls her finger in her hair. No one would take me seriously!"

He rubbed his forehead as if he were getting a headache. "So all this is because Blair and Bloodsworth both start with a *B*?"

I cast my gaze upward. "The light dawns."

"That's a load of bullshit."

"And the bulb just burned out." Aaargh! When would the avalanche of B-words stop? This always happens to me. When something starts bugging me (aaargh again!) I can't get away from the alliteration.

"Bloodsworth isn't a cutesy name, no matter what the first name is," he said, scowling at me. "It has *blood* in it, for God's sake. As

17

in blood and guts. That isn't cutesy."

"What would you know? You don't even know who Britney and Buffy are."

"And I don't care, because I'm not marrying them. I'm marrying you. Soon. Though I think I may need my head examined."

I wanted to kick him. He made it sound as if I were a trial, when I'm really very easy to get along with; just ask any of my employees. I own and operate a fitness center, Great Bods, and my employees think I'm great because I pay them well and treat them well. The only person I have trouble getting along with, except for my ex-husband's current wife who tried to kill me, is Wyatt, and that's only because we're still jockeying for position — Wyatt and I, that is. The problem is we're both alpha personalities, so we have to stake out our relationship territories.

Okay, I also didn't get along with Nicole Goodwin, a psycho bitch copycat who got murdered in the parking lot at Great Bods, but she's dead so she doesn't count. Sometimes I almost forgive her for being a psycho bitch, because her murder is what brought Wyatt back into my life after an absence of two years — don't get me started on *that* — but then I'd remember what a pain in the ass she was even when she was dead, and I get over that brain fart in a hurry.

"Let me save you the psychiatrist's bill," I said, narrowing my gaze at him. "The wedding's off."

"The wedding's on. One way or the other."

"I can't go through life as Blair Bloodsworth. Though . . ." I tapped my finger on my chin and stared out at my night-shadowed patio; the Bradford pear trees beyond the patio were lit with strings of white lights that made my tiny backyard into something special. It was a very pretty sight, and I'd miss it when I moved into Wyatt's house, so he had to make it up to me somehow. "I could keep Mallory as my last name."

"No way in hell," he said flatly.

"Women keep their own names all the time."

"I don't care what other women do. You're taking my name."

"I'm already established in the business community as Blair Mallory. And I like my last name."

"We're going to have the same name. Period."

I smiled sweetly at him. "Oh, that's so nice of you, changing your last name to Mallory. Thank you. That's such a perfect solution, and only a man who's really secure in his masculinity could do that —"

"*Blair.*" He got to his feet, towering over me, his level dark brows drawn together in a V over his nose. He's six-feet-two, so when he towers over someone, he does it right.

Not to be towered over, I got to my feet, too, scowling right back at him. Okay, so there's still that ten-inch difference in our heights, but I went on tiptoe and pushed my chin up so we were almost nose to nose. "Expecting me to change my name while you keep *yours* is *archaic* —"

His eyes were narrow, his jaw set, his lips a thin hard line that barely moved as he spit out words as if they were bullets. "In the animal kingdom, the male marks his territory by pissing on it. All I'm asking you to do is change your last name to mine. *Take. Your. Pick.*"

My hair all but stood on end, which is a really stupid expression, because how else would it stand? It isn't as if it can stand on middle. "Don't you dare piss on me!" I shrieked in outrage. Wyatt can push my buttons faster than anyone else, which I guess keeps things even, but that was why it took a few seconds before the mental image sank in and my shriek abruptly turned into a sputter of laughter.

He was so angry and frustrated it took him a second longer, but as he snorted his gaze dropped to where my robe had come completely open and his expression changed as he reached for me. "Don't bother," he growled as I reached for the belt to retie it.

Sex with Wyatt tends to be tempestuous. We have chemistry out the wazoo, or wherever chemistry comes from. I like the hell out of it, because that means I can pretty much count on an orgasm or two, but it also means that even though we've been engaged for a couple of months now the urgency hasn't slacked off much, and he'll take me down wherever we happen to be, unless we're in public, of course.

He didn't strip me out of the robe, since it wasn't in his way, just out of my underpants. The robe saved me from getting carpet burn on my butt, because he laid me on the dining room floor, spread my legs, and moved into position between them. His green eyes were glittering with lust and possessiveness and triumph and some other unnameable male things as he settled his weight on me.

"Blair Bloodsworth," he said in a tough tone, reaching down to position his penis. "No negotiation."

I caught my breath as he pushed into me, thick and hard and so damn exciting I could barely stand it. I dug my nails into his shoulders and tightened my legs on his hips, trying to hold him still even though my heartbeat was stuttering and my eyes were closing. He hooked his left hand around my knee and pushed my leg wider, allowing him to go deeper, all the way. He shuddered, his own breathing hard and raspy. No matter how shattered I was by our lovemaking, he was right there with me.

"All right," I gasped, with my last thread of sanity. "But you owe me! For the rest of our lives, you owe me." No negotiation, my ass; what did he think we'd been doing?

He growled something unintelligible, rocking against me while he bent his head to kiss my neck, and I literally saw stars.

We were both sweaty and exhausted and very happy twenty minutes later when he raised his head and smoothed a tendril of hair out of my face. "One month," he said. "I'll give you exactly one month from today. We're either married by then or we do it my way, regardless of where it is or who can be there. Got it?"

Huh. I know a challenge when I hear one. I also know he wasn't kidding. I had to kick things into high gear.

CHAPTER TWO

I called Mom first thing the next morning. "I lost an argument with Wyatt, and we're getting married within the month."

"Blair Elizabeth. How did that happen?" she asked after a shocked pause, and I knew she was asking about the first part of my statement.

"Strategic battle," I said. "Stupid of me, but I just realized last night that my name will be Blair Bloodsworth, so I told him I was keeping Mallory as my name and he hit the ceiling, and the upshot of the outcome is he either pisses on me to mark me as his territory, or I take his name."

She stopped laughing long enough to say "So now he owes you" before succumbing again. I love my mom; I don't have to explain anything to her. She gets me immediately, maybe because we're so much alike. Knowing Wyatt's stubbornness and the deviousness of his mind, plus some other characteristics such as possessiveness, etcetera, the outcome of our argument last night had never been in doubt unless I wanted to break up with him, which I didn't, so I had maneuvered to get the best terms possible. He *owed* me. Eternal debt was good.

"But . . . he gave me an ultimatum. We're either married within the month, or we'll do it on his terms."

"And those terms would be?"

"If I'm lucky, a courthouse wedding. If not, Las Vegas."

"Ugh. Not after Britney. That's tacky."

See? It's like I'm her clone.

"That's what I thought, but he made it a challenge. I have to kick the plans into high gear."

"First you have to *have* plans. 'Get married' isn't exactly a plan. It's an end result."

"I know. I was trying to be considerate of everyone's schedule, but that's out. Twenty-nine days from today — since this challenge officially started last night — we're getting married, and people can either reschedule whatever they have scheduled, or they'll miss it."

"Why twenty-nine, and not thirty? Or thirty-one?"

"He'll argue that since there are four months with thirty days in them, that constitutes a legal month."

"February has twenty-eight."

"Or twenty-nine. It can't make up its mind, so it doesn't count."

"Got it. Okay, twenty-nine days from today. That means you'll be getting married on the thirtieth day. Will he count that?"

"He has to give me the full thirty days, so, yeah." I grabbed the pad and pen I'd been using the night before and started writing down items. "Gown, flowers, cake, decorations, invitations. No attendants. No tux for him, just a suit. This is doable." A wedding didn't have to be fancy to be memorable. I could do without fancy, but I refused to do without pretty. I'd originally thought maybe one attendant for me and a best man for him, but I was paring as much as I could.

"The cake will be the problem. The other refreshments can be gotten anywhere, but the cake . . . ."

"I know," I said. We both took deep breaths. A wedding cake is a work of art. It takes *time*. And people who do good wedding cakes are usually booked solid, for months in advance.

"I'll take care of the cake," Mom said. "I'll call in favors. I'll get Sally on the job, too. She needs a distraction now, to get her mind off Jazz."

That was a sad subject. Sally and Jazz Arledge were on the verge of seeing a thirty-five-year marriage dissolve if they couldn't work out their problems. Sally was Mom's best friend, so we were solidly on her side, even though we felt sorry for Jazz because he was so clueless. Sally had tried to hit Jazz with the car and maybe break his legs, and really he should have let her do it instead of jumping out of the way, because then she would feel the scales had been balanced and she would have forgiven him for getting rid of her priceless antique bedroom furniture, but I guess survival instinct tripped him up and he *did* jump out of the way and Sally hit the house instead, and the airbag deployed and broke her nose, which made the situation even worse. Jazz was in big, big trouble.

"I'm opening today so Lynn is closing" — Lynn Hill is my assistant manager at Great Bods — "and I'm going shopping tonight," I told Mom. "Heavy shopping. Any suggestions?"

She named a few shops, and we hung up. I figured we'd talk several more times during the course of the day, as she kept me updated on how she had marshaled forces. My sisters, Siana and Jenni, would be called to action, that was for certain.

My immediate goal was plain: find a wedding gown pronto, so there would be time for alterations if any were needed. I'm not talking about a fairy-tale wedding dress; I've already had one of those, when I married the first time, and it didn't work: there was no fairy tale. What I wanted this time was something simple and classic that would make me look like a million bucks and make Wyatt go almost blind with lust. Hey, just because we were already sleeping together was no reason why I should forgo a memorable wedding night, right?

There had to be a way I could keep him away from me for the next month, to make damn certain he was blind with lust. So far, though, when it came to Wyatt I wasn't real great in the keeping-away department. He has a way of overcoming my few and pitiful defenses, mainly because I go blind with lust for *him*.

I thought I might have to go live with his mother for the duration. That would put a crimp in his sexual expectations — though he's perfectly capable of kidnapping me and carrying me away to his lair for a night of blissful raunchiness. God, I love that man.

It occurred to me that if he couldn't have sex, neither could I. Going an entire month without him . . . maybe I could get him to kidnap me more than once.

See? I'm truly pitiful, a fact he has used to his advantage more than once.

Oh, man, the next few weeks looked like *fun.*

Wyatt called my cell early that afternoon. I was in the middle of an intensive workout — because I own Great Bods, I have to keep in shape or people will think it must not be a great place — but I stopped to take the call. Not that I knew it was Wyatt, because I didn't until I saw his number in the Caller ID window; with all the activity that had been started that morning, Mom could have been calling.

"I think I can get out of here on time, for once," he said. "Want to go out for dinner?"

"I can't, I have to go shopping," I said as I went into my office and closed the door.

He had a man's normal respect for shopping, which means none at all. "You can do that later, can't you?"

"No, because there *is* no later."

Silence fell, because whenever I make statements like that he pauses, as if he's looking for hidden meanings or traps. It's heartwarming, the attention he has paid to me and my methods.

Finally he said, "If the end is nigh, why bother to shop?"

I rolled my eyes, even though he couldn't see. Excuse me, if the end was nigh, what else would you do but shop? Those hot shoes you've been eyeing but wouldn't buy because you didn't know where you'd wear them and they cost the earth anyway? Go get 'em, honey. It isn't as if you'd have to worry about the credit card bill, with the end nigh and all that. Maybe you really can't take it with you, but do you want to take that chance? What if you *can,* and you find out too late? There you'll be, without all the stuff you really wanted but didn't get because you didn't see the use in stockpiling.

I jerked my thoughts away from eternity and back to Wyatt. "I didn't say the world is ending. This is all about you and your precious deadline."

"Ah. I get it. My deadline." He sounded very self-satisfied about his deadline; it had accomplished exactly what he intended, which was to galvanize me into action so I would ride roughshod over everyone else's conflicting schedules. I knew him well enough to know he meant exactly what he said, too, otherwise his galvanizing tactics wouldn't have worked.

"Because of your deadline," I continued sweetly, "I probably won't have time to eat for the next month, much less go out for a leisurely meal. I have to find a wedding dress *tonight* so there'll be enough time for alterations. You do have a black suit, don't you?"

"Of course."

"That's what you're wearing for the wedding then, unless it has frayed cuffs, in which case you'd better go shopping, too, because if you wear frayed cuffs to our wedding none of us will ever forgive you for it, and I swear I'll make your life miserable."

"I could always divorce you if you tried." Lazy amusement was in his tone now. I could just imagine his green eyes glinting.

"You could always *try* to divorce me, because I'd fight it tooth and nail, and I'd hound you to the ends of the earth. Siana would hound you, too. And Mom would get all her sorority sisters to hound you." Siana's a lawyer and that maybe gave him pause, but he's around lawyers all the time so they're no big deal to him. On the other hand, he has a healthy respect for my mom, based on real fear. She *would* get all her sorority sisters to hound him.

"So you're going into this for life?"

"You bet your ass I am." I waited a beat and added, "Your life, anyway."

It was really annoying when he laughed at something I'd meant to give him food for thought. "I'll check those cuffs," he said.

"What color shirt?"

Okay, he *had* been taking notes, after all. "White or gray. I'll let you know." I didn't believe in the groom taking attention away from the bride. Yes, I know it would be his wedding, too, but all he cared about was making it legal so I'd finally consent to live under the same roof with him and have his kids, though I'm pretty sure the kid part wasn't his most immediate concern.

"Make it easy on me. I already have white shirts."

"Make it easy on *you?* After what you've done to me with your stupid deadline?"

"Other than having to shop tonight, exactly what have I done to you?"

"Do you think invitations order themselves? Or send themselves? Or that refreshments just magically appear?"

"So hire a catering firm."

"I can't," I said even more sweetly than before. "Catering firms are booked months in advance. I don't have that kind of time. Ditto on the wedding cake. I have to find someone who can do a wedding cake on a moment's notice."

"Buy one from a bakery."

I pulled the cell phone away from my ear and stared at it, wondering if it had somehow connected me to an alien. Putting it back to my ear I asked, "Did you do *anything* for your first wedding?"

"I showed up and stood where I was told to stand."

"You'll have to do more than that this time. You're in charge of the flowers. Get your mother to help you. I love you, gotta go now. 'Bye."

"Hey!" I heard him yelp as I ended the call.

I entertained myself for the rest of the afternoon imagining his panic. If he were smart, he'd call his mother right away, but even though he's a very smart man he's first and foremost a *Man,* so I figured he'd instead maybe ask the sergeants and detectives who were married if they actually remembered anything about their weddings, and if so what kind of flowers was I talking about? By the end of the day he'd have figured out the flowers in question weren't the kind planted in pots of dirt. He'd maybe think I was talking about my bridal bouquet, which I wasn't — no way would I leave that to a man, no matter how much I loved him. Sometime tomorrow one of the guys would remember some sort of arch with stuff on it, maybe roses, and sometime tomorrow Wyatt would also find out that I wasn't free tomorrow night, either, and the awful truth would be dawning on him: his sex life was ruined for the next month, all by his own doing.

I just love it when a plan comes together, don't you?

Not that I left something as important as flowers totally to chance. I called his mother, who is so cool I can barely believe my own luck in getting her for a mother-in-law, and filled her in on the details.

"I'll keep him hopping," she promised. "There'll be all sorts of emergencies and delays, but don't worry, I'll make certain everything is what you want."

With that taken care of, I finished my workout, showered and dried my hair, did a fast swipe with mascara and lipstick, and changed clothes. Lynn had everything under control, as usual, so I ducked out earlier than normal and drove to the better of our two malls. There were several formal-wear stores scattered around town, but I might find what I wanted in one of the higher-end department stores in the mall. The formal-wear stores took forever on alterations.

There was a parking deck at the mall, as well as ample outdoor parking. Everyone tried to park in the deck, of course, which usually left some prime parking spaces free in the outside lots. I cruised around, my little black Mercedes convertible taking the corners like an energetic cat, and located one of those prime spaces just outside one of the department stores. I whipped into the space, smiling a little at the handling. Nothing drives like a Mercedes.

There was a little skip to my step as I entered the department store. There's nothing like a challenge to get me revved, plus I had a mission that involved trying on clothes. Sometimes all the planets are in alignment or something, and these little bonuses just happen. Color me happy. I wasn't even particularly upset when the first store didn't have what I wanted, because I'd been prepared for a long search. I did find a pair of shoes that were just what I'd envisioned, strappy and comfortable, with a two-inch heel that I could wear for hours. Best of all, they glittered with gold sequins and crystals. I like a shoe with some pizzazz to it, plus I really needed the shoe I'd be wearing for the wedding so I'd know if the dress, when I managed to find it, would need hemming or not.

I was looking for a gown in a pale champagne color. Nothing white, not even off-white or cream, because, let's get real, shall we? White does still carry the traditional message, which seems really silly in a second marriage. Besides, I look really good in champagne, and since the whole idea was to make Wyatt blind with lust . . .

I gave it the old college try. I shopped myself into the ground, stopping only for a quick salad for dinner in the food court. Along the way I found some fabulous underwear sets, some earrings that I just had to have, another pair of shoes — killer black pumps, this time — a great pencil skirt that fit just right, and even a few Christmas gifts since my gift-buying this year would be double what it had been before, with Wyatt's family added in, so I needed to get an early start.

What I didn't find was a champagne-colored gown.

At nine-ish, I gave up for the night. I'd have to start hitting the stand-alone formal-wear stores tomorrow, and unless they had changed since my prom days in high school — okay, so that was fifteen years, roughly, and change was possible — even if I found a gown I liked it probably would have been tried on by so many people that a new one would have to be ordered, which took time, and time was what I didn't have.

As I left the mall, my thoughts were racing. A seamstress. I needed a seamstress. I'd try one more time to find a ready-made gown, which would be the easiest solution, but if I didn't find something tomorrow night I'd go with my fall-back plan, which was buy the material and have the dress made. That was more time-consuming, but doable.

I wasn't paying attention to my surroundings, I admit. I had important things on my mind. As I left the store I did notice that there weren't many cars left in the parking lot, but I'd parked close to the store, the light was good, no suspicious stranger was lurking around my car, other people were leaving at the same time, etcetera.

I juggled my packages so I could dig my car key from my pocket, and hit the unlock button on the remote as I stepped off the curb. A van was parked in the handicap slot, which of course was the first slot on the row, and I'd parked in the second slot. My beautiful little car flashed its lights at me in welcome.

I heard the smooth sound of a car accelerating and stopped a few feet from the curb; with a quick glance I judged I easily had enough time to cross ahead of the oncoming car, and resumed my asphalt trek.

Everything seemed normal. I didn't pay much attention to the car as it neared; my left hand had started aching from the weight of all the plastic bags I was carrying, and I adjusted my grip. Still, something — some whisper of instinct that said the sound of the car was getting too close — made me look up as the car seemed to surge right at me, as if the driver had floored the gas pedal.

The car looked gigantic, coming right at me. The headlights were glaring right in my eyes, blinding me; I had only a vague impression of the dark form behind the wheel, and that was due solely to the lights in the parking lot. There was plenty of room for the car to swerve around me, but it didn't.

I took a running step to get out of the way, and in the split second that followed I swear it seemed the driver adjusted direction, too, and *aimed* for me.

Panic exploded in my brain. All I could think — and this wasn't a fully-formed, coherent thought, just an *"Ohmigod!"* kind of realization — was that if the car hit me I would be crushed between it and the van.

Good-bye, wedding. Hell, good-bye *me.*

I jumped. Actually, I dived. And it was a world-class effort, let me tell you. There's nothing like thinking you're about to be turned into mush to put some spring in the legs. Even when I was cheerleading in college I couldn't get that kind of distance.

The car roared by so closely I felt the heat

of its exhaust; I was still airborne at the time, that's how close I came to being hit. I heard squealing tires, then I crashed to the asphalt behind the van and the lights sort of went out.

CHAPTER THREE

I didn't lose consciousness, or at least not completely. The world was nothing but a dark, tumbling blur. I remember the sharp, burning sensation as I sort of skidded and rolled across the asphalt. I remember thinking *"My shoes!"* as I tried desperately to hold on to my packages. I remember my ears ringing, and the sudden hot taste of blood in my mouth. And I remember what felt like a shock wave of pain slamming through me.

Then the movement stopped and I lay on the asphalt, which was still warm even though night had closed in, not quite certain where I was or what had happened. I could hear sounds, but I couldn't tell what they were or where they were coming from. All I wanted to do was lie there and try to contain my body's outrage at being injured. I was hurt. My head was pounding in a sickening throb, throb, throb, in time with my heartbeat. I felt hot, then cold, and wanted to throw up. I could feel the sharp aches, the burns, the throbs and jabs; I just couldn't isolate all the sensations and make sense of them, couldn't determine location or severity, or do anything about them.

At least I wasn't dead. That was a plus.

Then a very clear thought burned through my brain: *"That bitch tried to run me down!"*

My second thought was, "Oh, shit, not again!"

I even said the words aloud, and the sound of my own voice startled me, sort of jarred me back into my body, which, by the way, wasn't a happy place to be. I almost wanted to go back into that disconnected state, except I was afraid the driver would turn around and come back for another pass at me, and if I were just lying there zoned out I'd be roadkill. Literally.

Spurred by a panicked shot of adrenaline, I sat up and hastily looked around. That wasn't my smartest move ever. Well, maybe it was, because I had to make certain I wasn't about to become a greasy mess on the pavement, but my body immediately rebelled: my head gave a huge throb, my stomach heaved, my eyes rolled up in my head, and I collapsed back to the asphalt.

This time I just let myself lie there, because the eyeballs-rolling-up thing was weird.

Surely someone would come rushing to my aid any minute now.

Frankly, I was getting very tired of people trying to kill me. Read my previous book if you don't know what I'm talking about. I've been shot (by my ex-husband's current wife); my brake line cut (by my ex-husband), resulting in a multi-car accident; and now this. I was tired of pain. I was tired of the hell this played with my schedule. I was *damn* tired of not looking my best.

The pavement was rough under my cheek. From the various shrieks of pain coming from nerve endings all over my body, I thought I must have left large amounts of skin on the asphalt. Thank goodness I was wearing long pants, but really, only leather will protect your skin, so I suspected the pants hadn't been a lot of help. Road rash is an ugly thing. I began to worry; how would I look for the wedding? Was four weeks enough time to heal, or would I have to invest in some heavy body makeup, which is icky and would smear on my dress? Maybe the sleeveless, sexy column of silk I'd envisioned would have to go, and instead I'd wear something with more coverage, like a burka, or a tent — not that there's much difference between the two.

Well, for pete's sake, where *was* someone?

41

Were all those people going to stay in the frickin' mall until midnight? How long would I have to lie there before someone saw me and came to help? I'd almost been smashed to a pulp! I needed a little concern here, a little *something.*

I was getting very indignant. Hello . . . a body lying in the parking lot, and no one notices? Yes, it was night, but the parking lot was lit by those huge vapor lights, and I wasn't lying between two cars or anything. I was . . . I opened my eyes and tried to get my bearings.

My vision was blurred; all I could see were black shadows and patches of light, and those swam and ran together. Automatically I tried to rub my eyes, only to find that my arms, neither of them, wanted to obey. They would move, but reluctantly, and not very well — certainly not well enough to have fingers flailing away at my eyes; I might blind myself, and wouldn't that be adding insult to injury?

Okay, so I couldn't see exactly where I was. Still, I had to be lying in the end of the row closest to the mall, where *someone* should notice me. Eventually.

Dimly I heard a car start, somewhere. So long as it wasn't a car that would back over me, that was okay, but I figured in that case the driver would have had to step over my body to get to said car, so that scenario wasn't likely. On the other hand, there have been times when I was so rushed that if I had stepped over a body I might have thought, *I'll get to that later.*

Something else to worry about: being backed over by someone like me.

Was there any sort of record on how long someone could lie in the middle of a parking lot and no one notice? And — yuck — what if ants and things crawled on me? I was bleeding. Probably all sorts of little critters were crawling at top speed toward me, eager to feast.

This thought was so disgusting that if my head hadn't been aching so badly I probably would have bolted upright. No, I don't like bugs. I'm not afraid of them, but I think they're nasty and icky, and I don't want them anywhere near me.

Come to think of it, the parking lot itself was nasty and icky. Tacky, classless people spit on the pavement, and sometimes they spit more than just spit. All sorts of crap landed on pavements, including, well, crap.

Oh, God, I had to get up before I died from an overdose of the nasties. No one was coming to my aid, at least not on my timetable, which pretty much meant *NOW.*

I'd have to do this myself. I'd have to find my purse, dig out my cell phone — I hoped the damn thing still worked, that the battery hadn't been knocked out or something, because finding a battery and replacing it was beyond me at the moment — and call 911. I also had to sit up, to get most of my body off the nasty pavement, or my mental state would soon match my physical one.

On the count of three, I thought, I would sit up. *One. Two. Three.* Nothing happened. My mind knew what I wanted to do, but my body said uh-uh. It had already tried that sitting-up stuff.

That pissed me off, almost as much as did the lying-there-unnoticed. Okay, I'm lying about that. Lying-there-unnoticed came close to the top of the list. If I had to rate the things that pissed me off right then, someone trying to kill me — *again!* — would have to rate a ten. No one paying any attention to me was a nine. A disobedient body was a distant third, coming in at maybe a five.

Still, I'd been a cheerleader for years, all the way from junior high through college. I'd told my body to do painful things lots of times, and for the most part it had obeyed. It just didn't make sense that it wouldn't obey me now when the stakes were a lot higher than turning a cartwheel or something. My life could hang in the balance here! Not only that, it felt as if something was crawling on my face. No doubt about it, I had to get up. I had to get help.

Maybe I was trying to do too much. Sitting up all in one motion, without the spur of panic to push me, was more than I could manage. Maybe I should try moving my arm again.

That worked out pretty well. My right arm hurt, but it did just what my brain told it to do, which was laboriously (I didn't tell it that part, that was just the way it worked) bring my hand up so I could swipe at whatever was crawling across my face.

I expected to feel a bug. I was braced to feel a giant bug. What I felt, instead, was wet and sticky.

Okay, I was bleeding. I was vaguely surprised, though I shouldn't have been. It wasn't that I was surprised I was bleeding, but that I was bleeding from my head or face, or both. I knew I'd hit my head, hence the headache and nausea that likely meant a concussion, but the situation was getting worser and worser, as someone once said. If I'd cut my face, would that mean stitches? The way this was going, I would look like the Bride of Frankenstein by the time Wyatt and I got married.

That realization shot up to a seven on my Piss-O-Meter. Maybe an eight. My plans for Wyatt were totally screwed if my face was scarred and I was covered in peeling road rash, because how could he possibly go blind with lust looking at that?

At least he wasn't with me this time. He'd been right there both of the other times when someone tried to kill me, and it had played hell with him on all sorts of levels. As a cop, he'd been infuriated. As a man, he'd been outraged. As the man who loved me, he'd been terrified. Naturally, he had shown all this by becoming even more arrogant and overbearing, and considering what his base level was for both those characteristics, you can imagine how unbearable he became. It's a good thing I already loved him, or I'd have had to kill him.

Thinking about Wyatt wasn't going to get help to me any faster. I was really good at putting off unpleasant stuff, but I couldn't put this off any longer. It was going to hurt, but I had to force myself to move.

I was lying on my left side, with my left arm pinned beneath me. I planted my right hand about even with my shoulder and awkwardly levered myself up until I managed to get propped on my left elbow. Then I paused, fighting nausea, fighting the horrible pounding in my head, waiting until the worst of it passed before I struggled into an upright position.

Okay. Nothing was broken. Having had experience with broken bones, I could tell that much. Scraped, bruised, jarred, and concussed, but not broken. Probably if I'd been in fear of my life I could have jumped up and run like hell, but the bitch who had almost run me down had evidently taken her road rage to, well, the road. Not having that pressing need, I sat there and used the hem of my blouse to wipe the blood from my eyes so I could see. I also used that time to reassure myself that my head wasn't going to explode or fall off, though it felt as if it might do both.

With my vision less blurry, I found my purse. It was hanging from the bend of my right arm, and it was tangled with some of the plastic bags that I likewise hadn't dropped. The tangled straps had been hampering my efforts to move my arm, and the bags themselves were woven around and under my legs. How about that? My purchases might have provided my skin with a little extra protection. I took this as a sign that God wanted me to shop.

Buoyed by this spiritual support, I clumsily fished in my purse for my cell phone and flipped it open. The blessed little screen lit up, so I punched in 911. I've called 911 before, when Nicole Goodwin was murdered and I thought the shots were being fired at me, so I knew the drill. When the dispassionate voice asked the nature of my emergency, I was prepared.

"I've been injured. I'm in the mall parking lot —" I told them which mall, which store, and which entrance I was lying outside of, though technically I was now sitting outside of it.

"What is the nature of your injury?" the voice inquired, without the least bit of urgency or even concern. I guess the 911 operator figured that if I were calling, I couldn't be hurt that much, and I guess she was right.

"Head injury; I think I have a concussion. Bruises, scrapes, general battering. Someone tried to run me down, but she's gone now."

"Is this a domestic dispute?"

"No, I'm heterosexual."

"Ma'am?" For the first time, the operator's voice had some expression in it. Unfortunately, that expression was confusion.

"I said, 'she's gone,' and you asked if it was a domestic dispute, so I said no, I'm heterosexual," I explained patiently, which, considering I was sitting on the nasty pavement bleeding, was an example of my self-control.

I really try not to piss off people who might be coming to my rescue. I say "might" because so far the rescuing hadn't happened.

"I see. Do you know the identity of this person?"

"No." All I knew was that she was a psycho bitch who shouldn't be allowed to steer a wheelbarrow, much less a Buick.

"I'll dispatch a patrol car and medics to your location," the operator said, having regained her professional distance. "I need more information, so please stay on the line."

I stayed. When asked, I provided my name and address, my home phone number, and my cell number, which I think maybe she already had, because of enhanced 911, plus my cell phone is one of those with a GPS locator in it. I had probably been triangulated, located, and verified. Inwardly I winced. My name was already going across police radios, which meant one Lieutenant J. W. Bloodsworth would hear it and was probably already leaping into his car and turning on his blue lights. I really hoped the medics could get here before he arrived, and clean some of the blood off my face. He's seen me bloody before, but still . . . it's a vanity thing.

The automatic door of the department store opened and two women came out, chatting happily as they carried out their booty and started up the aisle of parked cars. The first one to see me shrieked and stopped in her tracks.

"Don't mind that noise," I told the operator. "Someone was startled."

"Oh my God! Oh my God!" The second woman rushed toward me. "Were you attacked? Are you okay? What happened?"

Let me tell you, it's really annoying when help shows up once you no longer need it.

The parking lot was full of flashing lights, cars parked at odd angles, and uniformed men mostly standing around chatting. No one was dead, so there wasn't any sense of urgency. One of the vehicles with flashing lights belonged to the medics; their names were Dwight and Dwayne. You can't make this stuff up. I don't like the name "Dwayne" because that was the name of the man who had killed Nicole Goodwin, but I couldn't say that to this Dwayne because he was a really nice man who was calm and gentle as he wiped away blood and bandaged my scalp wound. My forehead was scraped, but my face wasn't cut, which I guess meant that I'd sort of had my head tucked down when I landed. Good news for my face, bad news for my head.

They agreed with my diagnosis of concussion, which on one level was satisfying — I like being right — and on another disheartening, because a concussion would seriously interfere with my schedule, which was tight enough without having this kind of handicap thrown into the mix.

One of the patrolmen was Officer Spangler — I knew him, from when Nicole was murdered. I was lying propped on a gurney and he was taking my statement while the medics efficiently wiped and bandaged and got me ready for transport when Wyatt drove up. Even without looking I knew it was him, because of the way his tires squealed, punctuated by a slamming car door.

"There's Wyatt," I said to Officer Spangler. I didn't turn my head, because I was trying very hard not to move.

He glanced in the direction of the new arrival, and pursed his lips a little so they wouldn't smile. "Yes, ma'am, it is," he said. "He's been in radio contact."

There had been some conflict between Wyatt and some of the older guys in the police department, because he was promoted ahead of them. Officer Spangler was fairly new, and young, so he was free of that resentment. He stood and gave a respectful nod as Wyatt approached and stared down at me, his hands on his hips. He was wearing jeans and a long-sleeved dress shirt with the cuffs rolled up over his forearms. His service weapon rode in a holster on his right kidney, and his badge was clipped to his belt. He carried a cell phone/radio in his hand, and he looked grim.

"I'm okay," I said to Wyatt, hating that look on his face. I'd seen it before. "Kind of."

He immediately switched the laserlike focus of his gaze to Dwayne. Dwight was fiddling with their medic cases, putting stuff back, so Dwayne was the target. "How is she?" he asked, as if I hadn't even spoken.

"Probable concussion," said Dwayne, which was likely against some sort of regulation, but I supposed most of the medics and cops knew one another, and maybe cops could get all kinds of info that was supposed to be private. "A lacerated scalp, some contusions."

"Road rash," I said glumly.

Dwayne smiled down at me. "That, too."

Wyatt squatted beside the gurney. The bright light the medics had set up for their work threw harsh shadows on his face. He looked tough and mean, but his hand was gentle as he took mine in it.

"I'll be right behind the ambulance," he promised. "I'll call your mom and dad on the way." He shot a look at Spangler. "You can finish taking her statement at the hospital."

"Yes, sir," said Officer Spangler, closing his notebook.

I was loaded into the back of the ambulance — to be precise, the gurney was loaded in the ambulance, but since I was on it, the end result was the same. The guys closed the double doors, and the last sight I had of Wyatt was him standing there looking both cold and fierce.

Then we pulled out of the parking lot, lights flashing but no siren wailing, for which I was grateful because my head ached so much.

Well, this was familiar. And in this case, familiarity sucked.

CHAPTER FOUR

Wyatt was the last thing I saw before the doors to the ambulance were closed, and the first thing I saw when they were opened.

He looked so grim and cold and furious, all at the same time, that I reached for his hand again as I was unloaded from the back of the vehicle. "I really am okay," I said. Except for the concussion, I really was. Banged up, but okay. I wanted to sound brave, which would convince him I was fine and was putting on a false front to garner sympathy, but my head hurt too much for me to muster the energy, so instead I sounded sincere, so of course he didn't believe me.

The man/woman jockeying-for-position supremacy thing was too complicated for me to deal with right then. You'd think he'd be relieved, but no, I could tell by the way his jaw clenched that instead he was worried as hell. Men are so perverse.

I mustered my strength. "This is all your

fault," I said, with as much indignation as I could manage.

He was walking alongside the gurney holding my hand, and he gave me a narrow-eyed look. "My fault?"

"I was shopping tonight because of *your* stupid deadline. *If* you'd listened to me I could have shopped during the daytime, like civilized people, but no, you have to give me an *ultimatum,* which forced me to be in the parking lot with a road-rage-crazed psycho bitch in a Buick."

His eyes got even more narrow. To my relief, the grim look had relaxed somewhat. He figured if I could work up a head of steam, I really was all right. "*If* you had managed to plan something as simple as a wedding," he said with maddening disregard for the millions of details that go into a wedding, "I wouldn't have had to step in."

"Simple?" I sputtered. "*Simple?* You think a wedding is simple? A shuttle launch is *simple.* Quantum physics is *simple.* Planning a wedding is like planning a war —"

"An apt comparison," he muttered under his breath, but I heard him anyway.

I jerked my hand out of his. Sometimes I wanted to just smack him.

Dwight, pushing the gurney, laughed. Dwayne was much nicer than Dwight. I said,

"I don't want you pushing my gurney. I want Dwayne. Where's Dwayne?"

"He's taking care of the paperwork, bringing in your things, stuff like that," Dwight said easily, and he didn't stop pushing my gurney.

The night was just *not* going my way, but I perked up as much as possible at the news that Dwayne was bringing in my things. It's a measure of how much my head hurt that I hadn't given a single thought to my purchases, especially my new shoes, until now. "He has my shoes?"

"You're wearing your shoes," Wyatt said, flashing a quick, questioning look at Dwight over my head, silently asking if I could have a brain injury.

"I'm not going loopy, I mean my new shoes. The ones I bought tonight." As I explained, Dwight rolled me into a cubicle. Dwayne followed within thirty seconds, his hands full of clipboard, papers, my purse, and several plastic bags. I spied the bag from the store where I'd bought my shoes, and sighed in relief. They hadn't gone missing. Then an efficient team of nurses took over; Wyatt was evicted, Dwayne and Dwight gave their report on my condition, which was pretty much as I'd already figured out. Then they, too, were gone, the curtain was pulled, and my clothes were swiftly cut off me. I really hate the way emergency room personnel treat clothing, even though I understand the need for it. Even someone who is conscious might not be able to accurately gauge her own medical condition, and speed and efficiency are the name of the game.

Regardless of that, I really, really hate when my bra is cut with one callous snip of those big scissor blades. I love my underwear sets. This particular bra was a gorgeous mocha color, with little flowers in the satin fabric, and tiny pearls sewn in the middle. Now it was ruined. I sighed when I saw it, because it was ruined anyway, from blood.

Come to think of it, pretty much every stitch I had on was ruined, either from rips or blood, or both. Scalp wounds really bleed a lot. I sighed as I looked myself over, then surveyed the clothing that had been tossed aside, which I could do without moving my head much because the head of the gurney was raised and I was propped up. No, nothing was salvageable, except maybe my shoes. My black cargo pants were torn in several places, big, jagged tears that couldn't be repaired, never mind that the legs had been neatly cut lengthwise to allow the nurses to swiftly remove them. My bare legs were both dirty and bloody, confirming that my irrational fear of germs in the parking lot hadn't been all that irrational. Actually, most of me was dirty and bloody. I wasn't a pretty sight at all, which was depressing, because Wyatt had seen me like this.

"I'm a mess," I said mournfully.

"It isn't too bad," one of the nurses said. "It looks worse than it is. Though I suppose it feels bad enough to you, doesn't it?" Her voice was brisk, but comforting. Or rather, she meant it to be comforting, but what she said made me feel worse because *looks* were exactly what I was worrying about. Yes, I'm vain, but I'm also under a deadline for a wedding and I didn't want to look like a war refugee in my wedding pictures. My kids would be looking at them, you know; I didn't want them wondering what their father had ever seen in me.

I'm also not of a "victim" mentality, and I'm tired of being shot, battered, and bruised. I didn't want Wyatt to think he had to take care of me. I want to take care of myself, thank you very much — unless I'm in the mood for pampering, in which case I want to be in good shape so I can enjoy it.

I had just been sort of halfway stuffed into a hospital gown when a tired ER doc shuffled in. He checked me over, listened to the nurses, checked my pupils to see how they were responding, and sent me off for a head CT and what seemed like all-over X-rays. A few boring and painful hours later, I was admitted to the hospital for an overnight stay because the docs also agreed with my diagnosis of a concussion. All of my scrapes were cleaned and some of them bandaged, most of the blood was swabbed away — except out of my hair, which annoyed me because it felt so icky. Worst of all was that they shaved a patch at my hairline and put in a few stitches to close the gash in my scalp. I would have to get creative with my hairstyles for the next few months. At last I was deposited in a nice cool, clean bed and the lights were turned low, which was a relief. Have I mentioned how much my head was hurting?

What wasn't a relief was the way Wyatt and my entire family were ringed around the bed, silently staring at me.

"This isn't my fault," I said defensively. It was weird, having them all sort of aligned against me, as if I'd done this on purpose or something. Even Siana had a solemn expression, and I can usually count on her to be in my court no matter what. I did understand, though, because if Wyatt had gotten hurt as often in the past few months as I had, I would be demanding he change jobs and we move to Outer Mongolia to get him out of the danger zone.

Mom stirred. She had been as tight-lipped as Wyatt, but now she went into mom-mode and went to the miniature sink, where she wet a washcloth. Coming back to my bedside, she began gently washing away the dried blood that the nurses had skipped. I haven't had my ears washed by my mother since I was little, but some things never change. I was just glad she used water instead of spit. You know all the jokes about mom-spit removing everything from grease to ink? It's true. Mom-spit should be patented and sold as an all-purpose spot remover. Come to think of it, maybe it has been. I've never read the ingredients of a spot-remover. Maybe it just says *mom-spit.*

Finally Wyatt said, "We're getting the security tapes for the parking lot, so we may be able to get a tag number for the car."

I'd been hanging around him long enough now to understand some of the finer points of the law. "But she didn't hit me. When she floored the gas pedal, I dived out of the way. So it isn't a hit-and-run. It's a terrify-and-run."

"She?" He picked up on that immediately, of course. "You saw her? Did you know her?"

"I could tell it was a woman, but as to whether or not I know her . . ." I would have shrugged, but I was trying to keep movement to a minimum. "The headlights were shining in my eyes. The driver was a woman, and the car was a late-model Buick, that's all I know for certain. Parking lot lights do weird things to colors, but I think the car was that sort of metallic light brown."

"You're sure it was a Buick?"

"Please," I said with as much disdain as I could muster. I know cars. It's one of the weird genes Dad passed on to me, because all Mom can tell is the color and if it's a big car, little car, or pickup truck. Make and model mean nothing to her.

"If she says it was a Buick, it's a Buick," said Dad, taking up for me, and Wyatt nodded. At any other time I would have been annoyed that he would automatically take Dad's word for it after questioning mine, but right then I was, not down and out, because I obviously wasn't out, but I was definitely down, both physically and mentally. I felt drained, not just from the pain, but it was as if this was just one incident too many. I mean, how many times can people try to kill you before it gets a little depressing? It isn't as if I go around pissing people off and getting in their faces. I don't even flip off stupid drivers because you never know if they've taken their antipsychotics or if they're driving around with a loaded pistol and an unloaded brain. I was tired of it, I was hurting, and I really wanted to cry.

I couldn't cry, not in front of everyone. I'm not a crier, at least not that kind of a crier. I'll cry over a sad movie or when "The Star-Spangled Banner" is played at football games, but when it comes to the personal hardship stuff I generally just suck it up and go on. I had been hurt worse in my life, and I hadn't cried. If I cried now, it would be because I felt sorry for myself, which I did, but I didn't want to show it. It was bad enough that I looked like roadkill; I refused to add sniveling to my current list of unattractive qualities.

If I ever got my hands on the bitch who had caused this, I'd strangle her.

"We can talk about this later," Mom said. "She needs to rest, not rehash everything. Y'all go home, I'll stay with her tonight. That's an order."

Wyatt doesn't take orders well, even from my mom, and she generally scares the hell out of him. "I'm staying, too," he said with that no-nonsense cop tone of his.

Even with my eyes half-closed I could see them squaring off. At any other time I would have watched the battle with interest, but all I wanted now was some peace and quiet. "I don't need anyone to stay with me. You all have work tomorrow, so all of you go home. I'm okay, honest." Note: When someone says "honest" they're usually lying, just like I was.

"We'll both stay," Wyatt said, ignoring my brave offer and reassurance. I glanced down to see if I had a visible body, since everyone was acting as if I wasn't there. First I lay in the grungy parking lot for what felt like an hour without anyone noticing me, and now I was certain that, though I was speaking, no one was hearing me.

"I must be invisible," I muttered to myself.

Dad patted my hand. "No, we're all just really worried," he said quietly, cutting right through my bravado. He had a knack for doing that, but then he had a keen instinct concerning me, maybe because I'm so much like Mom. I'm afraid Wyatt has the same instinct, which will be fine when we've been married thirty-something years the way Mom and Dad have, but while we were still jockeying for position that sort of put me at a disadvantage and I had to stay on my toes. In this Wyatt is light-years ahead of Jason, my ex-husband, who never saw beyond the blond hair and tight ass — his own, by the way.

Jason is one of those people who is like a Slinky; you always smile when you think of watching him fall down the stairs.

Anyway, back to the hospital room. Mom quickly got everyone sorted out. Dad and my sisters were sent on their way, because it was almost two a.m. and no one had had any sleep. She and Wyatt were both showing the strain, with that tight, bruised look around the eyes — and they still looked way better than the other occupant of the room, namely me.

A nurse came in to see if I was asleep, and to wake me up if I was. I wasn't, so she took my blood pressure and pulse and left, with a cheerful promise to be back in two hours or less. Other than the sickening headache, that's the worst part about having a concussion: they — meaning the medical staff — don't want you to sleep. Or rather, it's okay if you sleep, as long as they can wake you up and you know where you are and stuff like that. What this means is, by the time they get finished taking vitals and asking you questions, by the time you get settled down and doze back off, a nurse is breezing through the door again to start the whole routine all over. I foresaw a long and unrestful night.

Wyatt offered Mom the chair that opened into a narrow, uncomfortable bed and she took it without argument, opting for whatever fitful sleep she could get. He pulled the tall visitor's chair to my bedside and sat down, reaching through the rail to hold my hand. My heartbeat skittered and jumped when he did that, because I love him so much and he knew how much I needed even that small, silent communication.

"Get some rest if you can," he murmured.

"What about you?"

"I can nap right here. I'm used to odd hours and uncomfortable chairs."

That was true — he was after all a cop. I squeezed his fingers and tried to get comfortable, which really wasn't possible because of the way my head was pounding and my various scrapes were burning. But I closed my eyes anyway, and my old knack of being able to sleep anywhere, anytime, kicked in.

I awoke in the darkness; after I'd gone to sleep, Wyatt had turned out the dim light. I lay there listening to the breathing rhythms of two sleeping people: Mom at the foot of the bed, Wyatt on my right. It was a comforting sound. I couldn't see the clock to know how long I'd slept, but it didn't matter, because I wasn't going anywhere.

My head still hurt as much as before, but the nausea was marginally better. I began

65

thinking of everything I needed to do: call Lynn and arrange for her to handle Great Bods on her own for at least a couple of days, get Siana to water my plants, get my car retrieved from the mall, and other pesky details. I must have stirred, because Wyatt immediately sat up and reached for my hand. "Are you okay?" he whispered, so he wouldn't wake Mom. "You didn't sleep long, less than an hour."

"Just thinking," I whispered back.

"About what?"

"Everything I need to do."

"You don't need to do anything. Just tell me, and I'll take care of it."

I had to smile to myself, which was the only way I could smile since it was dark and he couldn't see me. "That's sort of what I was thinking, trying to remember everything I need to get you to do."

He gave a faint snort. "I should have figured."

Because it was dark, I got the courage to continue. "I was also thinking that I don't know how you could look at the mess I am and ever want me again." I kept my voice very low, because, hello, my mother was right there in the room, but I was listening to her breathing with one ear and it hadn't changed, so she was still asleep.

Wyatt was silent a moment, just long enough for me to start feeling sick to my stomach, as if I needed that on top of how sick I already felt, then he gently stroked a finger down my arm. "I always want you," he murmured, his voice as warm and dark as the room. "How you look at any given time doesn't have a lot to do with it. It's you, not your body — though I like the hell out of your ass, and your tits, and your sassy mouth, and all the parts in between."

"What about my legs?" I prompted. Man, was I feeling better. I was improving by the minute. If he kept talking, I'd be walking out of this joint in another half hour.

He gave a low laugh. "I like them, too. I especially like them around my waist."

"Shhh," I hissed. "Mom's right over there."

"She's asleep." He lifted my hand and pressed a warm, damp kiss into my palm.

"You wish," came the sharp comment from the foot of the bed.

After a startled moment Wyatt began laughing, and he said, "Yes, ma'am, I do."

I love that man. I was considerably cheered by our little dark-time talk, which was a relief, because it's a lot of work to feel sorry for yourself. I squeezed his hand and happily went back to sleep. So what if my head still hurt? Everything was okay.

I hadn't been asleep more than ten minutes when a nurse came in and turned on the lights to ask if I was awake. Figures.

CHAPTER FIVE

Wyatt left shortly after dawn to go home, shower and change clothes, and then head to work, where I figured he would spend more time than he should looking at parking lot tapes trying to get a tag number for the Buick. He'd gotten some more sleep, though anything longer than a short nap was difficult with a nurse coming in every so often to make certain I wasn't dying from a brain bleed. I wasn't — a relief — but neither was I getting much sleep.

Mom stirred around seven, left the room and came back with a cup of coffee that smelled heavenly — but which she didn't offer to me — and got busy on her cell phone. I did the same, calling Lynn at Great Bods to inform her of my latest mishap and to make arrangements for her to fill in for me for at least the next couple of days. My head hurt so much, I figured it would take me at least that long to be functional.

Talking and eavesdropping at the same time is an art, one that requires practice. Mom can do it effortlessly. When I'd been a teenager, I'd been as good as she was at it, out of necessity. I was still good, but out of practice. From the conversations I overheard, I learned she had a closing on a house that day and was showing another house, and she was postponing the showing until later in the day. She also called Siana, but either she didn't mention Siana by name or I totally missed it, because I was surprised when Siana entered the room around eight-thirty, wearing a great-fitting pair of jeans and a slinky little chemise top with sequined straps, plus a leather blazer draped over her shoulders. That was so not what she would wear to work, that I knew she'd taken the day off. Siana's a lawyer — as I've mentioned — very junior in a firm full of rainmakers, but senior in attitude. I didn't think she'd stick with the firm for much longer, because she'd do better on her own. Siana was born to have her own firm and be a raging success. Who wouldn't hire her? She was brilliant, had killer dimples, and was ruthless, all of which are great things to look for in a lawyer.

"Why aren't you working?" I asked.

"I'm taking Mom's place so she can close on a house." She settled in the chair where

Wyatt had spent the night, eating an apple.

I eyed the apple. The hospital hadn't offered me anything to eat, just some crushed ice, evidently holding off on feeding me until some doctor somewhere decided I wouldn't need emergency brain surgery. Said doctor was taking his or her own sweet time, and I was starving. Hey! Surprised, I did a quick check of myself. Yep, the nausea had diminished. Maybe I couldn't handle eggs, bacon, and toast just yet, but I could certainly handle yogurt and a banana.

"Stop staring at my apple," Siana said placidly. "You can't have it. Apple envy is an ugly thing."

Automatically I defended myself. "I don't have apple envy. I was thinking more along the lines of a banana. And you didn't have to take off work, I should be released sometime this morning. It was just for overnight."

" 'Overnight' doesn't mean the same thing to doctors that it does to real people," Mom said, completely dismissing the reality of the entire medical profession. "The emergency room doctor won't be the one who releases you, anyway. Another one will eventually look at your test results, eventually look at *you,* and with any luck you'll be home by late this afternoon."

She was probably right. This was the first

time I'd actually been admitted to a hospital, though I'd visited the emergency department a few times and had found that time definitely had a different meaning there. "A few minutes" invariably meant a couple of hours, which was okay if you knew that, but if someone went in expecting to be seen literally "in a few minutes" she was bound to be frustrated and annoyed.

"Regardless of that, I don't need a babysitter." I felt honor bound to point that out, though we all knew I didn't want to be left alone, they weren't going to leave me alone, and discussion was fruitless. Though sometimes I enjoy fruitless discussions.

"Deal with it," Siana said, grinning at me and flashing her dimples. "I thought the firm needed a day without me, anyway. I'm being taken for granted, and I don't like it." She took another bite of her apple, then tossed the core in the trash. "I've turned off my cell phone." She looked pleased with herself, which meant the people who had been taking her for granted would probably try several times during the day to get in touch with her.

"I have to leave," Mom said, leaning over to kiss my forehead. She looked great, despite a night of very little sleep and her worrying about me. "But I'll check in during the day. Let's see, you need clothes to go home in. I'll swing by and pick them up before I go home, then bring them at lunch. No way will you be released before lunch. I'm also hot on the trail of a wedding cake maker, I've located an arbor, and late this afternoon I'm going to Roberta's house" — Roberta is Wyatt's mom — "and we're going to brainstorm emergency procedures if the weather is bad. Everything's under control, so don't worry."

"I have to worry; that's the bride's job. There's no way all the marks from the road rash will be gone by then." Even when the scabs were gone — euuu, scabs, how lovely — there would be pale pink marks left on my skin.

"You'll need long sleeves or some kind of wrap anyway, since it'll be October." North Carolina weather in October is usually wonderful, but it can turn chilly in a heartbeat. She examined my face with narrowed eyes. "I think your face will be fine by then, it isn't scraped much at all. If it isn't, that's what makeup is for."

I hadn't yet seen a mirror to assess the damage for myself, so I asked, "What about my hair? How does it look?"

"Pretty bad, right now," Siana answered. "I brought shampoo and a blow dryer."

I adore her. She has my priorities straight.

Mom assessed the stitches in my hairline — my former hairline — and the shaved patch. "It's manageable," she pronounced. "A change in hairstyle will cover the shaved part, which really isn't very big."

All right! Things were looking up.

A nurse about my age breezed into the room, fresh and crisp in pink scrubs, which looked great with her complexion. She was a pretty woman — very pretty, with almost classic features — but she suffered from a really bad dye job. When it comes to hair color, "bad" almost always equals "do-it-yourself." This particular dye job was a sort of flat brown, making me wonder what her real hair color was, because who colors her hair brown? My own hair crisis was making me very aware of hair, not that I'm ever really *un*aware, but my level of attention had been jacked up. When she smiled and came closer, placing cool fingers on my pulse, I studied her brows and lashes. No help there — her brows were brown, and her extra-long lashes were tinted with mascara. Maybe she'd gone prematurely gray. I envied the eyelashes and approved the mascara, which reminded me that my own mascara was probably giving me raccoon eyes by now.

"How are you feeling?" she asked, keeping

her fingers on my pulse and her gaze on her wristwatch. She was another multitasker, counting and talking at the same time.

"Better. Plus I'm hungry."

"That's a good sign." She smiled and flicked a glance up at me. "I'll see what I can do about some food for you."

Her eyes were that great mixture of green and hazel, and I thought she must look really hot when she fixed herself up for a night on the town. She was calm and collected, but there was also a controlled spark of fire in her that made me think all the single doctors, and maybe a few of the married ones, were probably doing their best to hook up with her.

"Any idea what time the doctor makes the rounds?" I asked.

She gave me a rueful smile and shook her head. "The time varies, depending on whether or not he has any emergencies. Don't tell me you aren't happy with our hospitality?"

"You mean other than the no-food thing? And waking me up every time I doze off to make certain I'm not unconscious? And shaving my hair *twenty-eight days before my wedding?* Other than that, I've had a really good time."

She laughed out loud. "Twenty-eight days,

huh? I was absolutely nuts for the last two months before my wedding. What a time to have an accident!"

Mom had retrieved my keys from my bag and waved on her way out. I waved back, then picked up the conversation. "It could be worse. I could be really hurt instead of just some scrapes and one little cut."

"The doctors must think your condition is a little worse than that, or you wouldn't be here." She sounded a little chiding, but then nurses probably ran into reluctant patients all the time — and, really, I wasn't *reluctant* exactly; I was just possessed of a sense of urgency. Twenty-eight days were left, and the clock was ticking.

Since presumably she'd read my chart, I didn't see the need to tell her that an overnight stay for observation didn't indicate a serious injury. Maybe she just wanted me to worry a little bit so I wouldn't bug her or the other nurses about when I was getting out. I wasn't in a bugging mood, anyway; if I hadn't had so much to do, I'd have been very content to lie in a hospital bed and let people bring things to me. The nausea had eased, but the pounding in my head hadn't. I'd had to go to the bathroom twice, and moving wasn't fun, but neither had it been as bad as I'd feared it would be.

The nurse — she probably had a name tag attached to her pocket, but the way she was leaning over the bed I couldn't see it — turned the sheet back to check out all my scrapes and bruises, all the while asking questions about my wedding. Where it would be, what my gown looked like, that sort of thing.

"It's going to be at Wyatt's mother's house," I said happily, glad of something to distract me from my headache. "In her flower garden. Her mums are gorgeous, and I usually don't like mums because they usually come with dead bodies attached. If it rains, which isn't that likely in October, we'll just move inside."

"Do you like her?" Her tone was a little clipped, which made me think she had trouble with her own mother-in-law. That was too bad; in-law trouble could really hurt a marriage. I had liked Jason's mother well enough, but I adored Wyatt's mother. She gave me inside information and was generally on my side in the man-woman things.

"She's great. She introduced me to Wyatt, and now she's giving herself big pats on the back because she said she thought from the first we'd be a good match."

"Must be nice, to have a mother-in-law who likes you," she muttered.

I started to suggest that maybe the bad dye job was a bit off-putting, but stopped myself. Maybe a do-it-yourself home job was all she could afford, though nurses generally make decent money. For all I knew, she could have three or four kids at home to feed and clothe, and her husband could be handicapped, or just plain no good. There had to be *some* reason for the hair.

She peeled back the bandage over the biggest scrape on my left thigh, and the peeling-back *hurt*. I gasped, knotting my fists against the pain.

"Sorry," she said, peering at the scrape. "This is a good one. What were you doing, riding a motorcycle?"

I managed to unclench my teeth. "No, some psycho bitch tried to run me down in the mall parking lot last night."

She glanced up, eyebrows arching. "Do you know who it was?"

"No, but Wyatt is probably looking at the mall and parking lot security tapes right now, trying to get a license plate number and I.D." If he could get them without a warrant, that is, because I doubted a judge would issue a warrant; the incident just wasn't serious enough.

She nodded and replaced the bandage over

the scrape. "Must be handy, having a cop for a boyfriend."

"Sometimes." Unless he was making me go to the police station when I didn't want to, or tracking me down through charges to my credit card. He can be a tad ruthless in getting what he wants. Of course, I couldn't complain too much, because what he'd wanted when he did those things was me — and he got me, too. Even with the headache from Hell, the memory of how he'd got me made me shiver. His testosterone almost reached the toxic level, but the benefits . . . oh, my, the benefits were wonderful.

The nurse made a note of something on a small pad she fished from one of her pockets, then said, "You're doing fine. I'll see what I can do about some food for you," as she left the room.

Siana hadn't said a word the entire time, which wasn't unusual; she likes to size up people before she commits herself to conversation. After the door closed, though, she said, "What's up with that hair?"

Siana could be arguing a case before the Supreme Court — which she hadn't, yet — and she would notice the hair of everyone in the courtroom, including that of the justices, which is a pretty scary thought when you look at some of them. Jenni and I are the same way, and we all got that gene directly from Mom, who got it from her mother. I've often wondered what Grammy's mother was like. I said that once to Wyatt and he'd shuddered. He'd met Grammy once, at her birthday party a month ago; I think she either impressed him or scared the hell out of him, but he'd held his ground, and after the party Dad had given him a double whiskey.

I don't see what's so bad about Grammy, except that she can out-Mom Mom, which, all right, is kind of scary. But I want to be just like her when I get old. I want to stay stylish, I want to drive sharp cars, and I want my children and grandchildren to pay proper attention to me. When I get *really* old, though, I'm going to trade my sharp car for the largest one I can find, and I'm going to hunch down in the seat until my little blue head is just peeking above the steering wheel, then I'm going to drive really slow and flip the bird at everyone who honks at me. It's plans like this that make me look forward to old age.

If I can live that long, that is. Other people kept coming up with different plans for me. It's annoying.

I waited, but no food magically appeared. Siana and I chatted. After a while another nurse came in and took my vitals. I asked about my food. She checked my chart, said "I'll see what I can do," and left.

Siana and I figured there would be a wait, and we decided to wash my hair. Thank goodness stitches no longer have to be kept dry, because there was no way I could go a week with dried blood and gunk giving me a gruesome Mohawk. The stitches weren't a problem, the concussion was. As long as I moved very slowly, though, the headache didn't spike. But I didn't want just my hair washed, I wanted *me* washed. Siana snagged a nurse who said, sure, the bandages could come off for a shower, and I carefully, but happily, showered and shampooed. I also let the bandages come off *in* the shower, instead of pulling them off.

Afterward Siana blow-dried my hair; she didn't bother with any actual styling, but that didn't matter because my hair is straight. Just being clean made me feel better.

Still no food.

I was beginning to think the hospital staff was in on those alternate plans for me and intended to starve me to death, and Siana was about to go down to the cafeteria and get something for me herself, when finally a tray was delivered. The coffee was lukewarm but I seized it gratefully, drinking half of it before I lifted the metal cover off my plate. Fake scrambled eggs, cold toast, and limp bacon stared up at me. Siana and I looked at each other, then I shrugged. "I'm starving. This will do." But I made a mental note to write the hospital administrator about the culinary offerings here. Sick people need food that will at least *tempt* them to eat.

After I'd eaten about half the food my outraged taste buds overcame the weakening whines from my stomach, and I replaced the cover over the plate so I wouldn't have to look at the eggs. Cold eggs are revolting. My headache had eased some, and I realized part of it had been due to caffeine deprivation.

Because I felt better, I began fretting about the passing time. No doctor had yet been in to see me, and it was almost ten-thirty, according to the clock on the wall.

"Maybe no doctor has been assigned to my case," I mused. "Maybe I'm just here, forgotten."

"Maybe you should get a regular doctor," Siana pointed out.

"Do you have one?"

She looked guilty. "Does a gynecologist count?"

"I don't see why not. I have one of those, too." Hey, you have to get your prescription for birth control pills somewhere. "Maybe I should call her."

A hospital stay is boring. Siana turned on the television and we tried to find something to watch. Neither of us is ever home during the day so we're unfamiliar with daytime fare. It says something when *The Price Is Right* is the best we could find, but at least it entertained us. Siana and I both did better than all the contestants, but, hey, shopping is a talent.

The noise from the hall was a distraction, because the lady who'd brought in my breakfast tray had left the door half-open, but we'd left it that way because the circulating air kept the room a little less stuffy. The bright blue sky outside my window told me summer hadn't quite loosened its grip yet, even though the calendar said autumn had officially arrived. I wanted to be out in that sunshine. I wanted to be out looking for my wedding dress. *Where was a doctor, any doctor?*

The Price Is Right was over. I said to Siana, "How did your date go last night?"

"Slowly."

I gave her a sympathetic look and she sighed. "He was a nice guy, but . . . no spark. I want sparks. I want a whole box of sparklers. I want what you have with Wyatt, some guy looking at me as if he could eat me up, and I want him to."

Just using the words *Wyatt* and *eat* in the same sentence made me feel warm and squirmy. No doubt about it, he had me programmed.

"I waited a long time for Wyatt. I even waited for two years after he dumped me." That was still a sore point with me, that he'd dumped me after just three dates because he thought I was high maintenance.

"You didn't exactly *wait*," she said, amused. "You went out on dates. A lot of them, as I remember."

Out of the corner of my eye I saw a flash of movement at the door. The movement stopped. No one came into the room.

"But I didn't sleep with any of them," I pointed out. "That's waiting."

Wyatt still didn't enter the room. He was staying just out of sight, listening. I *knew* it was him; I'd figured he would come visit around lunch, if he could get free. He had a sneaky streak that was a mile wide; he was such a cop, he couldn't resist eavesdropping just to see if he could hear anything interesting.

I caught Siana's eye, narrowed my gaze, and indicated the door. She gave a quick little grin and said, "You always said you wanted to use his SDS."

I hadn't, but the Southern Women's Code said that eavesdroppers of the male variety should always get their ears full. Siana's quick thinking delighted me. "His SDS was what interested me from the first. I really wanted access to it."

"It must be impressive."

"It is, but the responsiveness is at least as important. There's no point in having a large SDS if it won't do what I want it to do — sort of like a bank."

She muffled a snort of laughter. "I'm looking for a great SDS, too. I see no reason why I can't fall in love with a guy who has one and can handle my requirements."

"I don't either. I — Come in," I called, interrupting myself to answer Wyatt's abbreviated, belated rap on the door. He pushed the door the rest of the way open and came in, his expression set and unreadable. Anger made his green eyes even brighter, and I had to swallow an impulse to laugh. We hadn't been together all that long, but from the beginning getting the best of him had been difficult.

Siana was smiling as she got to her feet. "Great," she said. "I need to stretch my legs. I'm going down to the cafeteria for a bite to eat. Want me to bring something back?"

"No, I'm good," he growled. "Thanks."

The *thanks* was tacked on as an after-thought. Wyatt was mad, and he was determined to wring the truth about his SDS out of me as soon as Siana was gone. He didn't shy away from a fight, like most men did, and my having a slight concussion didn't mean he'd cut me any slack.

He firmly closed the door behind her, not noticing the sly wink she gave me just as she slipped out. Then he stalked to my bedside, all aggressive, menacing male. His dark brows were lowered in a fierce glare that he pinned on me.

"All right," he said evenly. "I want to hear all about how you were only interested in me because you wanted access to my SDS."

I thought *Wyatt* and *eat* and felt my cheeks begin to turn pink. Yep, it was foolproof. Wasn't that a useful thing to find out? I squirmed in delight. "Oh, you heard that?"I asked, glancing away from him and trying my best to look guilty.

"I heard." His tone was grim. He seized my chin; he didn't jerk my head, because even as angry as he was he was mindful of my concussion, but he made it plain he intended for me to look at him. I met his angry gaze, and let my own eyes go wide.

"I didn't say I was *only* interested in your SDS."

"But you wanted access to it."

I batted my eyelashes at him, thinking it was time to throw him a hint. "In a big way. I thought you knew."

"How could I know?" His tone was even darker, like a thundercloud about to break. "I —" Then he stopped, his gaze narrowing on me as the fluttering eyelashes and big innocent eyes registered with him. "Just what the hell *is* an SDS?"

I went with just the big eyes, savoring the moment. "Sperm delivery system."

CHAPTER SIX

He stalked away from me and stood looking out the window, his hands on his hips as he took deep, controlled breaths. I watched him, almost fizzing with glee. Teasing him like this was almost more fun than teasing him the other way — almost, because the pay-off was better with the other kind of teasing.

Finally he said, "You little shit," and swung around to face me. The glitter in his eyes promised retribution.

I grinned at him.

With deceptive mildness he asked, "You and Siana were discussing my dick?"

"Only because you were eavesdropping. I thought you should hear something interesting, since you went to so much trouble."

He didn't look the least embarrassed at having been caught, maybe because snooping was his stock-in-trade. Instead he came to the bed, bracing his hands on either side of me as he leaned down. If he thought I'd feel uneasy being sort of surrounded and trapped that way, I wasn't. For one thing, this was Wyatt. For another, well, this was Wyatt; I liked being surrounded and trapped by him. Fun and interesting things usually happened when he was this close.

I didn't raise my head from the pillow, but I put my hand on his face, feeling the hard structure of jaw and cheek, the warmth of his skin, the prickles of his beard even though he'd shaved just a few hours before. "Gotcha," I said smugly. Yes, I know it isn't nice to gloat, partly because Wyatt isn't a grin-and-bear-it sort of guy. He'd think of some way to pay me back, even if it was something as excruciating as finagling me into making a bet he could make certain I lost and forcing me to watch the World Series. I *so* don't like baseball.

He gave me a smug smile in return, which put me on alert. "So you didn't sleep with anyone for the two years we were broke up, huh? You were waiting for me."

"Not really. I'm just picky." Damn the man, he *would* find some way to turn this to his advantage.

"You were impressed by my delivery system."

"I said that stuff because I knew you were listening."

"You wanted access to it. You wanted to use it, if I recall correctly."

That's one of the bad things about cops: they remember stuff. He could probably quote verbatim my conversation with Siana. Besides, in various ways I'd made it plain I was *very* fond of his SDS. Please. If I don't like something, it does *not* go in my mouth — or anywhere else in my body, if you get my drift.

Okay, sometimes the only way to regain control of a situation is to completely and utterly surrender. I smiled at him and trailed my hand from his face down his chest, down his stomach, until I was cradling his SDS in my palm. I was delighted to feel that he already had a semi-erection. That's my Wyatt; mention sex and he's ready. Great, huh? "You recall very correctly. I wanted it, and now I have it." I shivered a little, because touching him was doing a number on me, too.

He leaned over me, his breathing faster, his eyes darkening as he pushed harder against my hand. There was no "semi" about him now, he was hard and ready. Then he said "Fuck" in a strained voice, straightening and moving away from me.

"Well, yeah," I said. Hadn't it been obvious?

He shot a burning glance at me as he turned back to the window. "You have a concussion," he said very tersely.

Groaning, I saw the problem. No jostling around for me, for the next few days at least, and if anyone has figured out how to have sex without even a little jostling I wish you'd let me in on the secret. No sex yesterday, no sex today, no sex tomorrow — no sex for as long as this headache lasted, which was probably several more days. Now I was *really* pissed at that psycho bitch in the Buick, for causing this unexpected deprivation — not that an expected deprivation would be any better, because it wasn't as if you could stock up on orgasms and keep them in the pantry until you needed one.

Which reminded me of something, and what better time to broach the subject than when I was hurt and he was in protective mode? It wasn't as if I had anything better to do. "I need to redo your house."

That brought him swinging around. The crotch of his pants was still tented, but his attention was riveted on me. From the wariness in his gaze you'd have thought I'd said, "I have a gun, and it's aimed at your heart."

He stared at me for several seconds, running our conversation through his mind. Finally he said, "I give up. How did we get from talking about my SDS and your concussion to you wanting to redo my house?"

"I was thinking about pantries." That wasn't all I'd been thinking about, but I didn't want to get into the whole stocking up on orgasms thing, when I was temporarily on the sidelines. Besides, he didn't need to know every little detail of how I got to where I was, conversationally speaking.

He gave up on trying to make the connection. "What about pantries?"

"You don't have one."

"Sure I do. It's that little room off the kitchen, remember?"

"You have your office in there, so it isn't a pantry. And your house is all wrong, anyway. Your furniture is all wrong."

His eyes narrowed. "What's wrong with my house? It's fine. It has good furniture."

"It has *guy* furniture."

"I'm a guy," he pointed out. "What other kind would I have?"

"But I'm not a guy." How could he be so oblivious to something so obvious? "I need girl stuff. So either I redo your house, or we'll have to move somewhere else."

"I like my house." He was beginning to get that digging-in-his-heels expression that men get when they don't want to do something. "I have things just where I want them."

I gave him a speaking look, which made my head hurt more, because you sort of have to roll your eyes to do a proper speaking look. "At what point is it supposed to become *our* house?"

"When you move in." He said it as if that were the simplest, most obvious conclusion in the world. For him, I guess it was.

"But you don't want me touching anything, buying a chair that fits *me*, fixing up an office for me, or anything like that?" My raised eyebrows told him what I thought of *that* idea — and again, raising my eyebrows hurt, but when you don't use Botox it's really hard to talk without any expression. For the next few days, though, I thought I might try really hard to imitate Nancy Pelosi.

He scowled. "Shit." He saw the point of the conversation, which was that no way in hell was I satisfied with the status quo regarding his furniture, and if he wanted me living with him some adjustments had to be made, but he didn't like it. His eyes did that narrowed, piercing thing again. "My recliner stays where it is. So does my television."

I started to shrug, then stopped when I remembered that moving was not a good thing. "That's fine. It isn't as if I'll be in there."

"What?" He not only wasn't pleased to hear that, he was getting pissed.

"Think about it. Do we watch the same things on television? No. You want to watch baseball; I hate baseball. You watch *all* sports. I like football and basketball, period. I like decorating shows, and you'd rather have splinters shoved under your fingernails than watch a decorating show. So if you want me not to go mad and kill you, I'll have to have my own television and a place to watch it."

The truth is, I don't watch much television, except for college football, which I'll actually go out of my way to catch. For one thing, some nights I don't get home until after nine o'clock, and even when I do I usually have paperwork. There are a couple of shows I'll TiVo and watch on Sundays, but for the most part I don't bother. That doesn't mean I'm willing to fight Wyatt for use of the television whenever I *do* want to watch something, and even less does it mean I'm willing to give up those few shows. Not that he needs to know how little I watch; it's the principle of the thing.

"All right," he said grudgingly, because after all fair is fair. "Though I'd rather have you with me."

"We'd have to watch what I want to watch half the time."

And what a disaster *that* would be. He knew it as well as I did. After a pause he abandoned that idea and gave in. "Which room will you use? One of the upstairs bedrooms?"

"No, because then I'd have to redo it again and move everything in a few years when the kids get their own bedrooms."

His expression didn't soften, but it filled with heat — the I-want-to-get-you-naked kind of heat, not the mad kind. "There are four bedrooms," he pointed out, thinking of the process of making babies to fill those bedrooms.

"I know. We'll have the master, we'll have two kids — I'm not ruling out three, but I think probably two — and we'll have a guest bedroom. I'm thinking the living room will work out best. Who needs a formal living room? Oh, and I'll need to redo all the window treatments. No offense, but your taste in window treatments sucks."

The hands were back on his hips. "What else?" he asked in a resigned tone.

Huh. He was giving in easier than I'd thought. Took some of the fun out of it. "Paint. Not that you weren't smart to go with neutrals, since decorating so isn't your thing," I added hastily. "It's just that decorating *is* my thing, so now you can relax and leave all those decisions to me. Trust me, a little color on the walls will do wonders for the house. Plants will, too." He had *no* houseplants, a point I'd already made. How could any sane human live without houseplants?

"I've already bought you a plant."

"You bought me a *shrub.* And it's planted outside, where it belongs. Don't worry, you don't have to do anything with the plants, other than move them where I tell you to move them, when I tell you."

"Why don't you just put them where you want them and leave them there?"

Was that a male point of view, or what? "Some I will. Some I'll put outside on the porch during warm weather and only bring them in for the winter. Just trust me on the plants, okay?"

He couldn't see how I could do anything sneaky with plants, so grudgingly he nodded. "Okay, we can have a few plants."

A few? He was so clueless. I loved him anyway.

"And some rugs."

"I have carpeting."

"The rugs go on top of the carpeting."

He shoved his hand through his hair in raw frustration. "Why in hell would you put a rug on top of carpet?"

"For looks, silly. And there should be a rug under the breakfast room table." The breakfast nook floor had the same tiles that were on the kitchen floor, and they were cold. A rug for there would be one of my first purchases. I smiled at him; smiling didn't hurt. "That's it." For now, anyway.

He grinned suddenly. "Okay, that sounds fairly painless."

A horrible suspicion began to form. Had I been played? Had he been *messing* with me? Now, as a general rule, at least half of what I said was because I enjoyed messing with him, pushing his buttons and trying to get a rise out of him, but that's part of the fun of dealing with a man as alpha as he was. Trust me on this. Teasing Woody Allen wouldn't be half the thrill that teasing, say, Hugh Jackman would be.

But just because I enjoyed pushing his buttons didn't mean turnabout is fair play.

"Have you been talking to Daddy?" I asked suspiciously.

"Of course I have. I know I'm taking on a big job, marrying you, so I'll take all the expert advice I can get. He told me to pick my battles, not to start feeling territorial over crap I don't really care about. As long as you leave my recliner and television alone, I'm okay."

I didn't know whether to sulk or feel relieved. On the one hand, Daddy wouldn't steer him wrong, and my life would be a lot easier if I didn't have to do all of Wyatt's training myself. On the other hand, well, I'm a button-pusher.

"You can just write a check for me to get started," I said cheerfully. "I'll let you know when I need more. I know this great carpenter, and though he probably won't be able to get started right away I can meet with him next week and show him what I want and let him get started on the plans."

He stilled, going wary again. "A check? A carpenter? What plans?"

One great big button, duly pushed. Life was good.

"You do remember how this conversation started, don't you?"

"Yeah. You and Siana were talking about my dick."

"Not that conversation, *this* conversation. The redecorating one."

"Got it. I still haven't made the connection between my dick and window treatments," he said wryly, "but I'll go with it for now. What about how this conversation started?"

98

"A pantry. You don't have one. I need one."

An incredulous look entered his eyes. "You're evicting me from my office? And you expect *me* to pay for it?"

"I expect you to pay for the lion's share, yeah. You have more money than I do."

He snorted. "I drive a Chevrolet. You drive a Mercedes."

I waved that away. Details. "I'm not *evicting* you. I'm moving you into a new office. We'll divvy up the space of the living room." It was a big room, and I didn't need all of that space for a home office for myself. The biggest portion of it, yes, but not *all* of it. "You need a bigger office anyway, you have so much crammed in the pantry you can barely get yourself in there."

That was nothing but the truth. It was a mystery to me why, when he'd done such an extensive remodeling of the house when he first bought it, he hadn't included an actual office for himself. The only explanation was that he was a guy. At least he'd put in an adequate number of bathrooms, though that could have been the building contractor's idea; certainly the idea for the pantry hadn't come from Wyatt.

I watched him wrap his mind around the idea of a bigger office, and realize I was right

— he needed more space, and I needed a pantry. "All right, all right. Do whatever you want, and I'll pay for it." He pinched the bridge of his nose. "I came here to tell you about the security tapes, and somehow I end up spending twenty thousand dollars, at least," he muttered, mostly to himself.

Twenty thousand? He wished. I kept that part to myself, though. He'd find out soon enough. "You got the parking-lot tapes?" I was a bit incredulous. "I didn't think you would, since she didn't hit me. Did the mall just hand them over?"

"As a matter of fact, yeah, but I could have gotten them anyway."

"You'd have needed a warrant, and no crime was committed."

"Reckless endangerment is a crime, honey."

"You didn't say anything about reckless endangerment last night."

He shrugged. In his view, cop stuff was his business, in sort of the same way keeping the lap pool at Great Bods properly chlorinated was mine; I didn't discuss every detail with him, and come to think of it, he discussed very little cop business with me. I didn't exactly agree, because cop business is way more interesting than pool chlorination, which was why I snooped through his files every now and then. Okay, whenever I got the chance.

I waved away his lack of communication, which, regarding his work, he had no intention of remedying anyway. "What did you find?"

"Not much," he admitted, frustration glinting in his eyes. "To begin with, the mall has an outdated system that uses tapes instead of being digital. The tape is worn out; I couldn't make out a tag number, just that the car was definitely a Buick. Our tech guys said the tape should have been replaced a month or so ago, it literally has holes in it. They couldn't pull anything really useful from it."

"The mall doesn't replace the tapes with new ones on a regular basis?" I asked indignantly. The *mall* was lax? I felt betrayed.

"A lot of places don't, at least until something happens. Then whoever is in charge of the surveillance system will catch hell, and for a while the tapes will be changed out the way they should be. You wouldn't believe some of the crap we're given to work with." His tone was hard. Wyatt didn't cut much slack for people who didn't do what they should.

He reached under the sheet and clasped the inside of my thigh, his hand hard and slightly rough, and oh so warm. "She missed you by inches," he said roughly. "I damn near had a heart attack, seeing how close it was. She wasn't trying to just scare you, she literally tried to kill you."

CHAPTER SEVEN

Mom came in shortly afterward with my clothes, hanging them in the minuscule closet and dropping my keys back in my purse. "I can't stay," she said, looking frustrated and harried and incredibly beautiful, because that's just Mom, she can't look any other way. "How are you feeling, sweetheart?"

"Better," I said, because it was true. I'd managed to eat those God-awful eggs, hadn't I? The "better" was qualified by a "marginally," but I'd take what I could get. "Thanks for bringing my stuff. Now go do your thing, and don't worry about me."

She gave me a wry, "yeah, sure" look. "Has a doctor been in yet?"

"Nope."

Her look of frustration increased. "Where's Siana?"

"She went to the cafeteria when I got here," Wyatt said, checking his watch. "She's been gone about twenty minutes."

"I can't stay until she gets back, I have to leave five minutes ago." She leaned down and kissed my forehead, gave Wyatt's cheek a buzz as she breezed past, and was out the door, tossing "Call my cell if you need me" over her shoulder as she disappeared from view.

"You didn't mention the parking-lot tapes," Wyatt observed. He was still working on deciphering our family dynamics. While he went with the belief that cold, hard reality is the most stable operating platform, Mom and I shared a tendency to go off on tangents so we wouldn't have to think about the bad stuff until we'd processed it and were ready to deal. I'd had all night to process, plus I'd *been* there and knew exactly how much danger I'd been in, so I'd already explored a few tangents and was now solidly squared with the cold hard stuff.

"She knows someone tried to run me over. There's no point in telling her how close the bitch came to actually doing it. She's already stressed, and that would just worry her more." The incident was *over* . . . except for the getting-well part. There was no way to track her down, so everyone might as well forget and move on. I was; I had to. I had shopping to do! This had already cost me a day, would likely cost me at least a couple more, and I didn't have the time to spare.

Wyatt checked his watch again. His days were incredibly busy, so I knew he'd been pushing to find time to come to the hospital. I reached for his hand. "You need to go, too." Hey, I can be understanding.

"Yeah, I do. You have your key to my house with you, right?"

"It's in my purse. Why?"

"So you can get in, if I can't shake free to come pick you up when you're released. Siana can drive you, can't she?"

"That isn't a problem, but I'm not going to your house, I'm going home." I saw his brows start to draw together and squeezed his hand. "I know you're feeling protective and I'm not trying to be difficult, honest" — hard as that was to believe — "but all of my paperwork and things are at home. I may not feel like shopping, but I can do some things by phone and computer. I'm not an invalid, this time around, so I don't need someone to stay with me. I also promise not to drive myself anywhere." There. I couldn't be any more reasonable than that, could I?

He didn't like it, mainly because he wanted me at his house permanently, right now — or rather, two months ago, and he didn't deal well with not getting what he wanted.

Here's a word to the wise: if you want someone who's laid-back, unaggressive, and nonarrogant, don't even *look* at a cop. When the cop in question also happens to be a former pro football player, you just have to know going in that you're dealing with a personality that can kick ass and take names.

Sometimes, I admit, I deliberately try to get him going, just because it's so much fun, but this time I was on the level. He knew it, too, so he reined in his natural tendency to issue orders. "Okay. After work I'll go home and get my stuff. I don't know what time I'll get to your place, though, so make sure you have something to eat before Siana leaves."

"You don't have to stay with me, I'll be fine by myself," I said, because it was the polite thing to say.

"Yeah, right," he said with something that sounded suspiciously like a snort. He was smart enough that he didn't even *think* of listening to me. I would have been so pissed if he'd left me to fend for myself when I had a concussion. Oh, Siana could have stayed with me, but I sort of looked at it as Wyatt's duty, part of the package deal that we'd agreed to by getting engaged. I took care of him, he took care of me. Simple. Though of course so far he hadn't needed taking care of, unless you want to count erections in that category, but that was okay with me because I shudder at the thought of him being hurt in any way. I loved him so much I couldn't stand the thought of that, plus he'd probably be a horrible patient.

Anyway, I let the sarcastic comment pass, so he kissed me and left. Siana, with her exquisite timing, came sauntering into the room a few minutes after he'd gone. "How'd he take it?" she asked.

"I think he thought we really *were* discussing his dick, as he put it." I made a little face. "As far as being caught eavesdropping, that didn't bother him at all. But I managed to work it into an agreement that I could remodel and redecorate his house, so that's good."

A look of admiration crossed her face. "I'm not certain how you segued from eavesdropping to decorating, but the end result is what counts."

Once again, I didn't want to explain about orgasms in the pantry, so I just smiled. Sometimes a younger sister just needs to look up to her older sister.

We passed the afternoon watching soaps, which was interesting. Siana told me she had heard that nothing happened in soaps except on Fridays, and I think that must be true. We watched one attempted murder, one kidnapping, and probably fourteen couples have sex, an impressive tally for just two hours.

We were in the middle of *Oprah* when a doctor came in and introduced herself. She was in her mid-fifties, tired, and you could tell only her intense focus was getting her through her rounds, so I didn't give her any grief about not being there sooner. The I.D. badge clipped to the pocket of her white lab coat read "Tewanda Hardy, M.D." She checked my eyes, read my chart, asked a few questions, then told me the nurse would give me a list of instructions and I could go home. She was out of the room before I could say more than a hurried "thank you."

Finally!

Siana got my clothes out of the closet, and while she called both Mom and Wyatt to let them know I was going home, I carefully eased into the bathroom to change. The outfit Mom had brought, pants and a blouse, was a very soft, flowing linen and rayon blend that wouldn't rasp on any of my scrapes, and the blouse buttoned down the front so I didn't have to pull anything on over my head. Having on real clothes again made me feel much better, even though exerting myself that much made my headache worse. I don't know how I could describe myself as feeling better, but I did. Clothes will do that for me.

A nurse came by with some paperwork for me to sign, a list of don'ts until the headache was completely gone, and that was pretty much it. I already knew how to take care of scrapes. No meds were prescribed; I could take over-the-counter stuff for the headache, if needed. *If* needed? Had no one ever told the members of the medical profession how a concussion *felt?*

I had to be wheeled out in a wheelchair, of course, but that was fine with me. Siana had taken my shopping bags and purse with her when she went down to get her car and pull it around to the entrance — or exit, as the case may be. When she stopped under the portico the nurse pushed the wheelchair out through the double set of automatic doors and a rush of chilly air washed over me.

"It's cold," I said in disbelief. "No one told me we're having a cold snap!"

"A front rolled in early this morning," the nurse said helpfully, as if I actually needed telling now. "The temperature dropped over thirty degrees."

I always enjoyed the first real cold snap of the fall, but I'm usually better dressed for it. The air even smelled fall-like, with a crisp scent of dry leaves even though the trees hadn't yet begun to turn color. It was Friday, the night for high school football. Soon people would be heading for the stadiums, dressed in sweaters and jackets for the first time since spring. I hadn't made it to a football game since opening Great Bods, and suddenly I really missed the smells and sounds and excitement. Wyatt and I would have to make a point of going to a game this year, either high school or college, it didn't matter.

I would have to hire another staffer at Great Bods, someone capable of filling in for either me or Lynn, I realized. If things went as I planned, I'd be pregnant by Christmas. My life would soon be changing, and I couldn't wait.

Getting into Siana's car and out of the wind was a relief. "This makes me want a hot chocolate," I said as I buckled up.

"Sounds good. I'll make some for us while we wait for Wyatt."

She drove carefully, no sudden starts or stops, and we made it to my condo without any major explosions of pain. My car was parked in its spot under the portico, which meant that while she'd had my keys, Mom had arranged to collect my car from the mall parking lot. I'd thought of it the night before, but then forgotten to mention it when everyone was awake.

Wyatt called on my cell as we were walking in the door, and I stopped to fish the phone from my bag. "I'm home," I told him.

"Good. I got away earlier than I thought I would. I'm on my way home to get my stuff now, so I'll be there within the hour. I can pick up something for dinner, so does anything appeal to you? And ask Siana if she wants to stay and eat with us."

I relayed the invitation and she accepted, then we had to decide what we wanted. An important decision like that can't be rushed, so I told Wyatt to call back when he left his house. Then I sat down and held myself very still until the head-pounding subsided. Ibuprofen, here I come.

My condo was chilly because the air-conditioning was on. Siana switched the thermostat over to "heat" but on a low setting, just enough to take care of the chill, then got busy with the hot chocolate while we discussed what we wanted to eat, and I used the chocolate to chase two ibuprofen tablets. Was that a winning combination, or what?

We decided on something simple and comforting for dinner — pizza. I knew Wyatt's tastes in the pizza department, so Siana called in the order. The phone rang a few minutes later and she handed the cordless to me. I expected it to be Wyatt, but the Caller ID window showed "Denver, CO." I'm on the national do-not-call list to stave off telemarketers, so I had no idea who could be calling from Denver.

"Hello."

Silence met my polite greeting. I tried again, slightly louder. "Hello?" I heard a click, then the dial tone; annoyed, I disconnected and set the cordless down on the table. "It was a hang-up," I told Siana, who shrugged.

Wyatt did call within five minutes and I gave him the pizza information. He arrived twenty minutes later, carrying his small duffel and one large and one small pizza box, and we fell on the pizza like starving hogs. Okay, that's an exaggeration, but I was hungry and so was he.

He'd changed clothes, into jeans and a long-sleeved Henley shirt in a dark green that made his eyes look lighter in comparison. "I've never seen you in cold weather clothes before," I said. "You've always been a summer romance." Knowing I was about to go through a winter with him was oddly fascinating.

He winked at me. "There's a lot of cold-weather cuddling coming up."

"Let me know ahead of time," Siana said

as she picked a black olive out of the gooey cheese and popped it in her mouth, "so I can clear out."

"Will do," Wyatt said, then, with a hint of sarcasm in his tone, added, "I don't want there to be any accidental SDS sightings."

Siana choked on her olive and I burst into laughter, which made my head give a sickening throb because I'd moved too suddenly. I stopped laughing and grabbed my head, which made Siana simultaneously choke and laugh — she's slightly perverted — and Wyatt regarded us both with a satisfied glint in his eyes.

The phone rang again and he picked it up, since we were both preoccupied, Siana with choking and I with holding my head. He looked at the Caller ID and asked, "Who do you know in Denver?" as he punched the talk button. "Hello." He did the same thing I'd done, repeating "Hello," in a louder voice, then disconnecting.

"That's the second time just since I've been home," I said, releasing my head and picking up my slice of pizza. "I don't know anyone in Denver. Whoever it was hung up the first time, too."

He checked the Caller ID again. "It's probably a prepaid calling card number; a lot of them are routed through Denver."

"Then whoever it is, is wasting minutes."

Mom called before we finished the pizza, and I assured her I was feeling better; the ibuprofen had kicked in so I wasn't lying, at least so long as I didn't make any sudden movements. She asked if Wyatt was staying the night, I said yes, she said good, and she was able to hang up knowing that her oldest chick was in good hands.

Then Lynn, my assistant manager, called. Wyatt grumbled, "What is this, Everyone-Call-Blair night?" but I ignored him. Lynn gave me the rundown on the day, told me she had no problem covering for me until I was able to get back to work, and said not to worry. I made a mental note to give her some extra vacation days.

The phone was quiet after that. Siana and Wyatt cleaned up the pizza remnants, then Siana hugged me and was out the door. Wyatt immediately lifted me out of the chair and sat down with me on his lap for some of the cuddling he'd mentioned. I relaxed against him, fighting a yawn. As tired and sleepy as I was, I didn't want to go to bed yet.

He didn't talk, just held me. I think I'd have to be dead not to physically respond to him, though, so I began to notice the heat of his body, and how good it felt for him to hold me, and how good he smelled. "It's been almost forty-eight hours since we had sex," I announced, unhappy with the growing total of minutes.

"I'm well aware of that," he muttered.

"No sex tomorrow, either."

"I know."

"And maybe not on Sunday, either."

"Trust me, I *know.*"

"Think you could put it in and not move?"

He snorted. "Get real."

That's what I'd thought, but it had been worth a shot. Still, when I felt better, it would be interesting to see how long he could go without moving. No, I don't consider that a human rights violation. Torturous, but not torture; there's a difference. I didn't mention my plan to him, but the anticipation made me feel better.

A woman always needs something to look forward to, right?

CHAPTER EIGHT

I took it easy on Saturday. I did feel better; the headache was still there, but thanks to the ibuprofen, less intense. Mom reported in that she hadn't yet been able to contact the wedding-cake maker; Jenni called to say she had located an arbor that was the perfect size but needed a coat of paint. It was in a yard sale of all places, and the owner wouldn't hold it if someone came by who needed an arbor right then. The price was fifty dollars.

"Get it," I told Jenni. Fifty dollars! That was such a steal, it was a wonder the thing hadn't been snapped up already. "Do you have enough cash on you?"

"I can swing it, but I need a pickup truck to haul the thing. Is Wyatt in his truck?"

I was upstairs in the second bedroom, on the computer surfing the upscale department stores looking for a wedding dress, and he was downstairs doing laundry, so I couldn't ask him unless I went to the stairs and yelled down. Going to the window and looking out was easier. Wyatt's huge black Avalanche, a mobile monument to manliness, sat at the curb. "Yep, it's here."

"Can he drive over to get the arbor, then?"

"Give me the address, and I'll send him over."

Now I *had* to go downstairs, but I held on to the banister, kept my head as still as possible, and tried to keep my movements slow and nonjolting. I didn't call Wyatt, because then he would stop what he was doing, and I wanted to watch him doing laundry. I get a kick out of seeing him do domestic stuff. He's so testosterone-laden that you'd think he wouldn't be good at it, but Wyatt handles household chores with the same competence that he handles his big automatic pistol. He had lived alone for years, so he learned how to cook and do his own laundry, plus he was good at repairs and mechanical stuff. All in all, he was a very handy man to have around, and it turned me on watching him hang up my clothes. Okay, so I'm easy; it pretty much turned me on watching him do anything.

I finally said, "Jenni's found an arbor at a yard sale. Could you go pick it up, please?"

"Sure. What does she want with an arbor?"

It struck me that, as much as I'd discussed my plans for the wedding with him, I'd done the discussing and he evidently hadn't even done the listening. "It's for our wedding," I said with remarkable patience, if I do say so myself. He was hanging up my clothes; I didn't want to piss him off before he was finished.

"Got it. *Jenni* doesn't want the arbor, we do."

Okay, so maybe he'd listened a little. More than likely, though, Dad had told him to just go along with whatever I planned for the wedding. Good advice.

"Here's the address." I handed over the slip of paper, plus fifty dollars. "She had to go ahead and pay for it to keep the lady from selling it, so here's fifty to pay her back."

He took the fifty bucks and stuck it in his pocket, giving me a sharply assessing look as he did so. "Will you be okay while I'm gone?"

"I'm not putting a toe outside. I'm not picking up anything. I'm not doing anything to jolt my head. I'll be fine." I was bored and frustrated, but accepted my limitations — for now. Tomorrow might be a different story.

He kissed my forehead, his hard, rough hand gentle as he cupped the back of my neck. "Try to be good, anyway," he said, as if I hadn't spoken at all. I don't know why he expects me to get into trouble — oh, wait, it could have something to do with being shot, in a car wreck, kidnapped, held at gunpoint, and now almost run down in a parking lot.

Come to think of it, since I'd been hanging out with him, my life had been almost non-stop turmoil, and . . . "Hey! *None* of what's happened to me has been my fault!" I said indignantly, catching on that he'd implied otherwise.

"Sure it has. You're a trouble magnet," he said as he strolled out the door.

I followed, of course. "My life was calm before you showed up! My life was *Lake Placid!* If anyone here is a trouble magnet, it's you."

"Nicole Goodwin got murdered in your parking lot before I showed up," he pointed out.

"Which had nothing to do with me. I didn't kill her." I felt really good about that, because there had been times when I could have, very cheerfully.

"You got in a fight with her, which was why she was hanging around your parking lot, which is why she was murdered there, which is what gave your asshole ex-husband's crazy wife the idea of killing you and blaming it on Nicole's killer."

Sometimes I just hate the way his mind works. He grinned at me as he got in his truck. I couldn't kick anything without making my head hurt — I couldn't do much of anything without making my head hurt, and he knew it — so I contented myself with closing the door on his grin and going in search of a pen and paper on which to start a list of his newest transgressions. I wrote "Baits and teases me when I'm injured" and left the list lying where he could see it. Then, on the principle that one item does not a list make, I went back and added, "Blames me for things that aren't my fault."

As lists went, this one was pretty anemic. I wasn't satisfied with it at all. I wadded up the paper and threw it away; it was better to have no list at all than to let the impact be watered down.

Frustrated, I went back upstairs and did some more Internet surfing, but it, too, was fruitless. Almost an hour later, I logged off. I wasn't having any fun at all.

The phone rang and I snatched it up on the first ring, not waiting to check the Caller ID, mainly because I was bored and frustrated.

"Too bad I missed" came a malevolent whisper, then there was a click and the call disconnected.

I pulled the phone away from my ear and stared at it. Had I heard what I thought I'd heard? *Too bad I missed?*

What the hell — ? If I'd heard correctly, and I wasn't certain I had, the only way that made sense was if the Buick-driving bitch somehow knew who I was, and since my little incident hadn't been reported in the paper — probably because it was too unimportant, which sort of ticked me off — that meant she knew exactly who I was. That put the whole thing in a new light — one I didn't like. But that was the only time anyone had "missed" me in any way, at least since the last time my ex-husband's wife, Debra Carson, had shot at me. The first time, she'd hit me; the second time, she'd accidentally hit her husband.

But it couldn't be Debra, could it? She was out on bail, they both were, but the last time I'd seen her she'd been ecstatic that Jason loved her enough that he'd tried to kill me, too, and since her original motive was jealousy, that pretty well took care of that, didn't it?

I checked Caller ID, but I'd answered the call too fast and the information hadn't been processed. The last call that showed was the one from Jenni.

Alarmed, I called Wyatt. "Where are you?"

"I just unloaded the arbor at Mom's. What's up?"

"I just got a call. A woman said *'Too bad I missed'* and hung up."

"Wait a minute," he said, and I heard some fumbling noises, then he said, "Repeat that." His voice was a little clearer, a little louder, and I could almost see him cradling the phone between his head and shoulder while he reached for his pen and notebook, which went everywhere with him.

"She said, *'Too bad I missed,'*" I repeated obediently.

"Did you recognize the name on Caller ID?"

That *would* be the first thing he asked. "I answered too fast for it to register," I replied.

There was a short silence. He probably always waits to see who's calling. Normally, so did I. He must have decided not to make an issue of it, though, because he merely said, "Okay. Are you certain that's what she said?"

I thought about it, replaying the words in my head, and honesty made me admit, "Not completely certain, no. She was whispering. But that's what it sounded like. If you want percentages, I'm eighty percent certain that's what she said."

"If it was a whisper, are you certain it was a woman, and not a crank call from a teenage boy?"

Asking questions like this was his job, and

I'd learned that cops almost never take things at face value, but I was getting annoyed. I stuffed the annoyance down — time for that later — and once again mentally reviewed what I'd heard. "I'm more certain of that, maybe ninety-five percent." The only reason I wasn't a hundred percent certain was that for a short time between childhood and adolescence, a boy's voice could sound like a woman's, and also because some women have deep voices and some men have light voices. You just can't be a hundred percent certain on something like that.

He didn't ask any more questions, didn't comment on the call, just said, "I'll be there in about fifteen minutes. If any more calls come in, don't answer unless you know who's calling. Let the machine pick up."

No more calls came in, thank goodness, and he was there in twelve minutes, not that I was clock-watching or anything. Twelve minutes was long enough for me to begin wondering if I'd overreacted, if maybe I was on edge from the parking-lot incident, added to the stress from the wedding deadline. The truth was, I was beginning to feel paranoid. I'd had crank calls before, and they hadn't made me wonder if someone was after me.

I met Wyatt at the door and went into his arms. "I've been thinking about it," I said into his shoulder, "and I think maybe the stress from your deadline is making me crack up."

He didn't even pause, just gently maneuvered me backwards. "I'm not even in the door yet and already it's my fault."

"No, it was your fault before that, but you're just now hearing about it."

He shut the front door and locked it. "Are you saying you think you overreacted?"

I didn't like the way he phrased that, even though I'd thought the same thing to myself. Overreacting sounds so . . . immature. "On edge," I corrected. "Not just from almost being hit by a car, but from being shot, being in a car wreck, then abducted at gunpoint by Jason the nitwit and almost shot *again* by his nitwit wife . . . It's as if I've started *expecting* stuff like this to happen."

"So now you don't think she said 'too bad I missed'?" He still had his arms around me, but his eyes were narrow as he studied my face, as if he wanted to read every little change of expression.

I couldn't say that, because I *did* think that was what she'd said. "I think it could have been a wrong number, or a crank call — either that or Jason's nitwit wife has gone off the deep end again and is working herself up for another shot at me."

Okay, so it isn't that easy to get over paranoia.

"If you think you can get a deadline extension out of this, forget about it," he said, his eyes going even more narrow.

I scowled up at him, ticked off. I'd been genuinely alarmed, and even though I could now see the probability that there was nothing to the call, not once had I thought about using any of this to get a deadline extension. He'd issued a *challenge* with his damned deadline; no way would I wimp out now. I'd make that wedding happen if I had to be pushed to the altar in a wheelchair, trailing bandages like some mummy out of a horror movie.

"Have I *asked* for an extension?" I snapped, pulling out of his arms a little too forcefully, which made my head throb.

"You've complained about the deadline plenty."

"Which is not the same thing! This wedding will happen even if it nearly kills me." And all the trouble and bad stuff would be held over his head for the foreseeable future. See how this works? Why would I give up an advantage like that, just because of a concussion and some scrapes? Not that he'd care about all the bad stuff being held over his head, because he's contrary that way, but he'd still have to deal with it whenever we had an argument.

I poked him in the chest. "The only way we won't get married in four weeks —"

"Three weeks and six days."

I glared at him. Damn him, he was right. "Four weeks" sounded much longer than "three weeks and six days" even though there was only one day's difference between the two. Time was ticking away from me. "Is if you don't get *your* stuff accomplished."

"My stu—" he started to ask, then memory surfaced. The flowers. "Shit."

"You forgot? You *forgot* the flowers for our *wedding?*" My voice started to rise. Can I play a situation, or what? If he stopped to think for a minute he'd realize no way would I leave something that important to any man who wasn't gay, but so far he hadn't had that minute. A little payback is a good thing.

"Calm down," he said testily, walking past me into the kitchen to get a drink of water. I suppose loading and unloading an arbor can be thirsty work, even though the cool snap had persisted. "It'll get done."

I followed him. "I'm calm. I'm pissed, but I'm calm. Calmly pissed. How's that?" I was getting a little testy, too. The last couple of days had been stressful. The proof of that was that we seemed to be getting into an argument, a real argument.

He slugged back a glass of water, then set the glass down with a definite clink. "Is it time for your period, or something?"

With unerring instinct, he'd found a great big red button, and pushed it. Wyatt fights to win, which means he fights dirty. I understand the concept because that's how I fight, too, but understanding it didn't stop me from reacting. I could practically feel my blood bubbling with steam. *"What?"*

He turned around, all controlled aggression, and damned if he didn't push the button again. "What is it about having a period that makes women so bitchy?"

I paused for a moment, struggling against the urge to leap on him and tear him limb from limb. For one thing, I love him. Even when he's being an asshole, I love him. For another, any attempt to leap and tear right now would hurt me way worse than I could possibly hurt him. It was an effort, but I said as sweetly as possible, "It isn't that we're bitchier, it's that having a period makes us feel all tired and achy, so we have less tolerance for all the *bullshit* we *normally SUFFER IN SILENCE.*" By the time the sentence ended the sweetness was long gone, my jaw was clenched, and I think my eyes were bugging out.

Wyatt took a step back, belatedly looking alarmed.

I took a step forward, my chin lowering as my eyes narrowed, watching him like a starving puma watches a wounded rabbit. "Furthermore, that's the kind of question that makes a normally sweet-tempered woman anticipate, with great pleasure, standing over a man's bloody . . . mutilated . . . *dismembered* body." It's really, really impossible to sound sweet when your teeth are clenched.

He took another step back, and his right hand actually went to his hip, though of course his weapon was upstairs on the bedside table. "It's against the law to threaten an officer of the law," he warned.

I paused, considered that, then gave a dismissive flip of my hand. "Some things," I growled, "are just worth eternal damnation."

Then, with Herculean effort, I turned around and left the kitchen, went back upstairs, and lay down on the bed. My head was throbbing, maybe because my blood pressure had shot up during the last couple of minutes.

He followed a couple of minutes later, lying down beside me and easing me into his arms so my head was pillowed on his shoulder. I settled against him with a sigh, the tension in me melting as I was surrounded by his heat and the hard solidity of his body. The scent of crisp air, the hint of approaching winter, still clung to his clothing and I buried my nose against him, sniffing in appreciation.

"Are you crying?" he asked suspiciously.

"Of course not. I'm smelling your clothes."

"Why? They're clean." He raised his arm, the one I wasn't lying on, and sniffed himself. "I don't smell anything."

"They smell like winter, like cold air." I snuggled closer. "Makes me want to cuddle."

"In that case, I'll hang all my clothes outside." His mouth curved as he turned on his side to face me, his hand going to my butt and urging my hips closer to his. Sure enough, a full erection prodded at me. Some things are as reliable as Old Faithful.

I love having sex with him. I wanted to have sex with him right then. And knowing that we couldn't, that the headache would be too severe for me to enjoy it if we tried, was in a way its own turn-on. Forbidden fruit, and all that. We couldn't make up after our argument the way we usually made up, which made the making out even more delicious.

He had me half-naked in no time, his hand between my legs, two big fingers gently moving in and out while his thumb took care of other business.

"Don't make me come," I moaned, pleading as I arched into his hand. "It'll make my head hurt." Oh, God, I was so close. Stopping now would be wonderfully frustrating and I would go nuts.

"I don't think so," he murmured, kissing his way down my neck and making sparks fizzle behind my closed eyelids. "No jostling. Just relax, and let me take care of you." Then he bit the side of my neck and forget "close," I was there, wave after wave of orgasm shuddering through me while he held me down and kept me from moving.

In a way, we were both right. My head hurt, but who cared?

"What about you?" I murmured as I began drifting off to sleep.

"I'll think of something extra you can do, to make it up to me."

Extra? What "extra"? We already did everything I was willing to do. Vaguely alarmed, I forced my eyes open. "What do you mean, 'extra?'"

He chuckled and didn't reply. I went to sleep wondering where I could get a suit of armor.

Wyatt has making up down to a fine art.

CHAPTER NINE

I felt much better the next day, Sunday. The headache had subsided from a pounding presence to just a presence, and one that I could almost ignore.

Wyatt drove me over to his mother's house so I could inspect the arbor; as Jenni had said, it needed a coat of paint — as well as scraping and sanding before it was painted. But it was the perfect size, and the shape was wonderful, with a graceful arch that reminded me of the onion domes on buildings in Moscow. Roberta was in love with the arbor and wanted it as a permanent addition to her garden. We agreed that sanding and painting the arbor was a perfect job for Wyatt, since he was in charge of the flowers.

I could tell from the faintly wary look in his eyes as he studied the arbor that he was beginning to realize "the flowers" meant more than a couple of vases and a bouquet. Roberta could barely hide her grin, but until he asked for help she was going to let him stew, while she quietly handled the flowers herself.

There was always a chance he wouldn't ask for help — his inborn aggressive, dominant streak might keep him from admitting he couldn't handle the job. We had agreed we wouldn't let the charade go on any longer than two weeks. That was long enough to let him share in the stress, without actually letting him do something that would interfere with our plans.

Yes, it was mean. So?

From there we went to my parents' house for lunch, to satisfy Mom's need to fuss over me and my need to be fussed over. We were grilling pork chops — grilling is never out of season in the South — so Dad and Wyatt immediately went outside, beers in hand, to see to the grill. I thought it was cute, the way they'd bonded, two guys trying to stay afloat in a sea of estrogen.

Dad's very philosophical and smart about it, but he's had years of experience with Mom *and* Grammy — Grammy equals, like, two of me. Plus, Dad had raised three daughters. Wyatt, on the other hand, was accustomed to being immersed in guy stuff: first football, then law enforcement. Even worse, he's an alpha personality, and has a hard time understanding the concept of "no." *Getting* me was a testament to all the dominant, aggressive facets of his personality; *keeping* me was a testament to his intelligence, because he'd seen right away that Dad was an expert in the war between the sexes. Okay, so it isn't really a war; it's more like different species. Dad speaks the language. Wyatt was learning.

Mom and I got everything ready for the grilling to start, all the while making more war plans — er, wedding plans — and when the men took over the pork chops we had a few minutes to rest. She'd found a dress online that she liked, which she'd ordered, and she showed it to me on the computer. I wasn't having any attendants, the wedding would be smaller and more informal than that, so I didn't have to deal with picking out bridesmaids dresses or anything like that, thank heavens. We looked some more for the gown I had in mind and once again came up empty, which was really annoying because it wasn't as if I wanted some over-the-top wedding dress with lace and flowers and seed-pearl embroidery. I'd had that the first time I got married, and didn't want to go through the experience again.

"I know!" Mom suddenly said, her face lighting up with inspiration. "Sally can *make* the gown, and this way you'll know it'll fit perfectly. Sketch the design you want, and we can go tomorrow to find the fabric."

"Call Sally first," I suggested, "to make certain she can do it."

Sally had her own troubles right now, what with Jazz being mad because she tried to hit him with her car, and her being mad because he ruined her bedroom by having it redecorated behind her back. They were living apart, after being married for thirty-five years, and they were both miserable. I was excited by the possibility that she could make the gown, though, because that was the perfect solution. Sally was a whiz with a sewing machine; she'd made Tammy's prom gowns, which had looked gorgeous.

Mom called Sally right then. Sally said of course she could do it, then Mom passed the phone to me and I described the gown I wanted to Sally, who, bless her, said it would be simple to make. It *was* a simple design, no frou-frou to it at all. The way I envisioned it, the magic would be in the flow of the fabric and the way it fit, and Wyatt wouldn't be able to think of anything except getting me alone and out of the gown.

I was so relieved I could barely stand it. I still had to find the perfect fabric, but finding fabric is much easier than finding the perfect ready-made gown. If I'd been prepared to settle for something that merely looked good I wouldn't have been so worried, but I'm not the best in the world at "settling." Sometimes I have to, but I don't like it.

Over lunch we told Dad and Wyatt how Sally was saving the day. "She needs something to get her mind off Jazz, too," Mom said.

Wyatt's gaze met mine and I saw his expression. It isn't that he doesn't get Mom's and my position on the matter, which is that Jazz deserved being hit with a car for what he did, because I've explained it to him; it's that his cop instincts are outraged. He looks at Sally trying to ram Jazz with her car as attempted murder, even though Jazz jumped out of the way and wasn't hurt, and he thinks Jazz should have reported the incident to the police and pressed charges against her. Sometimes I think his sense of right and wrong is a little warped by all those criminal justice classes he took in college.

He didn't say anything, but I knew he wasn't happy about Sally making my dress; I also knew he'd have plenty to say when we were alone, but he wasn't going to start an argument in front of my parents, especially when it was about Mom's best friend. The glint in his eyes, though, told me we'd be discussing it plenty when we were alone.

I didn't mind. I was in an unassailable position. No matter what decision was made about any part of our wedding, it was All His Fault, because his deadline was what had precipitated the rush. I just love unassailable positions — so long as I'm the one occupying them.

He barely waited until I was buckled into the seat of the Avalanche before he attacked. "Can't you find someone else to make your wedding dress?"

"There isn't enough time," I said sweetly.

He saw right away where that was going, and detoured. "She tried to kill her husband."

I gave a wave of my hand. "I don't see the connection between that and making my dress. And I've told you: she didn't try to *kill* him, she just wanted to maim him a little."

He shot me an unreadable glance. "Two days ago I watched a videotape of someone trying to hit you with a car. Don't talk to me about 'maiming a little.' A car is deadly. She was going so fast she couldn't stop before she hit the house. If Jazz hadn't jumped out of the way, he'd have been pinned between the car and the house. Do I have to find scene photographs to show you the damage that can be done to the human body in situations like that?"

Damn it all to hell and back, I absolutely hate it when he makes a point that overrides my unassailable position.

He was right. Viewed from his vantage point as a cop, which meant he regularly saw things that would give me nightmares, he was right. Sally had acted with complete disregard for Jazz's life and well-being. Not only that, I knew that if our positions were reversed and I'd watched someone try to kill Wyatt, I wouldn't be the least forgiving about it.

"Shit."

One of his level brows lifted. "Does that mean you agree?"

"It means I see your point." I tried not to sound sulky. I don't think I succeeded, because he hid a quick grin.

This was now a sticky wicket, because Sally had already agreed to make my dress; not only that, she was excited about it, because Sally loves my sisters and me almost as much as she loves her own kids. We're like family. I couldn't find someone else to make the dress now without really hurting her feelings. For that matter, in the short length of time I had, I probably couldn't find anyone else to make the dress, period.

I wasn't dumb enough to bang my head against the dashboard in frustration, but I felt like it.

Wyatt had caused this dilemma by using common sense. That's cheating. So I threw it back in his lap. That's only fair, right? "Okay, here's the deal: I'm really, really short on time. The odds are I won't be able to get the dress made by a professional, because they'll all already be booked. It's possible I can find what I want ready-made, but I didn't find anything in the mall and I haven't found anything online. If you insist, I'll somehow find a way to back out of letting Sally make my dress, *but,* you'll have to live with the consequences if I have to get married in whatever dress I can find at the last minute."

I was deadly serious in my tone and expression, maybe because I *was* deadly serious. I wasn't taking this lightly. I had a dream, a vision of how I wanted my wedding to him to be, and a big part of that dream was seeing the look in his eyes when I walked toward him wearing this killer gown. It was a moment something in me needed, something that had taken a big hit when I found out my ex was unfaithful. I didn't go around whining about it all the time, but I hadn't escaped my first marriage totally baggage-free; I had a couple of small carry-ons that had to be dealt with.

He gave me a quick, piercing look, gauging my sincerity. Really, I don't know why he didn't just take what I said at face value. Okay, so I do know. Probably it should bother me that the man I love doesn't trust me, but it would bother me a whole lot more if he were fool enough that he did trust me. I'm not talking about cheating on him sexually or emotionally because that wasn't going to happen, but in our own private little battle for relationship turf, all strategies were fair. He'd made that rule himself, with his damn-the-torpedoes, get-her-at-all-costs pursuit of me. Actually, he hadn't even pursued me; he'd grabbed me and refused to let go.

Remembering that gave me a little flutter, both in my heart and farther down, and I squirmed a little.

He swore under his breath, jerking his gaze back to the street. "Damn it, stop squirming. You do that every time you think about sex."

"I do?" Maybe I did. But he was . . . squirmworthy.

His hands tightened on the steering wheel, reminding me that we hadn't made love since Wednesday night, and it was now Sunday. He'd relieved some of my tension the night before, but as good as he was with his hands and mouth it just wasn't the same as his penis. Some things are made to go together, you know?

Wyatt, on the other hand, hadn't had any relief unless he'd taken care of the matter while he showered. Considering the whiteness of his knuckles, I didn't think he had.

"We were talking about Sally," he said, his tone rough and tense.

I fought to bring my thoughts back on subject. "I've told you what I think."

He took a couple of breaths. "Exactly what will be the consequences if you don't get married in this dress you want so much?"

"I don't know," I said simply. "I just know it'll hurt me."

"Shit," he muttered. He doesn't mind driving me nuts, making me angry, or frustrating the hell out of me, but he'll move heaven and earth to keep from hurting me. Every women should be loved like that. My heart swelled, or it felt as if it did. That's a scary sensation, too, because if your heart really swelled it could probably tear some of the plumbing lines loose, or something.

He was silent for about two blocks and I began to tense, wondering what he was thinking. Wyatt's too smart to let him think for long, or he'll come up with —

"Get them back together," he said.

My brain felt as if all the gray stuff was suddenly squeezed together. "What?" Damn it, damn it! Was he serious? I assumed he was talking about Sally and Jazz, but their own children couldn't even get them in the same room together. I should have interrupted him at least a block back, jerked the steering wheel or something, or maybe clutched my head and fallen over, except then he'd have taken me to the ER again, and I'd had enough of that place.

"Sally and Jazz," he said, confirming my fear that he was trying to completely derail me. "Get them back together. Make them sit down and talk this out. I figure if you can get Jazz to move past his wife trying to kill him, then I'll have to admit I'm taking this too seriously."

"Are you *nuts?*" I shrieked, rounding on him, which wasn't a good idea because the sudden movement shifted my headache from a mere presence into an attention-getter. I did clutch my head, but I didn't fall over.

"Be careful," he said sharply.

"Don't tell me to be careful after you throw something like that in my lap!" Just when I thought he couldn't get any more outrageous or demanding, he pulled something like that. He's a diabolical fiend.

"It's roughly equivalent to what you threw in mine." His eyes were glittering, sharp little green lights of mixed temper and satisfaction.

Oh. He'd noticed that, huh?

"You aren't incapacitated with a concussion! Or by a concussion. Whatever."

"You're recovering fast," he said with a notable lack of compassion. "I wouldn't be surprised if you went back to work tomorrow."

I had, in fact, been planning on just that. I scowled at him, which he took for an admission.

"I'm not a marriage counselor," I said in frustration. "Even worse, I'm almost like one of their own children. They won't listen to their kids, why do you think they'll listen to me?"

"That's your problem," he said, again with a notable lack of compassion.

"You don't think it'll be your problem if I'm not happy at our wedding? Didn't you hear me say I'm *short on time?* This will take time I don't have!"

"Make time."

He thought he was so smart. I narrowed my eyes at him. "Okay. I'll take the time we *would* have spent making love, and that's when I'll talk to Sally and Jazz."

He actually laughed out loud at that. Yeah,

I know my track record for refusing him anything is really pretty sucky, but he *laughed.*

One cannot flounce when one has a concussion, even one that's mild. I didn't even want to get out of his truck by myself, because it's a big truck and you have to climb down, and if I landed just a little too hard my head would be jarred and that was really no fun at all. So I had to wait for him to come around and lift me out of the truck, which he did with great pleasure because then he could let me slide all the way down his front, and I almost got caught on the parts that were jutting out, which made him smile with satisfaction.

This man was evil.

I said furiously, "*If* we ever have sex again, which right now is very much in doubt, we're doing it the tantric way."

He was grinning as he followed me up the steps to the front door. "I'm not chanting anything when we have sex."

"Oh, it doesn't involve chanting. I don't think. It involves discipline."

"I'm not letting you anywhere near a whip."

I scoffed. "Not that kind of discipline. Self-discipline. Tantric sex lasts a long, long time."

"Now that I can get behind," he said, looking interested.

Smiling sweetly I said, "Oh, good, we'll try that, then. You promise, don't you?"

"You bet," he said, his libido getting in the way of thinking clearly. That state of affairs wouldn't last for long, though, so I hurried in for the kill.

"By the way —"

"Yeah?"

"It lasts a long, long time because the man *doesn't get to come*."

CHAPTER TEN

Wyatt gave me an astonished look then burst out laughing, holding his sides as if the idea of tantric sex was the most hilarious thing he'd ever heard of in his life. He howled with laughter. Tears ran down his cheeks. He stopped laughing for a few seconds, then looked at my face and started all over again. He ended up collapsed on the sofa, still laughing.

I stood tapping my foot — very gently — for a while, my arms crossed. What the hell was so funny? I began to get annoyed. I like a joke as well as anyone, but first I have to know what it is. Then I began to get pissed, because I got the feeling he was laughing at me. I got this idea because he kept pointing at me, then breaking into fresh fits of mirth. Finally I was angry.

First, let me point out that if flouncing hurts, marching is out of the question. I had to settle for merely walking, but with attitude, over to glare down at him. "Would you *stop?*" I shouted, thinking seriously about pinching him. "What's so funny?" Things were not going my way, and that is so not on my list of favorite things. Evidently I'd overlooked something, and Wyatt is an expert at finding loopholes — or completely ignoring what I tell him. In retrospect, making him worry about the flowers for the wedding didn't seem mean at all.

"You," he wheezed, wiping tears from his eyes. He sat up and reached for me, but I hastily stepped back out of reach. I can't fight if he's touching me, because I get sidetracked. He fights dirty, using my weaknesses against me by going straight for my neck, like Dracula focusing on an open vein. Forget my breasts; touching them does nothing for me. But man oh man, my neck is a big-time erogenous zone, and Wyatt knows it.

"I'm so glad you find me amusing." I wanted to pout, and I also wanted to kick him. You'll notice I was having these violent thoughts, but I did not act on any of them. I'm not a violent person. Vindictive, maybe, but not violent. I'm also not stupid. If I ever get violent with someone, it isn't going to be a muscular, athletic guy who's ten inches taller than I am and about ninety pounds

146

heavier, if not more. That's if I have a choice.

His shoulders began shaking again. "It . . . it's just the very idea —"

"That some men believe their partners' pleasure is more important than their own?" I felt very indignant that he'd be laughing about this. I thought it was a great idea.

He shook his head. "N-no, not that." He took a deep breath, his green eyes brilliant from mirth and moisture. "It's just that — You came up with this idea as a way to pay me back because you thought I'd go nuts with frustration."

"Oh? You mean it won't bother you at all?" I couldn't believe him. I know Wyatt, and "horny" is his middle name. Not literally, of course, though wouldn't that be interesting on his birth certificate?

Lazily he got to his feet, hooking an arm around my waist before I could scoot even farther away. I was slower than usual, be-cause I had to be careful, and he moved with the quick grace of the true athlete. He pulled me close, wrapping his other arm around me, too, and lifted me on my tiptoes so my hips fit right against his. He had a hard-on, of course — big surprise there. The tingles that started zipping through me were no sur-prise, either.

"It would bother me," he drawled, "if it

happened. Picture this: I'm on top of you. We're naked. Your legs are around my waist. I'm kissing your neck. I've been fucking you for, let's say, twenty minutes or so."

Twenty minutes? Man, I need to turn on the air-conditioning, because the temperature in the condo was suddenly too high. My nipples were tingling now, because even though I don't much like having them touched, they weren't dead. Most of my parts were tingling. I took this to mean I was in trouble.

He bent his head down so his hot breath washed over my neck as he kissed the hollow below my ear. Somehow I was a little off balance, so I had to cling to his shoulders to stay upright — except that wasn't really working, because I wasn't exactly upright, but I just kept on clinging. "You wouldn't be able to *stop* me from coming," he murmured, kissing down the side of my neck. "You wouldn't even *think* of it."

Think of what? I wondered fuzzily, then jerked my wandering mind back on topic. See, this is what he does when we're fighting, he distracts me with sex. I admit to sometimes deliberately starting an argument because I like the way he fights; I'm *not* stupid. The problem is that he uses the same tactics when I'm serious. He likes that I have such a difficult time resisting him, because he isn't stupid, either. After we've been together a couple of years I figure the intensity will fade and we'll have to find another way to settle our arguments, but until then the best way to fight fire was to set a backfire.

I stopped clinging with one hand, and sent it roaming over his shoulder and down his arm, to his ribs, down some more — slowly, slowly, trailing my fingers, pausing to rub, then finally going for the bull's-eye. He shuddered as I stroked him through his jeans, his arms tightening around me.

"God almighty," he said in a strained voice, stopping his assault on my neck as he concentrated on my assault on him. He hadn't had any relief in a few days, and I figured he was more needy than I was, especially considering how generous he'd been with me the day before.

Yes, if I were fair-minded, I'd either give him the same relief or stop teasing him. Get real.

Probably our game of tease would have stopped being a game and we'd have ended up in bed — or on the couch — having the most careful, nonjostling sex we could manage, if his cell phone hadn't rung. He had it set to a real, old-fashioned ring-ring sound, just like an ordinary phone, and in my dazed state I thought my home phone was ringing. I fully intended to ignore it, but instead of continuing with what he was doing he immediately released me and pulled the phone from his belt.

The worst thing about being involved with a cop is the hours. No, the worst thing would be if he'd been on the street and in constant danger, but Wyatt was a lieutenant, which meant he wasn't involved in any dangerous stuff any longer — thank God — but it also meant he was on call just about all the time. Our city isn't a hotbed of crime, but still he got called out, on average, three or four nights a week. Weekends were no exception.

"Bloodsworth," he said in a slightly clipped accent, the result of his years spent playing football up North, his attention already completely focused on the situation being related to him. I started to move away from him and he caught my wrist, holding me in place. Okay, so maybe he wasn't completely focused.

"I'll be there in ten minutes," he finally said, and closed the flip-top on the phone.

"Hold my place," he told me, bending his head to give me a firm, warm kiss that involved some tongue. "When I get back, I want to pick up where we left off." Then he was gone, firmly closing the front door behind him. A few seconds later I heard the Avalanche roar to life and the wheels bark a little as he shot away from the curb.

Sighing, I went over to the door and locked it. Without him here distracting me, maybe I could think of some way to simplify my immediate future. Breaking a leg might work, because then the wedding would be put off until the cast was gone. Breaking *his* leg sounded even better. But I'd had enough of pain; I wanted to concentrate on the good stuff, on getting married, settling into our routine together, having a family.

Instead I had to concentrate on playing marriage counselor, a job for which I wasn't remotely qualified.

Manipulation, on the other hand . . . a little emotional blackmail here, a little guilt there . . . I could do that.

I called Mom. "Where's Jazz living now?" I asked. I didn't explain the problem to her — she was, after all, Sally's best friend. This was between Wyatt and me, our own private bone of contention.

"With Luke," Mom replied. Luke is the third Arledge son. The kids were refusing to take sides, which was annoying Sally and Jazz, who both felt misunderstood and completely justified in their actions. "I gather Jazz is putting a crimp in Luke's style."

Luke was also the wildest of the Arledge bunch. I don't mean wild as in drugs and getting into trouble, I mean wild as in definitely not tamed, uninterested in settling down, and with a social life that should have already caused permanent damage to his back. He wouldn't be at all happy to have his father living with him.

Why on earth had Jazz picked Luke to live with? Any of his children would have opened their homes to him. Matthew and Mark were both married and had families, but they also each had guest bedrooms, so the arrangement wouldn't have been horrible. John, the youngest, was working toward his master's degree and lived in a rented house with two other graduate students, so maybe living with him wouldn't have been so great. Tammy had been married about a year, and she and her husband had a large house in the country, but no children, so there was plenty of room there.

On the other hand, if Jazz wanted to make Sally fret about what he might be doing, living with Luke was the way to do it.

That gave me hope, because if Jazz was trying to make Sally jealous, then he hadn't walked away from the marriage. He was mad as hell, though.

Luke would be more than willing to help, I

thought. If Jazz was cramping his style, he'd want his father out of there, and what better way to accomplish that than by helping me? I was doing a good thing here; who wouldn't want to help?

I looked up Luke's number in the phone book, then thought better of the idea and called Tammy instead. Caller ID makes being sneaky more complicated, and I didn't want Jazz to see my name on Luke's phone. Therefore, I needed his cell number.

When Tammy answered I explained what I was trying to do — though not why — and she thought it was a good idea. "God knows *we* haven't been able to get anything accomplished," she said wearily, meaning her and her brothers. "Mom and Dad are so stubborn, it's been like beating my head against the wall. Good luck." She gave me Luke's cell number, we chatted for a while longer about the different arguments that had been used against her wayward parents, then hung up.

When Luke answered his cell phone, I went through the explanation again. "Hold on," he said, then I listened to a variety of noises that ended with the sound of a door closing. "I'm outside now, where I can talk."

"Jazz?" I asked, just to make certain. I didn't have to elaborate.

"Oh, yeah." He sounded weary.

"He won't be suspicious because you've gone outside to talk?"

"No, I've done that a lot lately."

"Is he seeing anyone? Making noises about actually filing for divorce?"

"Nada. For one thing, he can't live with me if he's going to cheat on Mom. And for another, he gets sick to his stomach and throws up when he starts talking about them not ever living together again. This whole fu—" He caught himself before the f-bomb exploded. "— situation is stupid. They love each other. What the hell this standoff is accomplishing is beyond me."

"They're showing each other how upset they are," I explained. I sort of understood it, except they were going to extreme lengths to make their separate points.

"They're also showing the world that they're idiots." Luke was definitely not a happy camper.

I bypassed that comment, not wanting to get into the question of idiocy. Personally, I was on Sally's side. Luke wanted his parents to work things out, but he was a guy; he probably thought his mother was taking interior decorating too seriously. I'm not sure it's possible to take decorating too seriously, but I'm not a guy.

"Has Jazz said anything that might hint how he wants this to play out? Does he want Sally to apologize, or just call and ask him to come back?"

"In a way, this is all he talks about, but he doesn't say anything new, you know? It's the same thing, over and over again. He was trying to do something nice for her and she blew up in his face, wouldn't listen to reason, then she went crazy, etcetera, etcetera. Anything useful there?"

Only that Jazz still had no appreciation for how hard Sally had worked collecting and refinishing her antique furniture. "Maybe," I said. "I have an idea, anyway. How about your mom? What has she said? What's your take, as a guy, on this whole thing?"

He hesitated, and I knew he was struggling to be fair, to not take sides. Luke's a nice guy, despite his hot sheets. As far as I was concerned, his sheets qualified as community property, and by that I mean an *entire* community. When he finally did settle down, I thought I should probably advise his chosen love to burn all his sheets, because that kind of nasty can't be boiled out.

"I kind of see both sides," he finally said, pulling my thoughts away from laundry problems. "I mean, I know Mom worked really hard refinishing the furniture, and she loves antiques. On the other hand, Dad was trying to do something nice for her. He knew he was clueless about decorating, so he went to an expert, and he paid a small fortune to have their bedroom redone."

Okay, this was interesting; my vague idea was getting firmer. I also had an ace in the hole I could pull out if my idea didn't work.

My phone beeped to let me know there was an incoming call. "Thanks, this has been a help," I said.

"No problem. Anything to get him back home."

We said our good-byes and I flashed to the incoming call. "Hello."

There was a pause, followed by click, then a moment of dead air, then finally the dial tone. Puzzled, I checked the Caller ID, but since I'd already been on the phone the call hadn't registered. Mentally I shrugged; if whoever it was wanted to talk, he or she could call back.

I spent the rest of the afternoon being bored out of my skull. I didn't have anything there I was dying to read, and it was Sunday, so of course there was nothing interesting on television. I played some games on the computer. I looked at shoes on the Zappos website, and bought a pair of snazzy blue boots. If I ever took up line dancing, I was set. I looked up some sea cruises, just in case we ever had a chance for a honeymoon, because so far this year it didn't look possible. Then I looked up birth control, to see how long it would take my body to return to normal after I stopped taking the Pill, because if possible I wanted to time my babies so I'd have them in months that had pretty birthstones. Mothers have to think about things like this, you know.

My interest in online things exhausted, I tried to find something on television to watch. Frankly, I'm no good at being a lady of leisure. The prolonged inactivity was eating at me, making me feel as if my muscles were getting cramped and stiff. I couldn't even do yoga because bending over wasn't a fun thing to do right now; the increased pressure made my head throb. I did some tai chi instead, flowing and stretching, which relieved some of the cramped feeling but still didn't give me the high I got from a really hard workout.

Wyatt still wasn't home by supper, but I hadn't really expected him. I've been involved in crime scene investigations, and nobody gets in a hurry, which I guess is a good thing when you're gathering evidence and taking statements. If he made it back by bedtime, he'd be doing good. I nuked a frozen dinner, and called Lynn while I was eating to assure her I would be back to work tomorrow. She was relieved, because Sunday and Monday are her normal off days. After pulling double duty on Friday and Saturday, she needed the rest.

And since Mondays are always long days for me — I both open and close at Great Bods, meaning I'm there from six in the morning until nine at night — I needed *my* rest, too. Even though I'd been doing nothing but lying around for three days, I was tired, or maybe that was because I'd been doing nothing but lying around. At eight o'clock, I went upstairs and took a shower, then carefully dried my hair.

While Wyatt was gone and I could concentrate, I got my pad of paper and sat down to work on my list of his transgressions. I thought of all the things he'd done to annoy me, but "Laughing at my idea of tantric sex" just didn't have much punch. The sheet of paper remained disturbingly blank. Good God, was I going soft? Losing my touch? Making lists of his transgressions was one of my greatest ideas of all time, and now that I couldn't think of a thing to write down I felt the same way Davy Crockett must have felt at the Alamo, when he ran out of bullets — sort of "Well, shit. Now what?"

Not that this was at all the same thing, because Davy Crockett died, but you know what I mean. Not only that, just exactly what else do you expect when you decide to fight to the death? You *die.* That's what the part about "fight to the death" *means.*

Big duh, there. Not to take anything away from ol' Davy.

I looked down at the paper and sighed. Finally I wrote, "Threatened to piss on me." Okay, so that was more funny than annoying. I chuckled just reading it. This wouldn't do at all.

I started to tear off the sheet and start fresh, but in the end decided to leave it. Maybe I just needed to prime the pump, and I had to start somewhere. Next I wrote, "Refuses to negotiate."

Oh, man, this was pitiful. He'd actually done me a favor by refusing to negotiate over the last-name issue, because now he owed me. I scratched out that item.

How about, "Takes the fun out of our wedding by putting too much pressure on me"? Nope, too long.

Inspiration struck. In big letters, digging the pen into the paper, I wrote: MADE FUN OF HAVING A PERIOD.

There. If that didn't nail his ass to the wall, I didn't know what would.

CHAPTER ELEVEN

I woke up when Wyatt got into bed beside me. He had his own key to my place, and the code to the security system, so he didn't have to wake me to get in, but he definitely woke me when he pulled me close against him because his skin was cold. The red numbers on the clock read 1:07.

"Poor baby," I murmured, rolling over to hold him. He wouldn't get much sleep; he was usually at work by seven-thirty at the latest. "Is it that cold outside?"

He sighed as he relaxed, lying heavily against me. "I had the air-conditioning in the truck on high, blowing in my face to keep me awake," he muttered. His hand slipped over the T-shirt I was wearing. "What the hell's this?" He didn't like for me to wear anything to bed; he wanted me naked, maybe for easy access, maybe because men just like naked women.

"I was cold."

"I'm here now; I'll keep you warm. Let's get rid of this damn thing." He was already pulling the hem of the shirt up, preparing to tug it over my head. I caught the shirt and took over the job, because I knew exactly where those stitches in my head were. "These, too." He had my pajama shorts down around my thighs before I got the shirt completely off, sitting up in bed to strip them the rest of the way down my legs. Then he lay back down and pulled me close again. He sort of automatically ran his hand over me, cupping my breast and thumbing my nipple, before reaching between my legs; it was as if he was reassuring himself all his favorite parts were still there even if he hadn't been able to avail himself of them. Then he sighed again, and went to sleep. So did I.

My alarm went off at five. I tried to turn it off before it woke him, but didn't succeed. He groaned and started to throw the covers back, but I kissed his shoulder and urged him down on the pillow again. "Just go back to sleep," I said. "I'll reset the alarm for six-thirty." He'd have to grab something to eat from a fast-food joint on the way to work, but he needed the sleep.

He muttered something that I took for agreement, burying his face in the pillow, and he was asleep again before my feet hit the floor.

I had put my clothes in the bathroom the night before, thinking he might be really late getting in, so I dressed in there. I didn't need makeup today, since I'd be in Great Bods all day; I brushed my hair but left it down — I wouldn't be working out today, either. The concussion headache wasn't quite gone, damn it. I'd really hoped it would be.

When I was dressed, I took my toothbrush and toothpaste with me downstairs, to brush my teeth after I'd had breakfast. The automatic timer had turned on the coffeemaker and coffee was waiting for me. I had a quiet twenty minutes at the table, eating breakfast and drinking coffee. Then I brushed my teeth in the downstairs half-bath, poured the rest of the coffee into a big travel cup, and prepared the coffeemaker again and reset the timer for Wyatt. I dropped an apple in my bag for lunch, grabbed a sweater, and was out the side door that opened into the parking portico. Well, almost. I had to stop and reset the alarm, because Wyatt was a fanatic about things like that.

The morning was cold enough that I needed the sweater. I shivered a little as I went down the steps, using the remote to unlock the car. The normal routine was comforting, a signal that things were indeed normal again, or getting there. I've been injured plenty of times; cheerleaders get hurt as often as football players do. It's always a pain in the ass. I've learned to be patient, because even though you *can* do stuff when you're injured, that doesn't mean you should — additional stress on an injured muscle or broken bone slows the healing. Since I always wanted to get back to performance level as quickly as possible, I'd learned to do exactly what I was supposed to do — and I hated every minute of it. I wanted to be at Great Bods, overseeing every little detail. The place is mine, and I love it. I wanted to be exercising, using the muscles I've worked so hard and so long to build and maintain. Besides, keeping myself in shape is great advertising for Great Bods.

There was almost no traffic on the streets; even in summer, opening Great Bods at six in the morning meant driving to work in the dark. In the middle of summer the sky would be beginning to lighten just about the time I arrived to unlock, but the drive itself was always in the dark. I kind of liked the emptiness of the streets, the early-morning quiet.

As I pulled into my parking space in the employee parking lot in the back, the motion sensor lights came on. Wyatt had installed those himself, just last month, after meeting me here one night and noticing how dark it was under the long awning that protected the employees' cars from the weather. I still wasn't used to those lights. They seemed unnaturally bright, as if I were standing on a stage as I unlocked the back door. I had a small LED light on my key chain that I'd always used before to see the lock, and to me it was perfectly adequate. Wyatt, however, wanted the place lit up like a runway.

The darkness under the awning had never bothered me. It had, in fact, concealed me from Nicole Goodwin's killer when she was murdered right there in the parking lot. I hadn't argued against having the lights installed, though — I mean, why would I? — and was glad when Lynn confessed she felt safer locking up at night, knowing those lights would come on the second she opened the door.

I unlocked, then went through the building turning on all the lights, setting the thermostat, starting the coffee both in the employee break room and in my office. I loved this part of my day, seeing the place come to life. The lights reflected in the polished mirrors, the exercise equipment gleamed, the plants were lush and healthy; the place was just beautiful. I even loved the smell of chlorine in the lap pool.

The first client arrived at six-fifteen, a silver-haired gentleman who'd had a mild heart attack and was determined to stay in shape and stave off any more attacks, so he spent some time on the treadmill every morning, then swam laps. Whenever he paused to chat, he'd tell me what his blood pressure and cholesterol levels were down to, and how pleased his doctor was. By six-thirty, three more clients had joined him, two employees had arrived, and the day was in full swing.

While Mondays were usually busy days for me, the added paperwork after missing two days kept me hopping. The headache rebounded a little so I tried to limit how much I moved around, but when you're the one in charge you can't just sit in an office.

Wyatt called to check on me. So did Mom, Lynn, Siana, Wyatt's mom, Jenni, Dad, then Wyatt again. I spent so much time on the phone assuring everyone that I was fine that it was almost three o'clock before I had time to eat my apple, by which time I was starving. I also needed to go to the bank and make a deposit, which should have been done on Friday. Things were a little slow right then, or as slow as they were going to get; the lunch rush was over, and the pace wouldn't pick up again until the after-school and after-work crowd arrived to work up a sweat, so I multitasked by going to the bank and eating my apple at the same time.

I admit, I was a little paranoid about watching for Buicks that were driven by women, but I think that's understandable. There was no way I could recognize the psycho bitch, but I wanted to give any possibles a wide berth. And because I was watching, things I likely wouldn't have noticed before got on my nerves, like the woman in the white Chevy who stayed on my bumper for a couple of blocks, or the one driving a green Nissan who changed lanes right in front of me, forcing me to slam on my brakes, which jarred my head and forced me to call her a fucking mongreloid. I hate when that happens, because people who aren't paying attention think I'm throwing off on people with Down Syndrome. Thank God my windows were up, you know?

I went through the drive-in at the bank, then threaded my way through traffic back to Great Bods. I kept an eye out for that green Nissan, and Buicks, which is why I noticed the white Chevy again. Well, a white Chevy, and it was driven by a woman, but that isn't uncommon, so I couldn't say it was the same white Chevy. What were the odds the same woman would be reversing her earlier path and would get behind me again? Not very high, but hey, I was reversing my path, wasn't I?

When I got to Great Bods I turned down the side street to go to the rear parking lot, and the white Chevy continued going straight. I breathed a sigh of relief. I either had to get over this newfound paranoia or start paying more attention so I'd *know* if the same car or just a look-alike turned up behind me. There was no point in imprecise paranoia.

My head was still pounding from being jerked around, so I went to my office and popped a couple of ibuprofen. Ordinarily I love what I do, but today hadn't been a great day.

Around seven-thirty, the end-of-the-day influx was beginning to outflux, to my relief. I got a pack of peanut butter crackers from the vending machine in the break room, and that was supper. I was so tired, all I wanted to do was sit down and not move for, oh, ten hours or so.

Wyatt showed up at eight-thirty, to stay with me until closing. He gave me a sharp look that made me think I probably didn't look my best, but all he said was, "How did you make it?"

"I was doing okay until I went to the bank, almost rear-ended a nitwit who cut in front of me, and had to slam on my brakes," I said.

"Ouch."

"How did your day go?"

"Pretty normal."

Which could mean anything from dead bodies turning up in a dump to a bank robbery, though I was pretty certain I'd have heard if one of the banks in town got robbed. I needed to get my hands on his paperwork to make sure I wasn't missing anything.

The last client left, and the staff began cleaning up and putting everything to rights. I employ nine people, counting Lynn, with at least three people on each seven-and-a-half-hour shift, and four on each shift on Fridays and Saturdays, the busiest days. Everyone gets two days off, except me. I get one. That would have to change soon, and with that in mind I wrote a note to remind myself to hire an additional person.

One by one the staff finished and called out their good-byes as they left. Yawning, I stretched, feeling the echo of soreness caused by my collision with the mall parking lot. I wanted a long soak in a hot tub, but that would have to wait because most of all I just wanted to go to bed.

I did a walk-through, checking that everything was in order, double-checking that the front door was locked. I always left a couple of dim lights burning in the front. Wyatt waited at the back door for me. I set the alarm, then he opened the door as I turned out the hallway lights and we stepped outside. The motion sensor lights came on immediately, and I turned to lock the door. When I turned back around, Wyatt was crouched beside my car.

"Blair," he said, his voice taking on that flat tone cops use when they don't want to give anything away. I stopped in my tracks, panic and fury both rising in equal force and making a potent mixture. I'd had enough of this crap, and I was damn tired of it.

"Don't tell me someone has put a bomb under my car!" I said indignantly. "That's the last straw. I've had it. What *is* this, let's-kill-Blair season? If this is just because I was a cheerleader, then people need to get a grip, there are a lot worse things in this world —"

"Blair," he said again, this time with rueful amusement.

I was on a roll, and I didn't like being stopped. *"What!"*

"It's not a bomb."

"Oh."

"Looks like someone keyed your car."

"What? Shit!" Furious all over again, I

169

rushed to his side. Sure enough, a long, ugly scratch ran down the entire driver's side of my car. The motion lights were bright enough to plainly see it.

I started to kick the tire. I'd already drawn back my foot when I remembered my concussion. The headache probably saved me from broken toes, because have you ever really kicked a tire, hard, as if you were trying to punt the car between the goal-posts? Not a good idea.

Nor was there anything else around that I could kick that wouldn't break my toes. The wall, the awning posts, things like that were my only available targets, and they were all even harder than the tires. I had no way of relieving my temper, and I thought my eyes would bug out from the internal pressure.

Wyatt was looking around, assessing the situation. His police-issue Crown Vic was sitting at the end of the row; the staff's cars would have been parked in the slots between his car and mine, effectively blocking his view of the damage, when he arrived.

"Any idea when this could have been done?" he asked.

"Sometime after I got back from the bank. That was about three-fifteen, three-twenty."

"After school was out, then."

It was easy to follow his line of thinking. A

bored teenager, walking through the parking lot, might have thought it'd be fun to mess up the Mercedes. I had to admit that was the most likely scenario, unless Debra Carson was on the warpath again, or the psycho bitch in the Buick had somehow tracked me down. But I'd been through those possibilities before, when I got that weird phone call that had creeped me out, and they were no more plausible now than they had been before. Okay, Debra was a stronger possibility, because she knew where I worked, and she knew which car was mine. The Mercedes had been a big sore point with her, because Jason had thought it would look good with the voters if she drove an American-made car.

She would be taking a risk, though, because she was already up on a charge of attempted murder — though God only knew when it would get to trial, given Jason's family connections — and harassing the victim wouldn't win her any points.

On the other hand, she was nuts. Anything was possible.

I said as much to Wyatt, but he didn't leap on it as a brilliant theory. Instead he shrugged and said, "It was probably some kid. Not a lot you can do about it, since there aren't any surveillance cameras back here."

Since he had mentioned surveillance cameras when he installed the motion lights, and I'd said there wasn't any need going to that expense, there was a slight edge to his tone.

"Go ahead," I said, and sighed. "Say 'I told you so.' "

"I told you so," he said with grim satisfaction.

I couldn't believe it. I gaped at him. "I can't believe you said that! That was so rude!"

"You told me to say it."

"But you weren't supposed to! You were supposed to be magnanimous and say something like there's no point in crying over spilled milk! *Everybody* knows you don't actually say 'I told you so'!" Well, there was an item for his troublesome list of transgressions: rude. And unsympathetic. No, I'd have to scratch "unsympathetic," because after all the man had just spent his weekend taking care of me. I'd settle for "Gloated about my car."

Rising from his crouch, he dusted off his hands. "I take it this means you've giving in on the surveillance system."

"Fat lot of good it'll do *now!*"

"If anything else happens, you'll be able to tell who did it. With your track record, I think you can pretty much count on another incident."

Wasn't that a happy thought? I glared at my beautiful little black convertible. I'd had it just a couple of months, and now someone had deliberately damaged it.

"All right," I said sulkily. "I'll have a surveillance system installed."

"I'll take care of it. I know what works best."

At least he hadn't said "If you'd listened to me before . . . " I probably would have screamed right in his face.

He said, "If you'd listened to me before —"

"*Aaaaaaa!*" I screamed, so frustrated I thought I'd explode. Now I could add "rubbing it in" to his list.

Startled, he jerked back a little. "What's that about?"

"It's about . . . it's about *everything!*" I shouted. "It's about nitwits, and jerks, and psycho bitches! It's about not having anything here I can kick without hurting myself! It's about having this stupid concussion so I can't even stomp around! I need to stomp. I need to throw something. I need a voodoo doll that I can stick pins in and set its hair on fire and pull off its little legs and arms —"

He looked mildly interested in my temper tantrum. "You do voodoo, do you?"

Just as a matter of information, you can't keep up a rant and snort through your nose

173

at the same time. I didn't want to laugh because I was mad about my car, but what the hell, sometimes a laugh is going to come out no matter what.

I had to pay him back, though. I said, "I'll need to borrow your Avalanche while my car is in the shop."

He stilled, thinking back over the track record he'd mentioned just a moment before. "Oh, shit," he said, sighing in resignation.

CHAPTER TWELVE

I wrote the new items on Wyatt's list of transgressions as soon as we got home, but I might as well have been using invisible ink for all the attention he paid to it. He didn't even glance at it, lying there on the counter that divided the living room from the kitchen, instead settling in a chair with the morning newspaper, which obviously he hadn't had time to read that morning, and asking me if I wanted the paper when he finished. Well, hell, it was my newspaper, wasn't it? Why would I pay for the thing if I didn't want to read it? And why was he reading the paper instead of paying attention to his list? Things were not right in my world.

But I was exhausted, and I was sick of that blasted headache. "I'll read it tomorrow," I said. "I'm going to take some more ibuprofen, shower, and go to bed." I was feeling grumpy, too, but most of it wasn't his fault, so I didn't want to take it out on him.

"I'll be up in a minute," he said.

I sulked in the shower, thinking about my car. There should be a security system you could put on cars that would electrify them, so when some punk scraped a key down the paint it would fry his ass. I amused myself visualizing bulging eyes, Einstein hair, and maybe even wet pants, so people could point and laugh. That would teach the little bastard.

In case you haven't noticed, I'm not much on turning the other cheek.

After showering I doctored my various scrapes and bruises — none of which needed bandages, so I just put stuff on them to help the healing process. I ran a little experiment on myself, by putting La Mer on one scrape, antibiotic ointment on another, and aloe gel on yet another, just to see which one healed best. I applied vitamin spray to my bruises. Maybe it helped, maybe it didn't. It was something to do.

I had just turned out the light and crawled into bed — naked, to save Wyatt the trouble of pulling off my clothes — when he came upstairs. I went to sleep while he was showering, roused enough to kiss him good night when he got into bed beside me, and didn't know anything else until the alarm went off the next morning.

Lynn always opened the gym on Tuesdays, so I didn't have to be there until one-thirty, though I usually was there before then. Today, however, I had a lot to do before getting to work. First I called the insurance company about my car, then I talked to Luke Arledge, then I made an appointment to get my hair cut — at eleven that very morning, if you can believe it — and finally I went shopping for the fabric for my wedding gown. On the way to the fabric store, I stopped at a place that refinished antiques to ask some questions, and as a bonus found a gorgeous Queen Anne desk that would look great in the office I was creating at Wyatt's house. All of this was by ten o'clock, so I was hustling.

I felt much, much better; the headache was nothing more than a twinge, and that was when I forgot myself and sort of skipped a little, just because it was a gorgeous sunny day. The weather was much warmer, the cool snap over for the time being, and everyone I talked to was in a good mood.

I had just enough time at the fabric store to look through their silks and satins and know they didn't have what I wanted. I was in a hurry, because of my appointment at the hair salon, so when I saw a woman who looked familiar I deliberately looked away, just in case I really did know her and would be obliged, if we made eye contact, to make small talk for at least a few minutes. Sometimes being a Southerner is a burden; you can't just nod and go about your business, you have to ask about family, and usually end the conversation with an invitation to come visit, which would really throw a monkey wrench in my schedule if, God forbid, someone actually took me up on it.

Shay, my hairdresser, was putting the finishing touches on a customer when I arrived, so I took a few minutes to look through some hairstyle books. Because it was one of those days when good things seemed to fall in my lap — it was about time I'd had one of those days! — right away I found a hairstyle I liked.

"This one," I said to Shay, pointing to the picture, when it was my turn in her chair.

"*Very* cute," she said, studying the lines of the cut. "But before I start cutting, be sure you want to go that short. You'll be losing five, six inches of hair."

I pushed my hair back to show her the shaved place in my hairline. "I'm sure."

"I guess you are. What happened?"

"I took a header in the mall parking lot." That version saved on explanations. Some other time I might have been in the mood for a lot of drama and sympathy, but right then I was moving on, and wanted to put all that behind me.

She wet my hair with a spray bottle of water, combed my hair back, and started cutting. I had a moment of panic when a half-foot-long strand of blond hair fell on the cape over my lap, but I was strong and didn't whimper at all. Besides, it was too late to turn back, and there's no point in wasting a whimper.

By the time Shay finished her magic with the blow dryer and curling iron, I was ecstatic. My new chin-length hairstyle was chic, swingy, and sexy. One side was pushed back and really showed off my earrings, while the other side sort of swooped down to cover the outside half of my eyebrow, which also, of course, meant it covered the stitches and shaved patch. I gave a tentative shake of my head, just in case the headache waited to pounce on me again, but I remained pain free and my hair did a very satisfying swing and bounce before settling back into place.

When you know you look good, the whole world seems a better place.

I called Wyatt as soon as I was back in the car. "I just got my hair cut," I told him. "It's short."

He paused, and I could hear background

noise that told me he wasn't alone. "How short?" he finally asked, his voice both wary and pitched low.

I've never known a man who likes short hair on a woman. I think their DNA is damaged by testosterone poisoning. "Short."

He muttered something that sounded like "shit."

"I knew you wouldn't like it," I said cheerfully, "so I thought I'd give you a blow job to make it up to you. Toodle."

I hung up, feeling very pleased with myself. If he was able to think of anything besides me for the rest of the day, I'd be surprised.

There was time to pick up something to eat before going to work, so I swung by my favorite barbecue restaurant and got a sandwich to go. Traffic was heavy because the lunch-hour crowd was scrambling to get back to work before one. I was the last in line in a left-hand turn lane waiting for the green arrow when a flash of white filled my rearview mirror.

Automatically I looked in the mirror. A white car was riding my bumper, so close I couldn't see what kind of car it was. The driver was wearing a baseball cap and sunglasses. A man? I couldn't be certain. A smallish man, maybe. I let my car roll forward enough to see the emblem on the front of the white car; it was a Chevrolet. The driver immediately pulled the Chevy close again, closer than before.

My stomach knotted. I had to get over this paranoia. I'd almost been hit by a beige Buick, not a white Chevrolet, so where was the logic? Just because I'd twice seen a white Chevrolet behind me yesterday? It wasn't as if white Chevrolets were rare; if I'd been paying attention, I probably had a white Chevrolet behind me at least once every time I went somewhere. Big deal.

My stomach wouldn't listen to logic, and it stayed knotted. On the traffic light, the green arrow lit and the line of vehicles began moving forward like a snake, the head moving first, then the next segment, until the entire line was moving. I put some distance between me and the white car, distance that it immediately closed. I looked in the mirror; I could tell that the driver had both hands on the wheel, which made it seem as if he or she was deliberately tailgating me.

I was driving an agile, responsive car with a powerful engine that didn't redline until it hit about seven thousand rpms. If I couldn't get away from a tailgating Chevrolet, then I might as well trade this baby in for a Yugo.

Giving a quick check to the traffic around me, I whipped the Mercedes to the right, into the middle lane, taking advantage of a space barely big enough to squeeze into. A horn blared behind me, terrifyingly close, but I swung into the far right lane then shot forward, passing three cars in as many seconds. A glance in the mirror showed the white Chevy trying to swerve into the middle lane, where it almost side-swiped a delivery truck before the driver of the Chevy jerked the car back into the left lane.

Oh my God. If it's really happening, then it isn't paranoia. That car *was* following me!

I braked hard and took the next right, then the next right again. I would have circled the block and got myself behind the white Chevy, but in their wisdom modern street planners almost never put streets in a grid anymore. Instead of a nice ordinary block, I found myself driving on a wide street that curved back and forth, with a lot of cul-de-sacs on it. The cul-de-sacs were filled with various businesses, so it wasn't even a residential area. Excuse me, but has no one ever told these stupid urban planners that *grids* are the most efficient means of moving traffic?

After several frustrating minutes, I gave up trying to work my way back to the street I wanted to be on and simply turned around and went back the way I'd come.

This was weird in the extreme. I don't mean the layout of the city streets, I mean this business with the white Chevrolet. I don't even know anyone who drives a white Chevrolet! I mean, maybe I do, but I don't know it. Like Shay, for instance; I have no idea which car in the parking lot at the hair salon is hers. Or my favorite clerk at the local grocery store. See what I mean? Any of them could drive a white Chevy and I wouldn't know it.

Was there something about me that tipped nutcases over the edge? Some undetectable attractant that sucked them into my orbit? And was there any way to spit them back out and send them on their way? There were other people out there who deserved stalking way more than I did.

Before I pulled back onto the main drag I took a good look around and saw four various models of white Chevrolets. I'm telling you, they were everywhere. None of the drivers paid me the least bit of attention, though, so I pulled into traffic and drove straight to the downtown area where Great Bods was located.

A white Chevrolet was parked at the curb directly across from Great Bods. Someone was sitting in the driver's seat, watching the driver's-side mirror. I saw the sunglasses reflected in the mirror and the bottom dropped out of my stomach.

I took the turn on two wheels, tires smoking, but I didn't go to the back because being alone back there didn't strike me as smart. Instead I pulled into the public parking area in front and skidded to a stop. Leaping out, I darted for the front door of Great Bods as I pulled my cell phone out of my bag. If that nut-case wanted a piece of me, he or she would have to attack me in front of witnesses, at least, and not in an empty back lot.

Maybe I should have called 911, but I didn't. I simply did the redial thing and called Wyatt, as I wheeled to stare through the front windows at the white Chevrolet parked across the street.

"Blair?" Lynn said behind me. "What's wrong?"

"Blair," Wyatt said in my ear, so my name came at me in stereo.

"Someone's following me," I said, my teeth chattering in reaction to all the adrenaline sizzling through me. "A white four-door Chevrolet Malibu . . . looks like a new model, a 2006 or maybe a 2005. It followed me yesterday, too —"

Across the street, the Chevrolet pulled out of its parking space and the driver sedately drove off, not speeding or anything, for all the world as if he or she had finished shopping and was just waiting for a break in traffic before pulling out.

"It just left," I finished, feeling as deflated as one of Mom's soufflés. Mom couldn't make soufflés worth a damn. Lynn came to stand beside me, peering out the window and looking puzzled.

"Did you get the tag number?" Wyatt asked.

"It was *behind* me." I'm pretty sure no one follows from in front.

He let that pass. Big of him. "What do you mean, it just left?"

"It was parked across the street from Great Bods. It just pulled out and left."

"This person followed you to Great Bods?"

"No, I did some juking and got away from them . . . her . . . him . . . whoever the hell it was, but when I got here to Great Bods they were waiting across the street."

Right away I saw the impossibility of that, even if the silence on the other end of the line hadn't been pointing it out, loud and clear. Again, you can't follow from the front; that car had been here before I arrived. There was only one way it could have been the same car, and that seemed just as impossible.

185

"They know me," I said, stunned. "They know who I am and where I work."

Lynn said, "Who does?"

Wyatt said, "Did you recognize the driver?"

I closed my eyes, feeling a little dizzy from hearing a different voice in each ear. Wyatt was the cop, so I concentrated on him. "No. He . . . she — damn it, I couldn't even tell if it was a man or a woman! Baseball cap, sunglasses. I could tell that much. The windshield was tinted."

"What about yesterday? Are you sure it was the same person?"

"A woman was driving yesterday. Long hair. She tailgated me."

"Did you recognize her?"

"No, but . . . she followed me here." Relief poured through me at being able to provide a logical explanation for the Chevrolet being here before I was. "That's how she knew where I work!"

"But you aren't sure it was the same person."

He was being thorough, and logical, the way cops had to be. I knew that on an intellectual level. On an emotional level, though, I wanted him to stop asking questions and round up all drivers of white Chevrolets and beat them bloody. Well, except for old people; I could tell the driver wasn't even middle aged. He shouldn't beat up young kids, either, because I was certain neither of the drivers I'd seen was a teenager. You can just tell, you know? Teenagers have that unfinished, still-growing thing going on. Big people were out, too, as well as teeny people. Okay, the people I wanted beat bloody were of regular size, ages twenty to maybe fifty. How hard could that be?

Taking my silence for a negative answer, which it wasn't, Wyatt asked, "Was there another person in the car with the driver?"

I'd been saying "they" and "them" so of course he would ask that, but the only reason I'd been so confused was because yesterday the driver had been a woman and today I couldn't tell, so there could be two different drivers, but how the hell would I know? "No."

"And you aren't certain it was the same driver both times?"

I was. The visceral part of me that had just been scared stupid was absolutely certain, because otherwise I'd have to believe that two days in a row someone in a white Chevrolet had tailgated me. Okay, so that wasn't much of a stretch. But the most plausible answer wasn't always the right answer.

Wyatt tried again. "Could you testify in a

court of law, under oath, that you're certain it was the same driver in both cases?"

Well, nail me to the wall, why don't you? Thoroughly pissed, I said, "No, not if I were under oath." Then I stubbornly added, "But it was the same driver." *So there.*

He sighed and said, "There isn't anything here I can pursue."

"I'd already figured that out."

Impatiently he said, "Next time, get the tag number."

"I will," I said politely. "I'm sorry I didn't think to do it this time." Yes indeedy, while I was sitting in that turn lane I should have gotten out, calmly walked past the nutcase to the back of the Chevrolet, and jotted down the tag number. The nutcase shouldn't have had any objection to that, right?

After a long silence he said, "I don't know if I'll get to Great Bods tonight in time for you to close."

"That's okay. No problem." I'd been closing Great Bods without him for a long time; I was pretty sure I still knew how. "You take care now, you hear? Good-bye."

He said "Fuck" with restrained violence, and hung up.

Beside me, Lynn said, "I guess what you're doing could be called smiling, because all your teeth are showing, but I have to tell you, it looks damn scary. Great haircut, though."

"Thank you," I said, fluffing my hair a little and then making it swing. I kept smiling the whole time, too.

CHAPTER THIRTEEN

Wyatt wasn't at Great Bods when it was time to close, nor was he at my place when I got home. I felt a little bad that I had bothered him, because he would have been there if he hadn't been tied up with work, which meant that somebody had been murdered or something. He didn't do detective work any longer, but he still had to oversee scenes, stuff like that.

I was also really kind of relieved that he wasn't there, because I was struggling to hold in check my annoyance with him. The only reason I was doing that was because I saw his point. He had to work within the framework of the law, and if I didn't have any concrete information to give him, there was nothing he could do.

But there's professional opinion, and then there's private opinion, like the difference between how I should feel and how I really feel. Regardless of what he could formally do, he could still have said something along the lines of "Look, I believe you. I can't do anything about it, but I trust your instincts."

He hadn't said anything of the sort, though, just as he hadn't really believed me about that crank phone call. He was probably right about the phone call, since there hadn't been any more, but the principle was the same. All I wanted was a little support in my time of need.

Okay, sometimes my thoughts make *me* laugh. What I really wanted was the sun, the moon, and the stars, but what's the point in dreaming little? I've never been one to aim for subpar. I wanted it all, and I wanted it right then; yesterday would be even better. What's wrong with that?

I let myself in, then locked the door and reset the alarm. Even though I knew I'd locked the car, I turned around and aimed the remote through the window in the back door and hit the "lock" button again, just to be certain. I felt uneasy in my own house and I didn't like it. Home was supposed to be a sanctuary, a place where you could relax and sleep in safety.

My sense of being secure here, though, had been damaged when Jason's wife was trying to kill me, and I'd never quite regained it. I'd be glad to move into Wyatt's house with him when we got married. Why didn't I move in with him now? Well . . . because. Number one, I didn't want him to take me being there for granted. He should feel as if he's achieved something when he finally gets me there. Not taking me for granted is probably my number two reason, too. And number three. When we're married and he looks at me sitting beside him at the table, he should feel as if he's fought a great battle and accomplished something — namely, winning me. He'll treasure me more. I like being treasured.

It's the same thing that makes young people take better care of a car they've had to work for and buy with their own money than they do of a car that's given to them. It's human nature. I wanted to be the car Wyatt had to pay for.

I was both anxious and sad to leave my condo behind. It was home — or at least, it had been home. I had decorated every inch of it, and it looked good, if I do say so myself. I should be able to sell it with no problem. In fact, I should probably go ahead and put it on the market, just to get the ball rolling.

Some of my furniture could be used at Wyatt's house — *our* house. I had to get used to thinking of it as ours. And Wyatt had to put my name on the deed with his. I wouldn't really think of it as "ours" until I'd put my stamp on it — repainting, remodeling, and redecorating. Thank God he'd bought the place after his divorce, because I couldn't possibly live there if his ex-wife had also lived there. No way in hell. That was the biggest mistake Jason had made after our divorce: when he remarried, he simply moved his new wife into the house where he'd lived with me. It drove her nuts, literally, though I think she'd already made part of the trip before they got married.

I'd already showered and was walking around the condo mentally placing pieces of my furniture in various rooms of Wyatt's house when he arrived. I was upstairs — all of my bedroom furniture could go, because he had two completely empty bedrooms — when I heard the door open, then the beep of the alarm system, followed by the beep-beep-beep-beep as he closed the door and reset the system.

My heartbeat picked up. Wyatt was here! No matter what, just being around him was as invigorating to me as a hard workout. We'd fight, because we were annoyed with each other, but then we'd make up with heart-pounding sex. We hadn't had sex in almost a week, and I was almost to the point of chewing his pants off.

I went downstairs. I wasn't naked, because I'm only naked in bed or when I'm bathing. Wyatt would probably like me naked all the time at home, but it just wasn't practical. I had on a cherry-red tank top — no bra, of course — and these really cute white pajama bottoms with little cherries all over them. When I fight, I want to look good, just in case I get so mad we *don't* have sex, and he'll really really regret it then.

He was in the kitchen getting a glass of water. His suit jacket was draped over the back of a chair; his white dress shirt was wilted and wrinkled from being worn all day in warm weather, and he still wore his weapon, a big black automatic, on his right hip. My heart squeezed, just looking at him. He was tall and muscular and dangerous looking, and he was *mine.*

Maybe we could forgo fighting, and move on to the sex. I said, "A really bad case, huh?"

He looked up, green eyes narrowed and glittering with temper. "Not especially. There were just a lot of them." He was obviously royally pissed. Wyatt didn't sulk; it was that aggressive, dominant streak in him. When he was mad, he was ready to fight. I liked that. Sort of. At least he didn't pout.

194

I'm a pouter, and two in the same house is one too many.

He set the glass down with a thunk and crowded into my space, looming over me. "The next time you get some nutty idea you're being followed, don't get pissy with me because I don't jump through hoops trying to find your imaginary stalkers. If I'm on my personal time and you get paranoid about something, fine, call me, but when I'm at work I'm dealing with real crimes and I'm not about to waste the city's resources on a wild-goose chase." His teeth were clenched, which was not a good sign.

I drew back a step, internally reeling a little. Wow! He'd let me have it with both barrels. Even though I'd been expecting something and could concede, reluctantly, that he had a point, there was so much in his opening salvo for me to take offense at that for a moment I just blinked my eyes, trying to decide which one to address first.

Imaginary? Paranoid? *Nutty?* "I'm not imagining things! I was followed by someone in a white Chevrolet, two days in a row." My voice rose with indignation, because even though I'd wondered myself if my recent experiences had made me paranoid, I at least knew there really had been a white Chevrolet — or a couple of different white Chevrolets — behind me.

"Well, hell, everyone who goes anywhere in this city has probably had a white Chevrolet behind him at some time or other!" he snapped. "There was one behind me on the way over here, but I didn't immediately assume it was the same vehicle you spotted behind you today. Do you have any idea how many white Chevrolets there are, just in this county, and not taking into account all the surrounding counties?"

"Three or four per square acre, probably," I said, goaded into real temper. He was right; if he'd shut up a minute, I'd tell him he was right. Damn it, doing the right thing is not easy.

"Exactly! So when you saw a white car behind you yesterday, and another one behind you today, and they're driven by different people, how the hell did you come up with the idea that it's the same car?"

"I know! I *know,* all right?" Trying to keep from yelling, because my neighbors had young school-age children who were probably in bed asleep, I took two more steps away from him and leaned against the cabinets, my arms crossed under my breasts. I also took a couple of deep breaths. "You have a point. I understand what you're saying." It galled me to admit it, but fair is fair. "Without a tag number or something concrete, there's nothing you can do, no way you can investigate —"

"*Blair!*" he yelled, evidently not caring about my neighbors' children. "Fuck! Write this down, so you can remember it: No. One. Is. Following. You. There's nothing to investigate! I'm not going to dance to your tune and spend city money because you're feeling nervous. Privately, yeah, I signed on knowing you aren't exactly maintenance free, but leave my fucking job out of it, okay? I'm a city cop. I'm not your private cop you can call on to check out every little thing that pops into your head. These dumb-ass tricks aren't funny. Got it?"

Okay. Okay. I opened my mouth to say something but my mind was curiously blank, and my lips felt numb, so I shut it again. I got it. I *so* got it.

Actually, there didn't seem to be anything *to* say.

I looked around the kitchen, and out into my tiny backyard where the trees were strung with white lights to make it look like a fairyland. A couple of the lights had burned out; I needed to replace them. The vase of flowers on the table in the dining alcove were wilting; I'd have to pick up some fresh ones tomorrow. I looked everywhere except at Wyatt, because I didn't want to see in his eyes what I was afraid I'd see. I didn't look at him because . . . because I just couldn't.

The silence in the kitchen was thick, broken only by the sounds of our breathing. I should move, I thought. I should go upstairs and do something, maybe refold the towels in the linen closet. I should do anything other than just stand there, but I couldn't.

There were arguments I could make. I knew there were. I could explain things to him, but somehow all of that was beside the point now. There were a lot of things I should say, things I should do . . . but I just couldn't.

"I think you should go home."

That was *my* voice saying those words, but it didn't sound like me; it was toneless, as if all expression had been drained away. I hadn't even been aware I was going to say anything.

"Blair —" Wyatt took a step toward me and I stumbled back, out of reach. He couldn't touch me now, he absolutely shouldn't touch me, because too many things were tearing me apart inside and I had to deal with them.

"Please, just — go."

He stood there. Walking away from a fight

wasn't in his nature. I knew that, knew what I was asking him to do. This was too important for me to finesse, too vital to my life for me to risk it for some cosmetic fix that would go only skin deep. I wanted away from him, I had to get away and be completely by myself for a little while. My heart was beating with slow, hard thumps that hurt all over my insides, and if he didn't leave soon I might start screaming from the pain of it.

I took a shuddering breath, or tried to; my chest felt constricted, as if my heart had got in the way of my lungs and wouldn't let them work. "I'm not giving back your ring," I said in that same thin, flat tone. "The wedding is still on —" *Unless you want it canceled.* "I just need some time to think. Please."

For a long, agonizing minute, I didn't think he'd do it. But then he wheeled and left, grabbing his suit jacket on the way out. He didn't even slam the door.

I didn't collapse to the floor. I didn't run upstairs to throw myself on the bed. I just stood there in the kitchen for a long, long time, gripping the edge of the countertop so hard my fingernails were white.

CHAPTER FOURTEEN

Eventually, moving slowly, I checked the doors to make certain they were locked. They were. Though I hadn't been aware of the extra beeps, Wyatt had also set the alarm system on his way out. As angry as he was with me, he was still careful with my physical safety. The realization hurt; this would be easier if he showed some lack of concern, but he didn't.

I turned out all the lights on the first floor, then laboriously climbed the stairs. Every move was an effort, as if there was a disconnect between my mind and body. I went to bed but didn't turn out the lights, just sat in bed staring at nothing as I tried to order my thoughts.

My favorite coping method is to concentrate on something else until I feel ready to deal with the important stuff. That didn't work this time, because my whole world felt filled with the things Wyatt had said. I was battered by them, suffocated by them, crushed under their weight, and there were simply too many of them for me to handle. I couldn't isolate any one thought, nail down any one issue — not yet, anyway.

The phone rang. *Wyatt!* was my first thought, but I didn't grab for the receiver and answer the call. I wasn't sure I wanted to talk to him just yet. In fact, I was certain I didn't. I didn't want him to muddy the water with an apology that would just gloss over the bigger problem I sensed, and that was assuming he thought he owed me an apology anyway, which was a big assumption.

I picked up the cordless phone on the third ring, just to see if it was him calling or someone else, and the Caller ID showed that weird number from Denver again. I set the phone down without answering it. The ringing cut off after the fourth ring anyway, as the answering machine downstairs picked up. I listened, but didn't hear a message being left.

Almost immediately the phone rang again. Denver again. Again, I let the machine get it. Again, no message.

When the third call followed closely on the heels of the second call, I got pissed. Obviously no survey-taker would be calling after eleven p.m., because that's a guaranteed way to not get your questions answered. I didn't personally know anyone living in Denver, but, hey, if someone I knew *was* calling, why not leave a message?

Wyatt had said the number and Denver location could be because someone was using one of those prepaid phone cards, in which case I guess someone I knew could be calling, trying to wake me up. I'd even seen a short item on the local news about phone cards, that the rates were so cheap some people were using them for all their long-distance calls. I might not know anyone in Denver, but I did know people who lived in other places, so the next time the phone rang, I answered it.

Click.

A minute later, it rang again. The Denver number showed on the phone.

These were obviously crank calls. Some piece of punk slime had learned these phone cards weren't traceable and was having fun. How was I supposed to concentrate on Wyatt with this almost constant ringing?

Easy. I got up and turned off the ringer on both my bedroom phone and the phones downstairs. This way the punk slime would still be burning money and minutes, and I wouldn't know a thing about it.

The calls were so irritating that they had

succeeded in breaking through my numb misery. I could think now, at least well enough to know this problem was too big for me to make any sort of decision tonight. I needed to think things through, one issue at a time.

Because writing things down helps me get things ordered in my mind, I got a notebook and pen and settled in bed with the notebook braced against my upraised knees. Wyatt had made a lot of accusations, both direct and indirect, and I wanted to think about them all.

I wrote down the numbers one through ten, and beside each number I wrote a bullet point, as I remembered them.

1. *Nutty*
2. *Did I expect him to jump through hoops, and get pissy when he didn't?*
3. *Paranoid*
4. *Imaginary*
5. *High maintenance*
6. *Dumb-ass tricks*
7. *Did I call him for every little thing that popped into my head and expect him to check it out?*

Try as I might, I couldn't think of anything for numbers eight, nine, and ten, so I crossed them out. Those seven were enough.

One item I knew was wrong. I hadn't been imagining anything. Someone driving a white Chevrolet had definitely been tailgating me today, had definitely tried to follow me, and had definitely been parked across the street from Great Bods. The ball cap, the sunglasses, the facial structure — I'd seen enough to know the person who had been parked waiting for me was the same person who had tried to follow me. Yesterday, a woman driving a white Chevrolet had definitely followed me to Great Bods. Whether or not the two drivers were one and the same was up in the air, but how else to explain how today's driver had known where I work?

Where my imagination bogged down was that I couldn't think of any reason why someone would be following me. I didn't carry large sums of money around. I hadn't robbed a bank and buried the money somewhere. I wasn't the contact for some spy, and, really, why would a spy be in western North Carolina anyway? Neither did I have a former lover or friend or relative who was a spy or a bank robber, and had escaped from prison, and the federal marshals had me staked out thinking that this former lover, friend, whatever, would try to contact me and . . . okay, this was stretching the limits even for Hollywood.

This was where my thinking parted company with Wyatt's, I realized. To him, there was no reason for anyone to follow me, ergo, I wasn't being followed. Where we differed was that I *knew* the driver behind me in the turn lane was also the driver who had been parked across the street, and had arrived ahead of me. I didn't have any proof, but proof and knowledge aren't the same thing.

It stood to reason that if I wasn't imagining things, then I also wasn't paranoid. I'd had my own doubts, because I couldn't see why anyone would be following me. But once I realized that I definitely had been followed then the reason didn't matter, at least as far as paranoia went — unless I was also delusional, in which case none of this mattered because it wasn't happening.

Two items down, five to go.

The "nutty" comment bothered me. I'm neither nuts nor nutty. Sometimes I'll use a convoluted means to get what I want, but that's either to lull someone into thinking I'm a mental lightweight so he'll underestimate me, or because I enjoy the means as much as I do the ends. Wyatt had never underestimated me. He saw the airhead act for what it was: a strategy. I like to win as much as he does.

So what was he calling nutty? I had no way of answering that. He'd have to supply his own answer.

The other four items were way too complicated and serious for me to attempt right then. I was too tired, too stressed, too emotional. Wyatt and I were on the verge of breaking up, and I didn't know what I could do about it.

I was just drifting off to sleep when I realized he hadn't said a word about my haircut. Coming on top of everything else, that did it: I cried.

I slept, but not well and not much. My subconscious hadn't provided any miraculous answers to my problems, either.

Common sense told me, however, that I couldn't act as if time had been suspended. The wedding was still going to take place, until Wyatt and I decided differently. That meant I had work to do. My enthusiasm level wasn't as high as it had been the day before — in fact, it was pretty close to zero — but I couldn't let my pace slack off.

My first stop that morning was Jazz's place of business, Arledge Heating and Air Conditioning. Jazz no longer did the installation work himself, he had employees to do that, but he did go around to new construction sites and figure how many units would be needed, how big, where they would be placed, where the vents would go for maximum effectiveness, that kind of thing. Because of some sneaking around Luke had done, though, I knew Jazz would be in the office instead of out at some site.

The office was a small brick building in an industrial section that was sadly in need of a beautification project — the whole section, not just Jazz's building. I'd never been here before, so seeing the building gave me a whole new slant on Jazz's side of his marital situation. Think plain and unadorned, not so much as a shrub planted by the cracked concrete walk that led from the gravel parking lot to the front door. The front windows did have blinds, but since the building faced west, if someone hadn't installed blinds the office staff would have been blinded every afternoon. Guess that's why they're called "blinds," huh?

There were two gray metal desks in the front room. At the first one sat a battleship in human form. You know the type: enormous gray beehive, glasses on a chain, enormous bosom that preceded her into every room. The woman at the second desk was younger than the first, but not by much; late forties to the other one's mid-fifties, I'd guess. As I entered I heard them gossiping away, but they stopped when they saw me.

"May I help you?" the battleship asked with a smile, her heavily beringed, red-tipped fingers not pausing as she flipped through a stack of papers.

"Is Jazz in?" I asked.

Both women turned to stone, the smile turned to ice, and hostility glared from their eyes. Belatedly I realized that by calling him "Jazz" instead of "Mr. Arledge" I'd given them the wrong impression. This was a little disconcerting, since I always thought of him as an uncle. And was Jazz making a habit of hooking up with women young enough to be his daughter?

I tried to thaw the ice. "I'm Blair."

No hint of recognition in the glaring eyes. In fact, they became even more hostile.

"Blair Mallory," I elaborated.

Nothing.

Well, hell, was this the South or not? Don't tell me these people didn't recognize their employer's wife's best friend's daughter's name! Please.

But nothing was sparking, so I hit them over the head with the information. "I'm Tina Mallory's daughter, you know, Aunt Sally's best friend?"

Realization dawned. It was the "Aunt

Sally" that did it. The smiles came out, and the battleship left its berth to come hug me.

"Why, honey, I didn't recognize you!" she said as I was attacked by a pair of gazongas as soft as your average inflated tire, and I realized she had those suckers hemmed up and packed down, so ruthlessly restrained they probably gave her whiplash when she unleashed them at night. The thought boggled. Even more frightening was envisioning the bra capable of holding them in restraint. It could probably be used as a launcher on an aircraft carrier.

The fastest way to be free of them was to show no fear, and play dead. So I stood there and let her hug me, blinking as I tried not to gasp for air, and all the while smiling the sweetest smile I could manage. When she finally released me I took a deep breath of precious air. "How could you recognize me? I've never been here before."

"Honey, of course you have! Sally and your mama came by one day not long after Jazz opened the business. Sally had Matt and Mark with her, and your mama had both you and your sister by the hand, and you were the two cutest little dolls I've ever seen. Your sister had just started walking."

Since I'm two years older than Siana, the visit this lady remembered would have made me around three. And she didn't recognize me? My God, what was wrong with her? I couldn't have changed that much between the ages of three and thirty-one, could I?

A village somewhere was missing its idiot.

"I don't really remember," I hedged, wondering if I should run for the hills. "I, uh, had a concussion a few days ago and my memory's really spotty —"

"A concussion? My word! You need to sit down, right over here —" My right arm was seized and I was steered to an orange vinyl couch, where I was all but plunked down. "What are you doing out of the hospital? Isn't someone watching you?"

Since when did "concussion" become synonymous with "irreparable brain damage"?

"I'm doing fine," I hastily assured her. "I was released from the hospital last Friday. Uh, is Uncle Jazz in?"

"Oh! Oh, of course he is. He's in the shop building."

"I'll page him," said the other woman, lifting her phone. She punched a button, then two numbers, and a loud buzzer sounded outside. After a minute she said, "Someone's here to see you." She listened, then hung up and smiled at me. "He'll be here in a minute."

It was actually less than that, because the

shop building was directly behind the office building and he had to walk maybe twenty yards. He came hustling in, medium height, bald, with the muscular build of a man who has worked hard all of his life, his face more careworn than I'd ever seen it. Before this problem with Sally he'd put on a little weight, but from what I could see now he'd lost that extra weight and then some. He skidded to a stop when he saw me, frowning in confusion.

"Blair?" he finally said, the word tentative, and I stood.

"You're looking good," I said, going to him for a hug, then kissing him on the cheek the way I'd always done. "May I talk to you for a minute?"

"Sure," he said. "Come on in my office. Do you want some coffee? Lurleen, is there any coffee?"

"I can always make some," said the battleship, smiling.

"No, I'm fine, thanks anyway." I smiled back at Lurleen.

Jazz led me into his office, a depressing space dominated by dust and paperwork. His desk was the same gray metal type as was in the outer office. There were two battered green filing cabinets, his chair — which was patched with duct tape — and two visitors' chairs in a shade of green that almost matched the filing cabinets. There was a phone on his desk, a metal in-out box, a coffee cup that held the usual collection of pens and one screwdriver with a broken handle — that was the extent of his office decor.

Clueless didn't begin to describe him. Poor man, he'd have been absolute putty in Monica Stevens's hands when he'd hired her to redecorate his and Sally's bedroom.

He closed the door, the smile vanished from his face as if it had never been, and he asked suspiciously, "Did Sally send you?"

"Good Lord, no!" I said, honestly surprised. "She has no idea I'm here."

He relaxed somewhat, and rubbed his hand over his head. "Good."

"Good, how?"

"She isn't speaking, but she'll send messages by people she knows I'll talk to."

"Oh, well, sorry. No messages."

"Don't be sorry." He did the head-rubbing thing again. "I don't want any messages from her. If she wants to talk to me, she can damn well act like an adult and pick up the phone." He flashed me a guilty look, as if I were still three years old. "Sorry."

"I think I've heard 'damn' before," I said mildly, grinning at him. "Want to hear my list of bad words?" When I was little, I would recite all the words I wasn't supposed to say. Even then I had lists.

He grinned, too. "I guess I've heard them before. So what can I do for you today?"

"Two things. One, do you still have the invoice from Monica Stevens, for the work she did on your bedroom?"

He winced. "You bet I do. That's twenty thousand dollars thrown up a wild hog's — uh, I mean, wasted."

Twenty thousand? I whistled, long and low.

"Yeah, tell me about it," Jazz muttered. "A fool and his money. I got part of it back from our old furniture that she sold in her shop, but still."

"Is it here?"

"Sure. I wouldn't have the bill sent to the house where Sally would see it, now would I? It was a surprise for her. Some surprise. You'd have thought I'd slit her throat." He got up and opened one of the drawers of the filing cabinet closest to him, rifled through the folders, then pulled out a sheaf of papers that he then tossed onto the desk. "Here."

I picked up the invoices and looked through them. The total wasn't quite twenty thousand, but close enough. Jazz had paid through the nose for the furniture, which was avant-garde, handmade, ugly as sin and twice as expensive. Monica had also replaced the carpeting in the bedroom, put in new artwork, which had also cost a small fortune — exactly what was "Luna," anyway? I knew it meant "moon," but had she hung a fake moon in their bedroom?

"What's this 'Luna'?" I asked, fascinated.

"It's a white vase. It's tall and skinny, and she put it on this lighted pedestal. She said something about drama."

Jazz had paid over a thousand bucks for that piece of drama. All I could say was that Monica had stayed true to her "vision." She liked glass and steel, black and white, weird and expensive. It was her signature.

"Could I have this for a little while?" I asked, already stuffing the invoices in my bag.

He looked puzzled. "Sure. What do you want with it?"

"Information." I hurried on before he could ask me what sort of information. "And could you do one other thing for me? I know this might not be a good time . . ."

"I'm not all that busy, this is as good a time as any," he said. "Just name it."

"Come with me to a furniture store."

CHAPTER FIFTEEN

Jazz was puzzled, but agreeable. He thought I needed his help with something, so he went with me, without even asking why I hadn't asked Dad or Wyatt for help — not that he knew Wyatt's name, but he knew I was getting married because our engagement announcement had been in the newspaper, not to mention Tammy would have told him. He asked when the big date was, and I said in twenty-three days.

Maybe, a little voice whispered in my ear, and my heart squeezed from a mixture of pain and panic.

I had set my cell phone on silent mode, so I wouldn't be distracted by the ringing, and as I drove I fished the phone out of my purse to see if any calls had come in. The message in the little window said I'd missed three calls. Looking back and forth between the phone and the road — yes, I know it's dangerous, blah blah blah — I accessed the incoming calls log. Mom had called, Wyatt's mom had called, and Wyatt had called.

My heart skipped a beat — literally. Wyatt had called. I didn't know if that was good or bad.

I didn't return any of the calls right then, because I had to concentrate on Jazz. I was so glad to have him to concentrate on, too, because I wasn't ready to think about the big stuff. I did keep an eye out for white cars, though; there hadn't been any white Chevrolets behind me on the drive to Jazz's, but that didn't mean I could relax.

When I pulled into the parking lot of the furniture refinisher's, Jazz sort of exploded on me. "No! Absolutely not! I'm not spending another penny buying something she wouldn't appreciate anyway. As she so kindly pointed out, I don't know my ass from a hole in the ground when it comes to decorating —"

"Calm down; I don't want you to buy a thing." I was kind of losing sympathy with both him and Sally, so my voice was a little sharp. It felt weird. I mean, Jazz and Sally really *were* like an aunt and uncle to me, so using my grown-up voice on him was a change of pace. He looked a little startled, too, as if in his head he still saw me as a kid.

"Sorry," he muttered. "I just thought —"

"And she was right about one thing: you *don't* know anything about decorating. One look at your office and I could have told you that. Which is why I'm going to have a long talk with Monica Stevens."

He thought about that for a second, then looked hopeful. "Do you think she'll get Sally's furniture back?"

I snorted. "Fat chance of that happening. It was heirloom stuff. Whoever bought it out of Monica's consignment shop wouldn't turn it loose on a bet."

He sighed, his expression changing back to depression. He looked at the refinishing place, which was really kind of cruddy, with pieces of junk piled haphazardly around the foundation. A rusted iron headboard leaned beside the front door. "Did you find something here that looks like something we had?"

"That isn't why we're here. Come on."

Obediently he followed me. I was beginning to get a read on him. Being stubborn by nature, he'd staked out his position and didn't intend to budge from it. However, because he also loved Sally to death, he desperately wanted someone to do something, anything, that would either force him from his position — so he could feel he had no choice — or would bring Sally around.

I didn't care who made the first move. I had a deadline, and I was desperate.

We went into the shabby place, which was just as piled up on the inside as it was on the outside. A bell over the door rang when we went in, alerting Mr. Potts, the owner, that someone was here. He stuck his head out of the back room, where he did all of his work.

"I'm back here! Oh, good morning, Miss Mallory." He came toward us, wiping his hands on a rag. Since I'd just bought my desk there, and had talked to him a good while, he remembered my name. A faintly puzzled look was on his face. "You look different."

"Hair," I said succinctly, moving my head and making my hair swing. A man I'd met only once had noticed my haircut — well, sort of — and Wyatt hadn't. My heart ached all over again. I pushed thoughts of him away and focused on the problem at hand, introducing Jazz and Mr. Potts to each other. "May we see what you're working on?"

I'd briefed him about the situation, so he fell right in. "Sure, come on back! I'm working on this great old armoire, but it's a handful, let me tell you. I've already got about sixty hours in just stripping off the old varnish and paint. Why anyone would paint a piece of furniture like this, I just don't know." He kept up a running commentary as he led us back to his workroom.

The workroom was more clutter, but it was well lit, with big windows marching down each side. He had all of the windows open for ventilation, as well as a big attic fan running. The smell was still pervasive. The floor was covered with a huge tarp; the tarp itself was a Neimanesque collection of stains and paint spatters. In the middle of the tarp sat the piece in question, a massive eight-foot-tall double-door mahogany armoire, with intricate scrollwork on the doors and around the frame.

Jazz blinked at the huge armoire. "How many hours did you say you've already been working on this?"

"About sixty. This thing is a work of art." Mr. Potts ran a rough hand lovingly over the wood. "Look at this scrollwork. Makes it harder to refinish, because you have to get the varnish and paint out of all these crevices, but that's the price you pay for something like this. People don't do much work like this anymore."

"How long will it take you to finish?"

"Can't say. Another two weeks, maybe. Getting all this crap off without damaging the wood is the hard part."

Jazz walked around the armoire, asking

more questions, then moved on to other pieces of furniture in the workroom, most of them in different phases of restoration. What Jazz knew about antiques, refinishing, and furniture in general was absolutely nothing — other than you sat in chairs, slept in beds, things like that — so Mr. Potts was able to elaborate to his heart's content. When Jazz learned that the armoire was two hundred seventy-nine years old, he turned and gave it a wondering look. "That thing was around when George Washington was born."

I've kept track of a lot of things in my life, but the year George Washington was born isn't one of them. Mr. Potts didn't blink an eye, though. "It sure was. Do you know of the Evers family?"

Both Jazz and I shook our heads.

"This was passed down from generation to generation. Emily Tylo inherited it from her grandmother . . ." He went on to explain how the armoire had ended up at its present home with Emily Tylo, whoever she was.

Finally Jazz got around to what interested him most. "How much is this worth?"

Mr. Potts shook his head. "Don't know, because it isn't for sale. I don't know what value an antique collector would put on it, but Emily Tylo values it plenty because it was her grandmother's. If I were selling it,

I wouldn't take less than five thousand for it, just because of the hours of work I've put in."

I could see the number forming in Jazz's head. Five thousand! Nothing gets a businessman's attention like a lot of zeros. Mission accomplished. The hard part now was getting him away from Mr. Potts, who was taking advantage of having such an interested audience. Finally I just took hold of Jazz's arm and started pulling him toward the door.

"Thank you, Mr. Potts, we've interrupted you enough," I called over my shoulder.

He waved good-bye, and went back to work rubbing on the mahogany armoire.

Jazz wasn't dumb. He knew exactly why I'd taken him to see Mr. Potts. When we got in the car he said, "That was a real eye-opener."

I didn't say anything, mainly because he was doing okay on his own, figuring things out. "I had no idea how much work refinishing is," he murmured. "Sally always had something down in the basement that she was working on, so I never paid much attention to it. She didn't seem to work on the stuff very much, though."

"That's because she wouldn't work on it while you were home. She always said she would rather spend the time with you." Salt is good for wounds. Keeps them from going putrid.

He winced, and spent several minutes looking out the window. We were almost back to his office before he spoke again. "She loved that old furniture, didn't she?"

"Yep. She'd spend months searching for the perfect piece."

His mouth worked a little, then he firmed it. After swallowing a couple of times he said belligerently, "I suppose you think I should apologize."

"Nope."

Surprised, he looked at me. "You don't?"

"I did before. I don't now. Now, I think she should apologize to you first. *Then* you should apologize to her." Okay, I was surprised myself. But it was true. Jazz had made a mistake in not paying more attention to his wife, then he'd made a mistake out of ignorance, but he hadn't deliberately tried to hurt her. Sally had deliberately tried to hit him with the car. Wyatt was right; this was two different kinds of wrongs. Hurt feelings just didn't equate with hurt bodies.

On the other hand, I'd much rather deal with a concussion than the way I felt now, as if the bottom had dropped out of my world and I was in free fall. *Heartsick* had a very real meaning. I wouldn't die of a decline if Wyatt and I broke up. I wouldn't neglect my business, I wouldn't become a nun; I save the dramatics for less important stuff, like getting my way, which, okay, is fairly important to me, but not life and death. But without him I wouldn't be as happy, and maybe wouldn't be happy again for a long time.

I couldn't do anything about that right now, but I could make some progress with Sally and Jazz.

I parked in front of his building and we sat looking at it. "Some landscaping would help," I finally said.

He gave me a blank look.

"The building," I prodded helpfully. "It's like an ugly little box sitting there. You need landscaping. And for God's sake, get rid of that couch."

I can only do so much in one day, and the morning was almost gone. I did take a chance that I might catch Monica Stevens, and stopped by Sticks and Stones.

Like I mentioned, glass and steel was her thing, her signature, and she was a popular decorator. I don't get it myself, but then I don't have to. Sticks and Stones, of course, was decorated in her style. I walked in and paused, giving myself time to stop shuddering before I actually spoke to anyone.

A stick-thin, very chic woman in her forties glided toward me. "May I help you?"

I gave her the full cheerleader smile, wide and white. "Hello, I'm Blair Mallory, owner of Great Bods. I'd like to speak to Ms. Stevens, if she's available."

"I'm so sorry, but she's out on a job. May I have her call you?"

"Please." I gave her one of my business cards, and left. There was nothing else to do until I spoke to Monica herself, and since she wasn't there I now had time for lunch, as well as returning phone calls.

I ate lunch first, on the theory that if I talked to Wyatt before I ate then I might not feel like eating. If I were going to be unhappy, then I'd need to keep my strength up.

When I was back in the car I sat in the parking lot and — yes, I was procrastinating — returned Mom's call first. Then Roberta's. Mom reported that she'd finally run the wedding cake maker to earth and was negotiating an emergency deal with her. Roberta reported that the flowers were well in hand, she had a florist friend who was making the arrangements in her spare time, and I needed to get with her about my bouquet.

I was almost in tears by the time I finished

talking to them, because I didn't know if the wedding would take place or not, but I had to pretend everything was hunky-dory. I couldn't let myself cry because I didn't want my nose to run, because if it did then I'd sound as if I'd been crying when I talked to Wyatt, which of course I would have been, but . . . never mind. It's complicated.

I hoped he wouldn't answer. I hoped he was in the middle of a meeting with Chief Gray, or the mayor, and had his phone turned off, except I knew he never turned his phone off, he just set it to vibrate. So then I hoped he'd dropped his phone in the john. Obviously, I wasn't finished putting off thinking about last night.

But I called him. By the third ring, I was getting my hopes up that he wouldn't answer. Then he answered. "Blair."

I'd sort of halfway planned what I would say, but when I heard his voice I forgot what I'd been planning. So I said something totally brilliant. "Wyatt."

He said drily, "Now that we have our identities sorted out, we need to talk."

"I don't want to talk. I'm not ready to talk. I'm still thinking."

"I'll be at your place when you get off work." He ended the call as abruptly as he'd answered.

"Jackass!" I yelled, sudden fury shaking me, and I threw my phone onto the floorboard of the car, which of course accomplished nothing because then I had to fish it out. It's a good thing I'm limber, because it's a small car.

I didn't want to talk to him yet. The four remaining issues I hadn't considered were so big I couldn't quite face them. What I was most afraid of was that Wyatt would convince me to put this fight behind us and move on, then later these big issues would bite us in the ass. He *could* convince me, because I loved him. And he'd want to convince me because he loved me, too.

That was what worried me. For the first time since realizing Wyatt loved me — I'd known for quite a while that I loved him, the jackass — I had real doubts that we could make a marriage work.

Love by itself isn't enough; it's never enough. There had to be other things, such as liking and respect, or love would get worn away by the realities of everyday life. I loved Wyatt. I adored him, even the things that got me most up in arms, such as that aggressive drive to win that had made him such a good football player and extended to every facet of his character. Wyatt was strong enough that I didn't have to rein in my own alpha tendencies; he could take anything I threw at him.

One of the issues I hadn't tackled yet was suddenly staring me in the face: Wyatt might not *want* to take everything I threw at him.

Two years ago he'd walked away after just three dates because he'd decided I was too high maintenance — that is, not worth the trouble. When Nicole Goodwin was murdered two months ago in my parking lot and for a little while he thought I was the victim, that had forced him to admit that what we'd had going on between us was damn special, like lightning in a jar. So he'd come back and convinced me that he loved me, and we hadn't been apart since, but — and this is a big "but," Hottentot big — for two years he'd been perfectly content not to be with me. That had always irritated me, like a rash, and now I realized why.

I hadn't changed. I was just as high maintenance as I'd always been.

He hadn't changed, either. We had compromised in some things, we'd adapted in other ways, but essentially we were still the same people we'd been two years before, when I hadn't been worth the trouble to him. These past couple of months, what I had seen as a deliciously fun jostling for position, maybe he'd just been enduring.

There was evidently a lot about me that he either didn't know, or didn't like. And facing that was breaking my heart.

CHAPTER SIXTEEN

"The security company called to set up an installation appointment," Lynn said when I got to Great Bods, handing me a list of calls. "And I've worked up an ad for the newspaper for the assistant assistant-manager, since I figured you'd be too busy to take care of it with the wedding so soon. It's on your desk."

"Thanks," I said. "Any complaints today?"

"No, everything's cool. What about you?" She gave me a shrewd look. "Anyone following you today?"

"Not that I've seen." Which was damn annoying, when you think about it. After following me for two days in a row, you'd think whoever was driving that damn white Malibu would show up the day after I had a big argument with Wyatt over whether or not it was really following me, right? I could then get Lynn to verify it was there, get a tag number, things like that. But no, there's no such thing as an accommodating weirdo.

After Lynn left, I forced myself to concentrate on the job. Being angry at Wyatt was good, so I focused on that feeling instead of the brokenhearted one, because anger is so much more productive. Angry people get things done. Brokenhearted people just sit around being brokenhearted, which I guess is okay if you want people to feel sorry for you.

I'd rather be angry. I blew through the rest of the day, mowing down responsibilities and chores. For whatever reason, the clientele was on the sparse side that afternoon and night, giving me time to catch up on stuff, plus some real free time.

For the first time since almost getting mowed down myself, I worked out; nothing jarring, no gymnastics or jogging, because I didn't want to make friends with the headache from Hell again. I did an intensive yoga routine, working up a sweat, then I lifted some light weights, then I swam. I was sort of afraid I'd work off my temper, but not to worry; it was still nice and healthy when I finished.

I wasn't in a hurry to close up and go home that night. Not that I deliberately dawdled, you understand; I just didn't *hurry*. If there was something that legitimately needed doing, I did it, and felt virtuous because I was so conscientious.

I had never before felt uneasy about leaving the gym by myself at night, but that night I opened the door and looked around, making certain no one was lurking nearby, before I stepped out. Thank you, weirdo stalker, for making me afraid at my own place of business. "Afraid" is not a natural state for me, and I don't do it well. It pisses me off.

My car was alone under the parking awning, the way it had been a thousand other nights — I'm guessing here; I worry about people who sit and count things like how many nights they've worked — but tonight I was jumpy, and deeply grateful those bright lights illuminated every inch of the parking lot. After locking the door I hurried to my car, then locked the car doors as soon as I got in. The doors automatically lock when I put the car in gear, but that leaves, what, maybe five seconds when you're vulnerable just sitting there? A lot can happen in five seconds, especially when you're dealing with weirdos. As a group, they're very fast. I guess it's because they're not weighed down with consciences.

I didn't take my usual route home, either. Instead of turning right when I left the parking lot, to hit the main drag in front of the gym, I turned left and wound my way into a residential area, where I'd instantly spot any car behind me, then took a circuitous route home. Nada, no one behind me, at least not in a white Chevrolet.

When I reached my neighborhood, Beacon Hills Condominiums, I did notice a few white cars parked in front of the various buildings, but as Wyatt had pointed out white cars weren't unusual, and, yeah, those white cars were probably always parked there this time of night because no one else was paying any attention to them. There's one lady in the condo next to mine who takes a progressive approach whenever someone unknown parks in her allotted space: she lets the air out of their tires. A guy in one of the other buildings will park his pickup behind the trespasser, so there's no way the offender can leave without hunting him up. As you can see, urban parking is akin to guerrilla warfare. I didn't see any warfare going on, so evidently there weren't any trespassers tonight.

Wyatt's big Avalanche was parked in front of my unit. I live in the third building, first unit on the end. The end units had more windows and extra parking, with covered porticos, so the end units cost more. I thought the cost was worth it. Having an end unit also meant I had neighbors on only one side, which can be a blessing, especially if we were going to have another argument that involved yelling.

I went up the steps and let myself in the side door. I could hear the television in the living room. Wyatt hadn't reset the alarm, knowing I'd be coming home, and though I locked the door I didn't reset the alarm, either — because he'd be leaving. I knew in my bones he hadn't come here tonight intending to spend the night. He would say what he wanted to say, then leave. Nor would I try to stop him, not tonight.

I dropped the bag containing my sweaty gym clothes on the floor in front of the washing machine, then went through the kitchen into the dining room. From there I could see into the living room, where he was sprawled on the couch watching a baseball game. His posture was relaxed and open — his long legs stretched out, his arms draped on each side of him, along the back of the couch. He did that, took command of a piece of furniture, a room, a scene, with his physical presence and confidence. At another time I would have gone into the living room and snuggled against his side, reveling in the feel of his arm coming around me and holding me tight, but I stayed where I was, rooted to the floor.

Somehow I couldn't go into my own living room and sit on any of my own furniture, not now, not with him there. I put my purse on the dining room table and stood there, at a safe distance, watching him.

He'd heard me come in, of course, had probably noticed my car lights reflected on the windows as I turned in. He lowered the volume on the television, then tossed the remote onto the coffee table before looking at me. "Aren't you going to sit down?"

I shook my head. "No."

His eyes narrowed; he didn't like that. The sexual attraction between us was already thick in the room, despite our current . . . was "estrangement" too strong a word? He'd been ruthless in using our sexual attraction when he'd been pursuing me, bringing every weapon he had into play to break down my defenses. Touch is a powerful thing, and he was accustomed to touching me — and being touched, because it went both ways — whenever he wanted, however he wanted.

He stood up, his powerful shoulders seeming to block most of the room. He'd been home and changed; he was wearing jeans and a button-up green shirt, with the sleeves rolled up on his forearms. "I'm sorry," he said.

The bottom dropped out of my stomach as

I waited for him to finish the sentence, to say "I can't do this, I can't marry you." Mentally I reeled, and I reached out and braced my hand on the table, in case my body imitated my mind.

But he didn't say anything else, just those two words; a few seconds clicked by before I realized he was apologizing.

The wrongness of it slapped me in the face, and I drew back. "Don't you *dare* apologize!" I flared. "Not when you think you're right and you're just saying it to . . . to *placate* me!"

His brows lifted in disbelief. "Blair, when have I ever placated you?"

Stopped dead by that question, I had to admit, "Well . . . never." The realization made me feel better, except for that teeny little diva part of me that would like to be placated every now and then. "Why are you apologizing then?"

"For hurting you the way I did."

Damn him, damn him, *damn* him! I turned away before he could see the sudden tears that burned my eyes. Right from the first he'd had an uncanny knack for slipping under my defenses with the simple truth. I didn't want him to know he'd hurt me, I'd much rather he think I was furious.

He wasn't saying he'd realized he was

wrong about all the things he'd said to me last night, just that he was sorry he'd hurt me. Nor had he said those things just to hurt me, to be deliberately spiteful. Wyatt wasn't a spiteful man. He'd said what he said because he believed it to be true — and, yes, that was what hurt so much.

I mastered the tears by deliberately thinking of something disgusting, like people who went shopping barefoot. That really works. Try it sometime. I totally lost the urge to cry, and was able to turn back to Wyatt with my feelings under control.

"Thank you for the apology, then, but it wasn't necessary," I said carefully.

He was watching me intently, focusing on me the way he used to focus on the ball-carrier. "Stop pushing me away. We need to talk about this."

I shook my head. "No, we don't. Not yet. All I'm asking of you is to just let things ride for a little while, let me think."

"About this?" he asked, leaning down to pick up an opened notebook from the couch where he'd been sitting. I recognized the one I'd used last night, with my list of the things he'd said — and I knew I'd left it on my bedside table.

I was horrified. "You snooped upstairs!" I accused. "That's *my* list, not yours! Yours is on the counter!" I pointed toward his list of transgressions, which hadn't been moved; he was still ignoring it. I didn't like him knowing I'd sat up last night obsessing about the accusations he'd made, although he probably didn't need to see that list to guess I hadn't got much sleep.

"You're avoiding me," he calmly pointed out, not the least bit uncomfortable. "I have to get information somehow. And since I don't deal with situations by running away from them . . ."

The accusation was obvious. I said, "I'm not running away from the situation. I've been *trying* to get everything sorted out in my head. If I were running away from it, I wouldn't be thinking about it at all." That was true, and he knew it. I have great avoidance skills. What I didn't say was that he was right, that there was a great deal I hadn't yet been able to face, because facing it might mean the end of Us, big U, us as a couple.

"But you are avoiding *me*."

"I have to." I met his gaze. I can't think when you're around. I know you; I know *us*. It would be too easy to end up in bed together, to gloss over this and not get anything settled."

"You can't think when you're at work?"

"I'm *busy* when I'm at work. Do you spend

all your time thinking about me when you're at work?"

"More than I should," he said grimly.

That admission made me feel a little better, but only a little. "There are too many interruptions at work. I need some quiet time, some alone time, to get things worked out in my head so I know where I stand. *Then* we'll talk."

"Doesn't it strike you that this is something we should work out together?"

"When I know exactly what it is . . . yeah."

Frustrated, he rubbed his hand over his face. "What do you mean — ? *This* is what it is," he said, holding up the notebook like Exhibit A.

I shrugged, unable to get into an item-by-item breakdown, which was probably exactly what he wanted.

"You thought about things last night, obviously, or you wouldn't have made this list."

"Some. The three obvious ones, anyway."

"And you had all morning to think about the other four."

Man, what was I, the suspect in a triple homicide? Any minute now he would be shining a light in my face. "As it happens, I was busy this morning. I was with Jazz."

His expression changed, softened a little. Being with Jazz meant I was still working on our wedding. "And?"

"And I'll be busy tomorrow morning, too." Looking for material for my wedding gown and, if possible, meeting with Monica Stevens.

"That isn't what I meant."

"That's all I'm prepared to tell you."

All this time we'd been facing each other like enemy soldiers, he in the living room while I still stood in the dining room, with twelve, maybe fifteen feet separating us. That wasn't far enough, because I could still feel the tug of chemistry between us, still see the heat in his eyes that meant he was thinking about jumping my bones. My bones were very happy at the idea of being jumped by him. Even with all this unfinished business between us, I wanted him.

The temptation to walk into his arms and forget about all this was strong. I know myself, know how truly, pathetically weak I am when it comes to him, so I looked away to break that eye-to-eye thing we had going on. The red light blinking on my telephone base caught my attention, and automatically I walked over to punch the button and hear the message.

"I know you're alone."

The whisper was barely audible, but it rasped along my nerve endings, made my hair stand up. I jumped back from the answering machine as if it were a snake.

"What is it?" Wyatt asked sharply, suddenly beside me and seizing me with a firm grip. From where he was standing, he hadn't been able to hear the message.

My first impulse was not to tell him, not after he'd accused me of calling him about every little thing that popped into my head. Hurt pride can cause people to do stupid things. When I'm scared, though, hurt pride can go hang itself, and this business of people following me around had me spooked.

I just pointed at the answering machine.

He hit the replay button, and obligingly the whisper came again. *"I know you're alone."*

His expression was hard and unreadable. Without a word he went back into the living room, picked up the remote, and turned off the television. Then he came back and replayed the message again.

"I know you're alone."

The little window gave the date and time of the message, as well as the name and phone number of the caller. The message had been left by that Denver caller, at 12:04 a.m., today's date.

He immediately accessed Caller ID. When the same person called more than once, it didn't show that call separately from the first one, it just showed the total number of calls from that number. The Denver weirdo had called me forty-seven times, the last time at 3:27 this morning.

"How long has this been going on?" he asked, tight-lipped, as he fished his cell phone from its clip on his belt.

"You know how long it's been going on. You answered the second call yourself, last Friday night after I got home from the hospital, while we were eating pizza."

He nodded as he thumbed a number on his cell. "Foster, this is Bloodsworth," he said into the phone, still keeping me hooked to his side with his free arm around me. "I have a situation here. Someone has been calling Blair, forty-seven times since last Friday —" He stopped and looked at me. "Or have you erased your Caller ID log since you got home from the hospital?"

I shook my head. Erasing Caller ID wasn't high on my list of things to do.

"Okay. Forty-seven times. Last night, the caller left a message that makes me think Blair's residence is under surveillance."

"Surveillance?" I squeaked, completely unnerved by the thought. "Holy *shit!*"

Wyatt squeezed me, either in comfort or to tell me to keep the comments down, take your pick. I picked comfort.

"The Caller ID log shows a number, and Denver, Colorado, which leads me to believe this is a calling card number," he continued. "How do we stand on tracing those numbers? That's what I thought. Shit. Okay." He listened a moment, then looked at my phone/answering machine. "It's digital. Okay. I'll bring it in."

He flipped his cell phone shut and hooked it back on his belt, then unplugged my phone from both the phone jack and electrical outlet, wrapping the cords around the base unit to hold the cordless receiver in place.

"Are you taking my phone into custody?" I demanded.

"Yeah. Damn it, I wish you'd said something before now."

Well, that did it. "Excuse the hell out of me!" I yelped indignantly. "I do believe I called you the first time she said something; remember last Saturday, and the woman who whispered, *'Too bad I missed'*? You said something about it being a crank call. As for all these other times, I think they were all last night, because I haven't noticed anything on Caller ID and there certainly hasn't been a message before now. After the fourth one last night, I turned the ringer off on all the phones."

He whipped around to glare at me. "Are you saying this is the same voice as before?"

"Yeah, I am," I said in a belligerent tone. "Yes, I know it's a whisper. The other time she whispered, too. No, I can't be one hundred damn percent certain, but I'm ninety-nine percent sure that's the same voice, and I think it's a woman! So there!" Mature and reasonable, that's me.

"Not only that," I continued, on a roll now, "a woman has been following me! Take it to the bank, Lieutenant! It was a woman who tried to flatten me in the mall parking lot, a woman who's been making harassing phone calls to me — gee, what are the odds that *three different women* have all of a sudden got it in for me? Not very high, right? My goodness, do you think it might be the *same frickin' woman?*"

One might reasonably add "sarcastic" to my list of characteristics.

"Might be," said Wyatt, grim-faced. "Who have you pissed off now?"

CHAPTER SEVENTEEN

"Other than you?" I asked sweetly.

"In case you haven't checked lately, I'm not a woman." He proved it, catching me to him with his free arm, still holding the phone in his other hand. I expected him to kiss me and I was prepared to bite, something I haven't done since the first time Mom took me to the dentist, unless you want to count the time I bit . . . never mind. Something of my intent must have shown on my face because he laughed and pulled me full against him, prodding me with his erection.

I shoved myself away, staring at him, my mouth open in shock. "I don't believe this! You just find out someone's *stalking* me, and you have a *hard-on?* That's *perverted!*"

He gave a one-shouldered shrug. "It's this little hissy fit you're throwing. Does it to me every time."

"I am *not* throwing a hissy fit!" I shouted. "I am *righteously angry!*"

"I like the hissy fits way better than you looking at me like I've slapped you," he said. "Now listen up."

I wasn't in any mood to "listen up." I stalked into the living room and sat down in one of the chairs, so he couldn't sit beside me.

He put the phone on the coffee table and leaned over me, bracing his hands on the chair arms and pinning me in. His gaze was hard and glittering. "Blair, you *will* listen to me. I sincerely, deeply apologize. You're a lot of things, but paranoid isn't one of them. I should have listened and put the pieces together."

I pressed my lips together, waiting for the comment that, if he'd had all the pieces, he might have come to that conclusion earlier. He didn't make it; he doesn't feel the need to state the obvious, as I often do.

"That said," he continued, "there's a strong possibility this nutcase has been watching your condo. How else could she know you were alone last night? We're usually together."

"I didn't see any strange cars when I got home."

"Do you know what everyone in these condos drives? I didn't think so. If she'd made any threats I wouldn't leave you alone, but she's stopped short of that."

"You don't think trying to run me down is a threat?"

"That person was driving a beige Buick, not a white Chevrolet. I'm not completely discounting it as part of the pattern, but it's entirely possible that was a stand-alone incident, and until proof surfaces that the driver of the Buick is also the driver of the Chevrolet, it'll be treated as stand-alone. These harassing phone calls are Class-Two misdemeanors, and if I can find out who's making the calls then you can press charges, but until then —"

"What you're saying is that this doesn't appear serious enough to warrant a great deal of police attention."

"You're getting a great deal of *my* attention," he said. "I'm not taking this lightly. I want you to pack your things and go home with me. There's no reason why you should be harassed and annoyed when you don't have to be."

"I can also just have my phone number changed, and get it unlisted," I pointed out.

"You're moving anyway, when we get married. Why not do it now?"

Because I wasn't certain we'd be getting married. His apology about the woman following me and my supposed paranoia was

246

gratifying, but didn't address our larger issues. "Because," I said. There. Short and to the point.

He straightened, looking incredibly annoyed, considering I was the injured party here.

For a minute I thought he would press the point, but instead he decided against an argument and changed subjects. "I'm taking your phone in to the department, letting one of our techno geeks see if he can do anything with that recording, maybe pull out some background sounds or enhance the voice. Don't answer the phone unless I'm the one calling. In fact, turn on your cell phone; I'll call it instead. If anyone comes visiting, don't answer the door; call nine-one-one instead. Got it?"

"Got it."

"There's a strong chance no one is watching you at any given time, just doing drive-bys to see if your car is here and if my truck is here, so I'm taking your car, and leaving my truck parked out front."

"How would she know you're involved with me at all if she isn't literally watching me?"

"If she knows where you work, then she's seen my truck parked at Great Bods on the nights when you're closing. It's a distinctive vehicle. She could easily have followed both of us here one night."

Something occurred to me and I gasped. "She's the one who keyed my car!"

"Probably." The readiness with which he agreed told me he'd already thought of that.

"That's vandalism! I hope that at least raises this to a Class A misdemeanor." I was a bit disgruntled at being a Class B, or whatever.

"Class-One misdemeanor," he corrected. "And, yes, it does. *If* this person actually did the damage, or had it done."

"Yeah, yeah, I know," I said impatiently. "Innocent until proven guilty, and all that crap. My ass."

He gave a brief laugh and bent to retrieve the phone from the coffee table. "I'm impressed by your sense of justice. And I love your ass."

Actually, I already knew that.

We swapped keys, or rather Wyatt did; I simply gave him my extra key to the Mercedes, which wasn't on a key ring, while he had to take the key to the Avalanche off his ring because his extra, of course, was at his house. I had once pointed out that having the extra at home did him no good if he lost his keys, to which he had smugly replied that he didn't lose his keys.

"I relocked the front door when I came in," he said as he let himself out the side door, into the portico. "Don't forget to set the alarm."

"I won't."

"It's already late, and I don't have clothes here for tomorrow, so I won't be back tonight unless you hear or see something, but if you do, call nine-one-one before you call me. Got it?"

"Wyatt."

"Call nine-one-one on the landline so they'll have your address, and use the cell to call me."

"Wyatt!" I said, getting more annoyed with every word out of his mouth.

He stopped and turned. "Yeah?"

"Hello, telephone expert here! I grew up with one attached to my ear. I also know how nine-one-one works. I think I can manage."

"Hello, cop here," he replied, mimicking my tone. "I tell people what to do. It's my job."

"Oh, great," I muttered. "You're turning into me."

He grinned, grasped me behind the neck, and pulled me to him for a quick, hungry kiss. I didn't have time to bite him, it was so quick.

"Three things," he said. "For the record."

"What?"

"One: it isn't just your hissy fits that turn me on. So far, pretty much everything does the trick."

I didn't look down at his crotch, but I wanted to.

"Two: I didn't think I would, but I love the haircut. You're cute as hell."

Involuntarily I touched my hair. He'd noticed!

"And three . . . "

I waited, unwillingly breathless with anticipation.

"You still owe me a blow job."

I double-checked every door and window, and made certain the alarm was set. I pulled the curtains over the double French doors leading from the dining alcove onto the covered patio. My small backyard had a six-foot privacy fence around it and a gate that could only be unlocked from inside, but a six-foot barrier isn't insurmountable. The fence was for privacy, not security. Big difference.

If I were going to break into a place, I'd pick the back, so there would be a much smaller chance of being seen. With that in mind, I turned on the little white lights that festooned the trees, and the patio light. Then

I turned on the light over the side door, in the portico. I turned on the front porch light. I felt a little dumb, lighting up the place like a Christmas tree, but I didn't want any entrance to my home shrouded in darkness.

As tired as I was, I was too uneasy to sleep. I also still needed to do some thinking about Wyatt, to figure out exactly which issues had been addressed tonight and which hadn't, but at the same time keep an eye out for some moron in a Malibu. I don't know if it's possible to deeply ponder issues and at the same time be hypervigilant. I'm guessing not.

I compromised by staying awake and not having the television on, or the earbuds of my iPod stuck in my ears, so I could hear any unusual noises, and doing mundane stuff that didn't need a lot of concentration. I got out the clothes I was going to wear the next day. I got my new shoes out of the closet and tried them on again, and they were as gorgeous as they had been last Thursday when I'd bought them. I walked in them to make certain they were comfortable, since I'd be wearing them for hours. They were. I was in shoe heaven.

That reminded me that my snazzy blue boots from Zappos should have arrived, but any delivery was left on the steps under the portico and there hadn't been anything there. I suppose some new delivery person could have left the box on the front porch, but in that case Wyatt would have brought it in. No delivery, then.

I was still carrying a summer purse, and it was time to switch to a more substantial autumnal bag, so I got my purse from downstairs, carried it up, and dumped the contents on my bed. Jazz's invoice from Sticks and Stones caught my attention, of course, and I went over it again item by item. Part of me was outraged by Monica Stevens, but part of me had to admire her; it takes guts to overprice things by that much.

I swapped everything over to a nice leather tote, and stored the summer bag on the top shelf of my closet. Then I checked Caller ID on the upstairs cordless to see if there had been any more calls from Denver. Nothing.

Finally I couldn't think of any other trivial things to waste time with, and I was yawning, so I crawled into bed and turned out the light. As soon as I did, of course, I was no longer sleepy. Every sound I heard seemed creepy, even those I knew.

I got up, turned the lights back on, and went downstairs to the kitchen where I selected the biggest chef's knife I owned. Comforted by the weapon — hey, it was better than nothing — I went back upstairs. Five minutes later, I was back downstairs digging in the closet under the stairs, where I unearthed my big black umbrella that looked like something out of *Mary Poppins*. I usually carry smaller, more colorful umbrellas, but I have the big black one just because I think everyone should have a serious umbrella. Closed, it was very sturdy; I figured it was strong enough to hold off a psycho stalker bitch while I whacked at her with my chef's knife. With my umbrella lying on the bed on top of the covers, and the knife on my bedside table, I felt as prepared as I was likely to be, short of buying a shotgun.

I turned out the lights, lay down, and promptly sat up again. This was not going to work. Getting up, I turned on the lights in the hall and on the stairs. That way I had light, but it wasn't shining directly in my eyes, plus anyone who came to the door would be silhouetted against the light but wouldn't be able to see me. Good plan.

As I drifted off to sleep, I wondered why I didn't own a shotgun. Single woman, living alone; a shotgun made sense. Every woman needs a shotgun.

I woke an hour later to roll over and look at the clock. Fifteen after two. All was quiet.

I checked Caller ID again; no calls had come in.

I should have gone to Mom and Dad's, I thought. Or to Siana's. At least then I'd have been able to sleep. Now I'd be exhausted all day tomorrow.

I dozed off again, and woke a little after three. No crazy was silhouetted against the light. I didn't check the phone, because by this point I didn't care if the crazy bitch had called. Sort of half dozing, I tried to get comfortable in bed. My knee banged the umbrella. I felt hot and uncomfortable, and the flickering light was annoying.

Flickering light? If the electricity went out, I would so freak.

My eyes opened and I stared at the hall, where the light seemed to be steady enough, but the light in my bedroom was definitely flickering.

Except I hadn't left any lights on in my bedroom.

I sat up and stared at my windows. Beyond the pulled curtains, red lights danced.

From below came a huge crash as something broke the windows, and my alarm began its cautionary beeping, warning that it was about to erupt into full shrill. "Shit!" I leaped out of bed, grabbed the umbrella and chef's knife, and bolted into the hall, only to reel back as a blast of heat and fiery sparks rose to meet me.

"Shit!" I said again, retreating to the bedroom and slamming the door against the heat and smoke. Belatedly, my fire alarm began its piercing shriek.

I grabbed the phone and dialed 911, but nothing happened. The phone service was already gone. So much for that plan. I had to get out of here! Roasting alive was so not on my schedule. I grabbed my cell and punched in 911 as I ran to the front window and looked out.

"This is the nine-one-one emergency operator. What is the nature of your emergency?"

"My house is on fire!" I screamed. Shit! The whole front of the condo was leaping with flames. "My address is three-one-seven Beacon Hills Way!"

I ran to the other window, the one overlooking the portico. Flames were already eating through the slanted roof right below the window. Shit!

"I've dispatched the fire department to your address," said the calm operator. "Is anyone else in the house with you?"

"No, I'm alone, but this is a condo and there are four units in this building." The heat and smoke were building at a terrifying speed, and all of my windows were blocked by fire. I couldn't go downstairs and out through the French doors in back because whatever had been thrown through the windows had ignited the entire living room, by the looks of it, and the stairs ended there by the front door.

The second bedroom! Its windows overlooked the back, which was secured by the privacy fence.

"Can you get out, and direct the fire department to the correct building?" the operator asked.

"I'm upstairs and the whole downstairs is on fire, but I'm going to give it the old college try," I said, coughing on the smoke. "I'm going out the window. Bye now."

"Please stay on the line," she said urgently.

"Maybe you didn't understand," I yelled. "I'm going out the window! I can't do that and talk on the phone at the same time! The fire department will be able to spot the condo just fine, tell them to look for the one with flames shooting out the windows!"

Flipping the phone shut, I tossed it in my bag, then darted in the bathroom and wet a towel, which I tied over my nose and mouth, then I wet another one and draped it over my head.

All the experts say don't bother getting your purse or anything, just get out, because you have only seconds to do it, I didn't listen to the experts. I not only grabbed the tote, which held my wallet and cell phone and Jazz's invoices from Sticks and Stones — the invoices seemed horribly important — I also grabbed the chef's knife and dropped it into the tote bag, too. The plan was, when I got out of this death trap, if I saw some psycho bitch out there, leaning against a white Malibu and gloating, I intended to gut her.

I made it to the bedroom door, then turned and made a swooping dive at my closet. Grabbing my wedding shoes, I stuffed them in the tote bag, too. Then, barefoot, I wrenched open my bedroom door. With a great *whoosh* the flames in the living room seemed to rush up the stairs. Sparks danced in the air, and black smoke already obscured the hallway. I knew exactly where I was, though, and exactly where the door to the other bedroom was. Getting down on my hands and knees, with the braided handles of the tote looped on my shoulder, I crawled as fast as possible down the hall. The smoke burned my eyes like all the fiends in Hell, so I simply shut them. I couldn't see where I was going anyway. I knew by feel when I reached the doorway, and raised on my knees to search for the doorknob. I found it, turned, and pushed inward, then all but fell into the relatively clear air of the bedroom.

Relatively clear. Smoke boiled in the open door and I hurriedly shut it again, coughing as the evil black stuff sifted around the edges of my wet towel and through the fabric. At least it wasn't so thick I couldn't see the lighter rectangle of the window. I crawled to it, pushed the curtains aside, fumbled with the latches — "Damn it!" I said hoarsely, when one wouldn't give. "Son of a bitch!" I was *not* going to let that bitch burn me to death.

Unslinging the tote from my shoulder, I reached into it and by some miracle didn't cut my finger off on the razor-sharp blade of the chef's knife. Grabbing the heavy knife by the handle, I began whamming the butt of it against the stubborn latch.

From downstairs I heard more glass shatter from the heat. I whammed harder, and the latch began giving. Two more whams, and it slid open.

Gasping for breath, coughing, I shoved the double-hung window open and hung over the sill, trying to stay below the smoke that poured out of the room so I could find some fresh air. My lungs were on fire, despite the wet towel protecting my mouth and nose.

I heard sirens, I thought, but maybe my own fire alarm was still valiantly shrilling an

258

alert. Maybe the neighbor's alarm had gone off. Maybe the fire department had arrived. I couldn't tell, but I wasn't waiting to see.

I threw the comforter off the four-poster guest bed and stripped both sheets off so fast I pulled the mattress half off the bed with the force of my tugging. Working as fast as I could, I knotted one corner of the sheet around the leg of the footboard, then tied the other sheet to the opposite corner of the first sheet, making a sheet rope that reached from the bed to the window, and down the side of the condo.

I didn't stop to see if the sheet rope was long enough, I just tossed my tote out the window, then grabbed the sheet and went out the window.

It's funny how the body works. I didn't consciously think about how I was going out the window, but my body knew what to do from all those gymnastic exercises. I climbed out feet first, then automatically caught the sill and turned so I was facing the outside of the building and could brace my feet against the wall.

Holding tight to the sheet, I began lowering myself hand over hand, my feet "walking" down the wall — until I ran out of both sheet and wall. I hung there for a minute, panicked; to my left, flames were breaking through the kitchen window. The guest bed-room was built to overhang the bottom floor, the bedroom floor providing the cover for the small patio. I had no more wall to walk down, and below me was an eight-foot drop.

What the hell. I'd been higher than that when I was at the top of a cheerleader pyra-mid. And, correct me if I'm wrong here, but I'm five-four. With my arms stretched over my head I can probably reach six and a half feet, give or take a few inches. That left just a foot and a half to the ground, right?

Not that I was hanging there doing math. I just looked down, thought, "How far can it be?" and let my legs swing down. When my arms were fully extended, I let go.

I think it was farther than a foot and a half.

Still, I landed with my knees bent the way I had trained, the cool damp grass absorbing some of the impact, and rolled.

I came to my knees and stared at the spec-tacle before me. Sparks were shooting into the air like obscene fireworks. The fire made a roaring sound, as if it were alive. I'd never heard a fire before, never been close to a burning building, but it's this . . . this own thing in itself, something with a whole new identity. For now, while it burned, it was alive, and it wouldn't die without a fight.

I was still trapped, there in the tiny fenced backyard with the flames devouring my home, looming over me, blackened walls threatening to collapse. Scrabbling around on the ground, I located the dark tote and this time looped the straps diagonally over my head and shoulders, then darted for the gate. I shoved the heavy latch open, pushed on the gate — and nothing happened. It wouldn't budge.

"Son of a *bitch!*" I shrieked hoarsely, so furious I could barely stay in my skin. Forget the knife; if I could get my hands on that moronic psycho nutcase bitch, I wouldn't need a blade, I'd do the job with my bare hands. I'd tear her throat out with my teeth. I'd set her hair on fire and toast marshmallows in the flame.

No, wait. That could get icky. Forget the marshmallows.

After climbing out a second-story window, a six-foot fence wasn't about to get the better of me. Reaching up, I caught the top of the fence and hauled myself up far enough to hook my right leg over, then I pushed upright, swung my left leg over, and vaulted to the ground.

Red lights were flashing everywhere. Men in yellow turnout suits were moving with urgent purpose, stringing out thick fire hoses, attaching them to pumps and fire-plugs. People in their nightclothes were spilling into the street, some of them with pants hastily pulled on over pajamas, the fire and flashing lights throwing weird shapes and shadows over them. A fireman grabbed me and yelled something but I couldn't understand him, because the fire trucks themselves made a god-awful amount of noise, added to the roar of the fire and sirens from other emergency vehicles that came racing toward us.

I guessed he was asking if I was hurt, so I yelled, "I'm okay!" Then I yelled, "That's my condo!" and pointed to it.

With one arm he literally lifted me off my feet and rushed me away from the fire, away from the showers of sparks and exploding glass, away from the blasting streams of water, the sagging electrical lines, and didn't let go until I was safely on the other side of the street.

I still had the wet towel tied over my mouth and nose; I'd lost the one I'd thrown over my head, somewhere between dropping and rolling. Whipping the towel free, I sank to my knees and sucked in fresh air as deeply as I could, coughing and gagging at the same time. When the coughing subsided a little and I could stand up, I began working my way through the crowd of people, pushing when I had to, wiggling my way through when I could, looking for a psycho bitch who would, obviously, be dressed in regular clothes instead of a nightgown or pajamas.

CHAPTER EIGHTEEN

Wyatt!

His name flashed in my brain and I paused in my woman-hunt to fish in the tote for my cell phone. This time, damn it, I did nick my finger on the knife. Snarling, I stood the knife, blade down, in one of the inside pockets — why hadn't I thought to do that before? Oh, yeah, preoccupied with trying to escape a burning building — and stuck my finger in my mouth. When I pulled my finger out to examine the damage, there was nothing but a thin hairline of red on the pad of my finger, so no great harm done.

I found the cell phone, and when I flipped it open the little window lit up and told me I'd missed four incoming calls. They were probably all from Wyatt, because someone would either have recognized the address and called him, or he'd been sleeping with the police radio beside him. I dialed his cell.

"Blair!" he yelled furiously as a greeting.

"Why haven't you been answering your fucking phone?"

"I didn't hear it ring!" I yelled back. My voice was so hoarse I didn't recognize myself. "A house fire and all the alarms make a lot of noise, you know! Besides, I was busy climbing out the upstairs window."

"God almighty," he said, sounding shaken. "Are you hurt?"

"No, I'm all right. My condo's a goner, though." I looked across the street at the scene of destruction and a horrible realization sank in. "Oh, no! Your truck!"

"Never mind the truck, I'm insured. Are you sure you're all right?"

"I'm sure." I understood why he was double-checking. With my recent history, he was no doubt expecting me to be in critical condition. "Other than cutting my finger on the knife in my purse, I don't think I have any injuries at all."

"Find a police officer and stick to him like glue," he ordered. "I'm almost there, another five minutes at the most. I'm betting this isn't an accident, and the stalker may be right behind you."

Startled, I spun around and stared right into the face of an elderly gentleman who had been standing behind me, watching the fire with wide-eyed interest and horror. He jumped back in surprise.

"That's why I have the knife," I said, fury roaring through me again. "When I find that bitch —"The old man's eyes got even bigger and he began backing away.

"Blair, *put the knife away and do only what I told you to do,*" he barked. "That's an order."

"You weren't in that fire," I began in hot defense of myself, but the sound of dead air told me he'd disconnected.

Phooey on him; I wanted some face-to-face time with her. I closed my phone, dropped it in the tote, and resumed my weaving pattern through the crowd of on-lookers, staring at their clothes instead of their faces. Men were automatically not in the running. She might not be here. She might have left immediately after throwing her firebomb or whatever through the window, but I'd read that killers and arsonists often hung around afterward, mingling with the crowd of onlookers, so they could enjoy the uproar they'd caused.

Someone touched my arm and I whirled. Officer DeMarius Washington stood there. We'd gone to school together, so we knew each other from way back.

"Blair, are you all right?" he asked, his dark face tense under his baseball cap.

"I'm fine," I said for what seemed like the hundredth time that night, though my voice was becoming more raspy by the second.

"Come with me," he said, taking me by the arm, his head swiveling as he constantly looked around. Wyatt must have radioed in, told them I was in danger. With a sigh, I gave in. I couldn't very well hunt for a psycho with DeMarius at my side, because he was sure to prevent me from gutting her. Cops are weird that way.

He led me away from the crowd, toward a patrol car. I tried to be careful where I stepped, because there was so much debris on the ground and I was barefoot, but with him pulling on my arm I didn't always have a choice. My left foot came down on something sharp and I yelped with pain; DeMarius whirled, his hand moving toward his service weapon as his gaze darted around, looking for the threat.

"What happened?" He had to half yell, because of the din.

"I stepped on something."

He looked down and for the first time noticed my bare feet. He said, "Oh, hell," which wasn't very professional of him, but like I said we've known each other forever — since we were six, in fact. I took another step and yelped again as soon as my left foot touched down. Held upright by his grip, I sort of hopped around as I lifted my foot to peer at it. All I could tell was that the bottom of my foot was dark; God only knew what I'd stepped in.

"Hold on," said DeMarius, and he half carried, half hustled me to the patrol car. Opening one of the rear doors, he set me down sideways on the seat, with my legs and feet on the outside, and took his flashlight from his belt as he hunkered down.

The flashlight revealed that the bottom of my foot was red, and wet. A sliver of glass protruded from just behind the ball. "I'll get the first-aid kit," he said. "Sit tight."

He returned with both a first-aid kit and a blanket, which he draped around my shoulders. I hadn't been aware of being cold; there's something about fighting for your life that throws you into high gear. Now the early-morning chill was sinking in as my adrenaline level dropped, and for the first time I was aware of my bare arms and shoulders. All I was wearing was my usual tank top — no bra, of course — and thin drawstring pajama pants that hung low on my hips and showed my belly button. Not what I would have chosen to escape a burning building in, but I hadn't had time to change clothes; I'd barely managed to rescue my wedding shoes.

Those were now the only shoes I owned.

I pulled the blanket tight around me while I twisted to stare at my burning home. The urgency of escaping had taken priority over everything else, but now I realized that I had lost everything: all my clothing, all my furniture, my dishes, my cookware, my *stuff.*

DeMarius whistled sharply, and I looked up to see him waving a medic over. I said, "It's just a little sliver of glass, I can probably pull it out with my fingernails."

"Sit tight," he said again.

So the medic came over, and DeMarius held the flashlight while the guy — he was neither Dwayne nor Dwight — poured antiseptic over my foot, then extracted the sliver using a pair of tweezers. He slapped a gauze pad over the puncture wound, wound some of the crinkly stuff that sticks to itself around my foot, and said, "You're good to go."

"Thanks," said DeMarius, leaning down to scoop my feet and legs into the car; then he closed the door.

For a minute I just sat there, suddenly so exhausted all I could do was slump against the seat, glad to be out of the cool air, not able yet to absorb the complete enormity of the fire and everything it meant.

I watched a small black car approach the

entrance to the condos, roll to a stop as a patrolman held up a hand to stop, then a familiar face appear in the window as it slid down. The patrolman stepped back and waved him forward, and Wyatt zipped my sharp little convertible past him, parking it on the grass a safe distance from the fire. As he unfolded his long legs and got out, I reached for the door handle so I could get out and go meet him. Suddenly I wanted nothing in this world so much as I wanted his arms around me.

My searching fingers found only smoothness. No door handle, no window control, nothing.

Well, duh. This was a *patrol* car. The whole idea was that whoever was put back here wouldn't be able to get out.

I knocked on the window. DeMarius turned and looked at me, his eyebrows raised. "Let me out," I mouthed, and pointed toward Wyatt. He turned and looked, and I swear an expression of relief crossed his face. He signaled Wyatt, Wyatt saw him — and me — and my dearly beloved gave a single sharp nod of his head before turning away.

Realization left me speechless. Wyatt had radioed in and told them to put me in a squad car and hold me there. That *sneak.*

That complete and utter *sneak!* How dare he? Okay, so I'd been stomping around barefoot, armed with a chef's knife, searching for the sow who tried to turn me into a crispy critter; that's an understandable reaction, right? Turning the other cheek is one thing, but when someone burns down your house, what are you supposed to do? Turn the other house? I don't think so.

I tapped on the window again, harder. De-Marius didn't look around. "DeMarius Washington!" I said as sharply as possible, given my throat felt like sandpaper. If he heard me, he made no sign, but he took a few steps away from the squad car and turned his back.

Thwarted and furious, I flung myself back in the seat and grumpily pulled the blanket tight around me again. I thought about calling Wyatt with my cell phone and giving him what-for, but that would mean *speaking* to him, and right now I wasn't. I might not speak to him for the next *week.*

I couldn't believe he'd had them lock me in a squad car. Talk about misuse of power! Wasn't this illegal, or something? Unlawful detainment? Only criminals were supposed to be closed up in the back of one of these things, which, come to think of it, did smell sort of *criminally.*

My nose wrinkled, and automatically I lifted my feet from the floorboard, holding them in the air. God only knows what kind of germs were back there. People puked in the back of squad cars, didn't they? I was pretty certain I also smelled urine. And feces. He knew what sort of things went on in the back of squad cars, and still he'd had me put in one. The callousness appalled me. I was thinking of *marrying* this man, a man who would jeopardize the health of his future wife for a power play?

My God, the things I could put on his list of transgressions.

Because I'd been so worried about the list, the thought of its revival almost cheered me up. Almost. This was so bad not even the list could make up for it.

I beat on the window with the side of my fist. "DeMarius!" I yelled — or rather, croaked. My voice was getting so bad I sounded awful. "DeMarius! I'll make you a Krispy Kreme doughnut bread pudding if you'll let me out of here."

From the way his shoulders stiffened, I knew he heard me.

"Just for you," I promised as loudly as I could.

He barely turned his head, but I saw the agonized look he rolled my way.

"I'll give you your pick of rum glaze, buttermilk glaze, or creamed cheese icing."

He stood frozen for a few seconds, then heaved a big sigh and came over to the door. *Yes!* Happily I began preparing to leave my stinky prison.

DeMarius bent down to the window and looked in, his dark eyes mournful. "Blair," he said loudly enough for me to hear, "as much as I love your doughnut bread pudding, I don't love it enough to cross the lieutenant and get demoted." Then he turned his back and returned to his previous position.

Well, damn. Bribery had been worth a try, but I couldn't blame DeMarius for not falling for it.

With nothing else to distract me from what I'd been trying not to think about, I arranged the blanket beneath me, got on my knees in the seat, and turned to look out the back window at my home. The firemen were putting up a valiant effort to prevent the fire from spreading to the next apartment, but I knew my neighbors would have massive smoke and water damage at the least. Wyatt's truck and the car next to it were both scorched, the heat had been so intense. As I watched, the front wall collapsed with a roar, sending sparks cascading up and out like the fireworks at Disney World.

The sudden flare of light illuminated a face — a woman's face, in the midst of the crowd. She wore a hoodie, her hands tucked in the pockets and the hood pulled loosely around her head. I noticed the paleness of her blond hair first, then I looked at her face. A twinge of uneasiness snaked up my spine. There was something vaguely familiar about her, as if I'd seen her somewhere else but just couldn't place her.

She wasn't staring at the spectacle of fire, though. She was staring straight at the patrol car, and at me, and for a split second there was nothing but triumph in her face.

It was *her.*

CHAPTER NINETEEN

I began beating on the window again, as hard as I could, screaming, "DeMarius! *De-Marius!* There she is! Tell Wyatt! Do something, damn it, *stop her!*" That is, I was trying to scream.

His back remained stubbornly turned, and though he could hear my fist thumping against the window he very likely couldn't hear anything I said because my voice was almost gone. My throat caught and I began coughing violently, the force of the spasms doubling me up and making my eyes water.

The rasping in my throat hurt; I felt as if I were raw on the inside, from the back of my nose all the way down into my lungs. Even breathing hurt. I must have inhaled more smoke than I'd thought, even with the wet towel over my face. Screaming hadn't helped any, either — as well as accomplishing exactly nothing.

When I could sit up straight again, I

looked for her, for the bitch who had burned down my home, but she was gone. Of course she was; she'd wanted to admire her handiwork, gloat a little bit, but she wasn't going to stick around.

Tears of fury and pain began to drip down my face. Furiously I wiped them away. I would *not* let that bitch make me cry. I wouldn't let any of this make me cry.

I dug my cell phone out and called Wyatt.

I half expected him not to answer, which would have made me so much angrier at him I'm not certain I'd have been over it by the time I filed for Social Security. Going to my knees again, I looked for him while I listened to the ringing. Then I saw him, taller than most of the other men, his head bent a little as he listened to the fire chief yelling something over the noise, and I saw him reach for his cell. He must have had the phone set to vibrate, which was smart considering the noise level. He said something to the fire chief, checked to see who was calling, then flipped open the phone and held it to one ear while he pressed a finger to his other ear.

"Be patient a little while longer!" he yelled into the phone.

I opened my mouth to blast him, to screech at him that he was letting her get away — and not one sound would come out.

Not even a squeak.

I tried again. Nothing. I had completely lost my voice. Frantically I pecked on the microphone with my fingernail, trying to get him to at least look at me. Damn it, there was no way he could hear that little bitty noise. Both frustrated and inspired, I began banging the phone itself against the window.

Note to self: Cell phones are not sturdy.

The damn thing came apart in my hand, the battery cover coming off, the front piece flying into the floorboard — where it could stay, as far as I was concerned, because no way was I rooting around in that particular floorboard to look for it. Some other electronic little doohickey went askew. All in all, it was a futile effort.

Aaargh! I watched Wyatt close his phone and hook it back on his belt. Not once did he glance in my direction, the jackass.

What else did I have in my tote? The knife, of course, but slicing up the upholstery wouldn't gain me anything and would cost me big-time, because I'm fairly certain the city takes a dim view of having its squad cars sliced and diced. The knife wouldn't help me. My wallet was in there, my checkbook, lipstick, tissues, pens, my appointment book — all right! Now we were cooking. I tore a page out of the back of my appointment book, got a pen, and in the otherworldly, flickering, uncertain light wrote: TELL WYATT THE STALKER IS HERE I SAW HER IN THE CROWD.

I plastered the note to the window, then frantically began knocking on the glass again. I knocked and knocked and knocked, and DeMarius, damn his stubborn hide, refused to turn around and *look.*

My hand began to hurt. If I hadn't been afraid of giving myself another concussion, I'd have beat my head against the window; I already felt as if I were beating it against a wall. If I'd had on shoes, I'd have started kicking the window. There were a lot of ifs, and all of them worked against me.

I put the note down and tugged on the metal cage thingie that separated the backseat from the front and protected the officers. They weren't meant to be budged; if they had been, I'm sure there are a lot of people stronger than I am who would already have budged them. So much for that effort.

There was nothing I could do. I pressed the note against the window again, rested my head against the paper to hold it in place, closed my eyes, and waited. Eventually, someone would let me out, and then they'd all know what stupid assholes they were.

For all the attention anyone was paying me, the psycho stalker bitch could walk up to the car from the other side and shoot through the window. As soon as the thought popped into my head I sat up and took a panicked look around, but no psychos were in sight. Well, that particular one wasn't, anyway.

I remembered putting some of that clean-your-breath gum in the tote. I felt around in the tote until I found it, punched out a piece, and began chewing. While I chewed I tore another page out of my appointment book and wrote: FORGET JAZZ AND SALLY THE WEDDING IS OFF!!!! When the chewing gum was thoroughly chewed I took it out of my mouth, pinched it in half, and used one half to stick the Stalker note to the window, and the other half held the Jazz and Sally note right below it.

Then I punched out more gum, and tore another sheet out of the appointment book.

Because the back window sloped, I needed both halves of that piece of gum to do the job. That note said: ASSHOLE MEN.

The pack of gum held ten pieces. I used all of them.

By the time anyone noticed, I pretty well

had the back window and both side windows plastered with notes.

Through one of the bare places — not that there were many — I saw a patrolman glance over, do a kind of "What the hell?" look, then nudge someone else and point. A couple of others noticed the pointing, and they looked, too. DeMarius noticed *that,* even though he'd ignored my beating and yelling — when I could still yell, that is — and he turned around to look. He grinned and shook his head, pulling out his flashlight as he approached.

I turned my back on him and crossed my arms. Damned if I'd beg to be let out now, when it wouldn't do any good.

He shined his flashlight on my notes, or at least on the two in the side window. A second later, I heard him yell. He jerked the door open, yanked the stalker note free of the gum, and *slammed the door closed again.* Even if I could have said a word of protest he wouldn't have heard it, because he was sprinting toward Wyatt.

The bare spot on the window was aesthetically unpleasing. I hadn't run out of things to say, so I wrote another note and stuck it up. I had to use the same piece of gum that had held the stalker note, but it was still pliable enough. Good thing; no way would I have put it back in my mouth to chew it again.

I didn't watch Wyatt to see what his reaction was. I didn't care, because no matter what he did now, he was too late. She was long gone, and I was so far beyond pissed there were no words for it.

I saw Wyatt coming toward the squad car, his face grim. I moved to the center of the seat, clutching the blanket around me, and faced forward.

He came to the left door. As he opened it, I scooted all the way to the right. He leaned in and barked, "Are you sure? Can you give me a description? Where was she?"

There was so much I wanted to say, beginning with Why bother now, she's long gone, thanks to you being such an asshole, but I couldn't say anything right now so I didn't even try. Instead I grabbed my appointment book again, furiously scribbled "blond hair, wearing a hoodie, WAS in the crowd," tore out the page, and extended my arm to give him the note. Looking for her now was a totally useless effort, no way was she still hanging around, but he wasn't going to be able to accuse *me* of not cooperating. She had escaped, it was totally his fault, and I intended to keep it that way.

Sometimes being morally superior is the

only way to go.

Wyatt quickly scanned the note, handed it to DeMarius, and began spitting out orders *as he slammed the car door closed again.*

There are no words.

CHAPTER TWENTY

Eventually Wyatt came back to the squad car, but by then dawn was beginning to lighten the sky, which meant I'd been in that damn car for *hours*. Nothing was left of my condo except debris, stench, smoke, and some dully glowing embers that one unit of the fire department was hosing down. Wyatt's truck was a goner, no doubt about it; so was the car parked next to it. The family who had lived next door huddled together, the little kids' faces solemn and big-eyed, the parents clutching each other and the kids. Their place wasn't a total loss, but they wouldn't be living there again anytime soon.

What had I done to make someone hate me so much that she'd not only try to *kill* me, but didn't care if she also killed innocent people in the effort? Well, I mean *other* innocent people, because I couldn't think of a thing I was guilty of that warranted killing. I try not to break any major laws, I don't cheat on my taxes, and if someone gives me back too much change I always give them back the correct amount. I also tip twenty percent. There was no logical reason I could see for this kind of malice and destruction.

Which meant the reason had to be illogical, right? I was dealing with a psycho. Their thought processes are warped.

Wyatt strode through the mess and debris, his frustration and temper evident when he viciously kicked at a chunk of wood and sent it flying. I knew they hadn't caught the blonde, because I hadn't seen anyone being escorted into the back of any of the other squad cars — no, that honor was reserved for me, *the victim* — but then I hadn't expected her to be caught because she was long gone by the time anyone paid any attention to me. Wyatt's badge was clipped to his belt, he was armed, and his face and arms were black with soot. A fire is not neat. I could just imagine what I looked like — after all, I'd been *in* the place. Let's just say it's a wonder DeMarius had recognized me in the crowd, though maybe it had been my soot covering that gave me away.

Opening the door, Wyatt leaned in and extended his hand. "Come on, let's go home."

I didn't have a home, thank you very much, and I wasn't inclined to go to Wyatt's.

I wasn't inclined to go anywhere with him. I thought I'd just go back to the police department with DeMarius, seeing as how I was in his squad car already.

I didn't say anything, of course, because I still couldn't make a sound. I sat against the right side door, wrapped in the blanket, and stared resolutely ahead.

"Blair —" His tone was heavy with warning but he bit off whatever he'd been about to say and instead leaned in and dragged me, blanket and all, out of the car, then simply swung me up in his arms. Wrapped up as I was, I couldn't do anything to ward him off so I continued staring straight ahead.

"Someone get those signs off the windows," he ordered, and DeMarius leaned into the car and began plucking my messages free from the wads of gum. The gum, of course, remained behind. He also handed out the pieces of my cell phone as well as my tote, which had been knocked to the floorboard when Wyatt dragged me out, giving both to a female officer I didn't know.

"What happened to your phone?" Wyatt asked, frowning at it.

I didn't answer. Well, I couldn't, could I?

DeMarius straightened from the squad car, my chef's knife in his hand and a stunned look on his face. "Holy hell," he blurted.

The knife must have fallen out of my tote when it had been knocked to the floorboard. A group of cops, both plainclothed and uniformed, had gathered in a loose knot around us and they all stared at my knife. The wide blade itself was a good eight inches long, and the entire thing measured about fourteen inches. I was proud, because it was an impressive sight.

Wyatt sighed. "Just drop it in the bag," he said.

The patrolman with my tote pulled it open so DeMarius could deposit the knife, then said, "Wait a minute." Reaching in, she pulled out my wedding shoes.

They were beautiful, sparkling with rhinestones, the straps delicate works of art. They so obviously weren't shoes you could wear to any job, unless you were maybe a Las Vegas showgirl, that looking at them was almost like disconnecting from reality. They were magic. They were a fantasy come to life, as if Tinker Bell had suddenly lit in her hand.

"Don't want to take the chance of cutting these babies," she said in a properly awed tone. "Put the knife on the bottom."

Omigod, I hadn't even thought of that. I was stricken. What if I'd accidentally scarred my shoes?

DeMarius placed the knife in the bottom

of the tote, then the female officer reverently put my shoes on top. DeMarius began shuffling through the notes in his hand. Sunrise was close enough now that they could be easily read without needing a flashlight. His eyes widened, and he made a choking sound.

"What is it?" asked someone I recognized, Detective Forester, reaching to take the notes. He quickly flipped through them, his eyes widening, too, then he broke into a guffawing laugh that he tried and failed to convert to a cough.

Wyatt sighed again. "Hand them over," he said wearily. "Just stick them in the bag with the weapon and the fashion statement. I'll deal with them later."

DeMarius grabbed the notes and hurriedly stuffed them into the tote; Wyatt sort of swung me around so he could take the tote into the hand that was clasping me under the knees. I glared at both DeMarius and Detective Forester. I'd been making various points with my notes, and they were *laughing?* Maybe it's a good thing I couldn't make a sound right then, because if I'd said what I was thinking, it's pretty likely I'd have been arrested.

"Good luck," Forester managed to choke out, clapping Wyatt on the shoulder. He didn't say "you'll need it," but I was pretty sure he was thinking it.

As Wyatt carried me to the car I refused to look up at him. Instead I watched the fire department units coiling up their hoses, while two men with "Fire Marshal" lettered on the back of their Windbreakers were poking around in the blackened rubble. The crowd of sightseers was slowly dispersing, some of them going to jobs, others hurrying to get their children ready for school. I also needed to be doing a bunch of things but just about all of them required talking, as well as clothing, so I foresaw a couple of problems there.

I didn't want to talk to Wyatt at all, but as he was currently my only means of communication, at least until I got to his computer, I'd have to at least write notes to him. This not-being-able-to-talk thing could get old in a hurry.

He put me on my feet when we got to the car, keeping his left arm around me while he opened the car door with his right hand. I rewrapped the blanket loosely enough that I was able to get into the car under my own steam, though I did have to fight with the fabric a little. By the time Wyatt slid into the driver's seat, I'd worked my arms free and reached for the tote.

He pulled it out of my reach. "I don't think

so," he said grimly. "I saw the size of that knife."

I needed my appointment book, not the knife — not that the knife wouldn't have tempted me. Accepting the inevitable, I made a pad with my left hand and pretended to scribble on it with my right. Then I pointed at the tote.

"I think you've written enough notes," he muttered, putting the key in the ignition.

I slapped his arm, not hard, just enough to get his attention. I pointed to my throat, shook my head, then used emphatic gestures for the pad and pen again.

"You can't talk?"

I shook my head. Finally he was getting it!

"Not at all?"

I shook my head again.

"Good deal," he said with satisfaction, cranking the engine and putting the car in gear.

By the time we reached his house I was so spitting mad I could barely sit still. As soon as he stopped the car I unclipped the seat belt and bolted, making it into the house before he did. I zipped straight into his pitiful excuse of an office and grabbed a notebook and pen. He was right behind me, reaching to take it away from me, when he saw that I was writing instructions instead of insults.

CALL MOM! was my first directive. I under-lined it three times, and put four exclama-tion points after it.

He regarded me with narrowed eyes, but saw the wisdom of what I wanted. He nod-ded and reached for the phone.

While he talked to her, giving her the bad news that I'd been burned out of my home but the good news that I wasn't hurt, I was writing down more stuff.

First and most important, I needed clothes, just something to wear today so I could go buy more. I listed bra, panties, jeans, shoes, and blouse, as well as a blow dryer and hairbrush. I gave that list to Wyatt, and he read it to Mom. I knew she'd handle it from there.

The next call on my list was Lynn at Great Bods. I might be late today.

Wyatt snorted and said, "You think?" But he made the call.

Next on my list was my insurance com-pany, but it wasn't open yet. Because I wanted to be fair, I also listed Wyatt's insur-ance company. He had things he had to deal with, too. Then I started listing everything I needed to buy. I'd just started on the second page when Wyatt jerked the notebook away from me and pulled me out of my chair.

"You can organize your shopping spree later," he said, physically shepherding me toward the stairs. "You should see yourself. We both need to shower."

No argument there. What I didn't need to do was shower *with* him. I jerked away from him, almost stumbling from the effort, and held up my hand like a traffic cop. My jaw set, I pointed at him, then at myself, then emphatically shook my head.

"You don't want to shower with me?" he asked innocently. Damn him, he knew how mad I was, and he was deliberately taking advantage of my laryngitis.

All right, let him see what he could make of this. I pointed to both of us again, then made a circle with the thumb and first finger of my left hand, and thrust the first finger of my right hand back and forth really fast in the circle, then dropped my hands and shook my head even more emphatically than before.

He grinned. "You don't have a clue how bad you look, or you wouldn't think my mind is on sex. Let's get cleaned up, then we'll go to the station and you can answer some questions, make a statement." Then he corrected himself. "*Write* a statement."

I had some idea how I looked, because I could see him. That didn't make me any less wary of his intentions. This was Wyatt, Mr. Perpetually Horny. I knew how he operated. We'd had sex in the shower more than a few times.

There were three bathrooms upstairs, but in typical Wyatt decorating only the master bath had towels in it. I went in ahead of him, grabbed two towels and a washcloth from the linen closet in the bathroom, shampoo and conditioner from the shower, one of his shirts and a robe from his closet, and headed out again.

"Hey! Where are you going?"

I pointed in the direction of the other bathrooms, and left him to shower alone. He needed to meditate on the enormity of his sins.

But he was right about how I looked. Once I was safely behind the locked door of the bathroom, I looked in the mirror and would have moaned if I'd had a voice. The rims of my eyelids were red and swollen, I was covered in oily soot, and my nostrils and around my mouth were completely black with the stuff. My hair was stiff with ashes and soot. There was no way one lathering with shampoo and soap would take care of this mess — at least, not this kind of soap.

I went back downstairs and stood a moment, considering. Dish detergent, or laundry detergent? I decided dish detergent would be less corrosive, but still good on oil and grease. I grabbed the bottle from underneath the kitchen sink and returned upstairs.

Thirty minutes later, even though I'd used only lukewarm water and turned it completely off while I was lathering, the hot water was gone, but then with two of us showering I wasn't surprised. The Palmolive had done an admirable job removing the soot, though it had left my hair with a texture like straw, so I'd had to shampoo and condition it, which had taken even more water. As I toweled dry I checked my face in the mirror. My eyes were still red-rimmed, but I couldn't see any soot. My hands and feet still showed some dark spots, but I didn't want to scrub my skin raw getting rid of them; they could wait.

I didn't have any underwear, of course; I hadn't left any clothing at Wyatt's house any of the nights I'd spent there. Feeling ridiculously naked, I put on Wyatt's shirt, then his robe over that. Finally, my wet hair wrapped in a towel, I went downstairs to wait for someone to deliver my requested clothes.

Wyatt was in the kitchen; he was freshly shaven and dressed in a suit and tie as he always was for work. He'd put on a pot of coffee — I blessed him for that, even if I was angry at him — and was standing with my sheaf of notes in his hand, looking through them.

He looked up when I appeared in the doorway. The expression in his eyes was a little disbelieving. He glanced back at one of the notes.

I could see it from the doorway, because I'd written all the notes in big block letters. That particular one proclaimed:

WYATT IS A JACKASS

CHAPTER TWENTY-ONE

I circled around him, giving him a wide berth, and headed to pour myself a cup of coffee while he continued pondering my notes. He chose another one, held it at arm's length, and cocked his head as if he'd never seen a note before. " 'I need a shotgun.' Now, there's a thought that probably has all my men on high alert."

I thought it was a good idea. I needed one right now. Peppering his ass with buckshot would make me feel ever so much better. Turning my back on him, I reveled in the fantasy as I took my first sip of coffee, which was a lot more work than I'd expected. My throat didn't want to cooperate, didn't want to do the swallowing thing. The coffee felt good going down, bathing my sore throat in heat. Drinking hot stuff usually helps a sore throat, and I wanted my voice back. I had a *lot* I wanted to say.

I needed to make a list of everything I

wanted to say, so I wouldn't forget any of it. I also needed to get started on Wyatt's list of transgressions, because this was going to be a good one.

His arms came around me from behind and he eased me back against him, resting his chin on top of my towel-wrapped head. "You were talking to me on the cell phone, and now all of a sudden you can't make a sound. Is something really wrong with your throat, or are you just not talking to me?"

Carefully I sipped more coffee. What was I supposed to do, answer him?

I thought about slinging an elbow into his ribs, but all that cop training he had made getting physical with him sort of dangerous, plus he never let me win, which is just so snotty of him I can't believe it because letting me win every now and then would be the gentlemanly thing to do. Besides, all I had on was his shirt and his robe, both of which were way too big for me. If we started tussling, the robe would come off in a heartbeat, and the shirt would be pushed up to my neck, and, well, that's just what happened when we started tussling.

Instead, because I knew this would worry and annoy him more, I set down the cup and calmly removed his arms from around me. After topping the cup with more coffee, I took it with me to the table, where I sat down, and then was momentarily distracted by my tote bag sitting in the middle of the table. I hadn't noticed it before, because I'd been so intent on battling with him, which tells you what a horrible effect he had on me. I hadn't forgotten the tote — or my shoes — while fighting for my life, but throw Wyatt into the equation and I lost all sense of concentration. Scary.

Briefly I wondered if he'd left my knife in there, or disarmed me. I'd check later. Right now I had some communicating to do. I pulled the notebook toward me and began writing. After I finished the note, I twirled the notebook around and pushed it to the other side of the table.

He poured himself more coffee and came to the table, frowning a little as he read. *Both. I coughed a lot from smoke inhalation, then strained my throat even more screaming to get SOMEONE'S attention when I saw her in the crowd. Plus I'm not speaking to you, and the wedding is OFF!!*

"Yeah," he said wryly. "I saw the note about the wedding." He glanced up, his green eyes narrow and glittering, intently focused on me. "Let's get something plain between us. Whatever I have to do to protect you, to keep you safe, I'll do it, no matter

297

how pissed off you get. Putting you in a patrol car *and keeping you there* was the best way to keep you out of trouble and out of danger. I won't apologize for doing that. Ever. Got it?"

He had a real knack for turning the tables, I'll give him that. He could make a point and turn a phrase so only someone small and petty could disagree with him. That's okay; I don't mind being small and petty. I reached out and pulled the notebook to me again.

I'm not your problem anymore. As soon as someone gets here with some clothes for me, I'm so out of here.

"That's what you think," he said calmly, after reading the note. "Your little ass is staying right here so I can keep an eye on you. You can't stay with any of your family, you'd be endangering them if you did. Someone's trying to kill you, and she doesn't care if other people get hurt so long as she gets to you."

Damn, damn, *damn!* He was right about that.

I wrote: *So I'll stay in a hotel.*

"No, you damn well will not. You're staying here."

There was an obvious point to be made here, so I made it. *And if she somehow follows me here? You'd be in just as much dan-*

ger as anyone else I stayed with. And you're called out a lot at night.

"I'll handle that aspect," he said, after pausing only enough to read what I'd written, certainly not long enough to have given it any thought. "You have to trust me on this. An arsonist leaves clues behind, plus it's standard procedure to videotape the bystanders at any murder or arson scene, and I clued everyone in while I was on the way that this was likely arson. A patrolman had the crowd on tape way before you spotted her. All you have to do is point her out to us, and we'll take it from there."

That was a relief. He had no idea how big a relief, because he hadn't been in that condo with me. I would have been much more relieved if she were already in custody, though, which she would have been if he hadn't had me locked in that stinky squad car.

I wrote, *I know her face, I've seen her somewhere, but I can't place her. She's out of context.*

"Then someone else in your family, or even one of your employees, might recognize her. Of course, you saw her when she was following you, so that may be what you're thinking about."

That was logical, but . . . wrong. I shook

299

my head. I hadn't been able to tell that much about her when she'd been following me, only that the driver was a woman.

The sound of a car in the driveway caught our attention and Wyatt got to his feet. The sound continued around to the back, which meant it was either family or a friend; everyone else went to the front door. He opened the door into the garage and said, "It's Jenni."

Wyatt had called Mom less than an hour ago, so I was surprised anyone had gotten here with clothes so soon. Jenni bounced into the kitchen with two Wal-Mart bags in her hands. "You have the most interesting life," she commented, shaking her head a little as she placed the bags on the table.

"Never a dull moment," Wyatt agreed drily. "She also has complete laryngitis, from smoke inhalation, so she's writing notes."

"So I see," said Jenni, picking up the one that said ASSHOLE MEN. She studied it for a moment. "And very upset, too. It isn't like her to be redundant." Her back was to Wyatt, so he couldn't see the mischievous wink she gave me.

His only response was a snort.

"Moving right along," Jenni said breezily, opening the bags. "I was already awake and dressed, so when Mom told me I went straight to Wal-Mart. This is basics only, but that's all you need today, right? Jeans, two cute tops, two sets of underwear, blow dryer and round hairbrush, mascara, gloss, and a toothbrush and toothpaste. And moisturizer. Oh, and a pair of loafers. I can't vouch for their comfort, but they're cute."

I dug out the sales receipt, nodding my liking for each item, and got out my checkbook to reimburse her. Because she was standing, she caught a glimpse of my wedding shoes in the tote, and gasped.

"Oh. My. God." Reverently she took one shoe out and balanced it on her hand. "Where did you get these?"

I paused in writing the check, and on the notebook, I obediently scribbled the name of the department store. She didn't ask how much they'd cost, and I didn't volunteer the information. Some things are irrelevant. Those were my wedding shoes; cost wasn't a factor in the decision to get them.

"You are so lucky they were in your tote," she breathed.

I finished the check and tore it out, then shook my head and scribbled, *They weren't. I had to go back and get them.*

Of course, Wyatt saw me shake my head, and he strode over to see what I'd written. He stared at me in disbelief for a moment, then his brows snapped together. "You risked your life for a pair of *shoes?*" he thundered.

I gave him an exasperated look and wrote, *Those were my WEDDING SHOES. At the time, I still thought I'd marry you. Now I know better.*

"Ooookay," Jenni said, grabbing the check and turning on her heel. "I'm outta here."

Neither of us paid any attention as she went out the door. Wyatt said furiously, "You went back into a fucking burning building to get a pair of shoes? I don't care if they're gold plated —"

I grabbed the notebook and wrote, *Technically, no. I was still IN my bedroom when I remembered the shoes, and I went to the closet to get them.* Then I slammed the pen down, gathered up my new clothing and paraphernalia, and took everything upstairs. And not to the master bedroom, either.

Safely locked in the bathroom I'd used before, I mentally blessed Jenni for remembering the smaller items. I brushed my teeth, moisturized — my skin badly needed it, after being exposed to all that heat and soot, then being scrubbed with dish detergent — and dried my hair. By the time I was dressed, I felt human again. Very tired, but human.

Wyatt was still waiting for me when I returned downstairs, not that I had truly expected him to leave without me. His expression lingered on the grim side, but he gave me a searching look and abruptly said, "You need to eat something."

My stomach agreed. My throat said no way. I shook my head, pointing to my throat.

"Milk, then. You can drink some milk." He always had milk on hand, for cereal. "Or oatmeal. Sit down and I'll nuke us some oatmeal."

He was determined, and he was probably right; we both needed to eat, after the night we'd put in. It seemed *days* ago that he'd taken my answering machine to the police department for analyzing, when it was really fewer than twelve hours. Time flies when you're jumping from the second story of a burning building, climbing fences, looking for psycho bitches to gut, and getting locked in a stinky squad car for hours while she makes faces at you.

He took off his suit jacket and efficiently nuked two bowls of instant oatmeal, adding enough sugar and milk to mine to make it a little soupy. Cautiously I took a bite; it was nice and hot, and soft enough that I managed to swallow it even though it made me cough. Coughing wasn't fun. I kept at it until I'd managed to eat half of the oatmeal, but the coughing that followed each bite was too rough on my throat, which already felt sand-blasted, so I gave it up after that. Maybe I should live on milk shakes, yogurt, and Jell-O for a few days.

We cleared the table together, not that there was a lot of work to it: two bowls, two spoons, two coffee cups. When everything was stowed in the dishwasher, I got my tote — yes, he'd removed my knife — then looked at him and pantomimed turning a key in the ignition.

"They're still in the car," he said, meaning my Mercedes. He'd be driving his city-issued cop car, the Crown Vic. I hated what had happened to his Avalanche. I'd seen one of the front tires flame up, so even though the fire department had immediately sprayed it with water I knew the damage was beyond repair. That close, the heat scorched the paint off, melted the headlights and top of the engine, did all sorts of nasty things. He was calm about losing the truck, but I guess he'd known from the beginning, having been to a lot of fire scenes, that it couldn't be salvaged.

Forget about the truck, he'd said. *Are you sure you're all right?*

Damn it. It wasn't easy, staying angry at a man who loved you as much as you loved him.

And then the sneak further undermined me by pulling me close for a long, hungry kiss. When he lifted his head he looked at my face, sort of half smiled, and kissed me again. "Oh, yeah," he said. "The wedding's still on."

CHAPTER TWENTY-TWO

Wyatt stayed behind me all the way to the police department, not that there was much chance I'd be followed anywhere from his house. No one had followed us there after we'd left the fire scene and he wasn't listed in the telephone directory, so locating him wouldn't be as easy as locating me had been. I've never had an unlisted number, never tried to hide from anyone. Of course, if someone knows where you work, he or she always knows where and when to find you.

Which made me wonder if all of this was somehow connected to Great Bods. The woman I'd seen in the crowd was someone I'd seen before. She wasn't a total stranger; she had a connection to me. I just couldn't place her face, couldn't put a name to her. I don't personally know all the members of Great Bods but I do recognize their faces, which, when I thought about it, eliminated Great Bods as the connection. When you see

306

someone who looks familiar but you don't know where you know them from, it's because they aren't in their accustomed place. When I put that face at Great Bods, there still wasn't any ah-ha moment of recognition, which meant that wherever I'd seen her, it wasn't at work.

Which meant she likely worked at one of my other regular points of contact: the grocery store, the mall, the post office, the bank, maybe even UPS or FedEx. Try as I might, though, I couldn't place her.

When we exited the elevators into the busy, noisy squad room, heads turned our way and wide grins bloomed on most of the faces. Well, the people who were handcuffed to the chairs didn't grin, and neither did the people who were there filing complaints and whatnot, but the cops grinned.

I was a little hurt. What was so funny about my condo being toast?

I glanced up at Wyatt, to see if he'd noticed all the grins. His gaze was focused on his office door, which bore a sign. He didn't pause until we got close enough to read it: WYATT IS A JACKASS AND THE WEDDING IF *OFF!* It wasn't one of my notes, but it definitely incorporated elements from two of them.

Wheeling, I glared at the room at large. Some of the cops were almost choking as they tried to stifle their laughter. They were making fun of my notes. "Not *one* of you," I announced loudly, "let me out of that car, *either.*" Or rather, I tried to announce it, because I'd forgotten I couldn't talk. Not a single sound came out of my mouth. Standing there with my mouth open was humiliating.

But I intended to make up a shit list, and put all of them on it.

Wyatt reached out and calmly removed the sign. "The wedding is back on," he said, and there was a smattering of applause because, being mostly men, they assumed he'd sexed me out of my temper. I glared up at him, but he just smiled as he opened the door and ushered me through it.

"I need that scene tape," he said over his shoulder before closing the door.

His office wasn't very big, and was cluttered with filing cabinets and paperwork. The sight of that paperwork perked me up a little. If he'd just leave me alone in here, I could catch up on my clandestine reading.

Sulkily I took one of his visitor's chairs while he settled in the big leather chair behind his desk. "Amazing," he said, a quirk to his lips as if he wanted to grin.

I raised both hands in an impatient "what is?" gesture.

"I'll tell you later," he said, tossing the sign

on his desk. "We have a lot of work to do right now."

He wasn't kidding about that. First I had to give a statement about what had happened last night, or rather, early this morning. Wyatt didn't take the statement, Detective Forester did, and to be accurate I didn't *give* the statement, of course, I wrote it out.

The detective had been busy, but the fire marshal had immediately ruled the fire an arson; evidently there hadn't been any attempt to disguise it. The fire dog had alerted him to gasoline all around the front and right side of my condo. When the fire had been ignited, the flames had immediately blocked my exit from both of those doors. There were still the double French doors in the dining alcove, but by throwing the gasoline bomb through the living room window and spreading the fire all over the living room, my route from upstairs had been blocked. As further insurance, the fence gate had been blocked. If by chance I'd made it out to the backyard, the arsonist had intended for me to be trapped there. As rapidly as the fire had spread to the Bradford pear trees in the tiny yard, if I hadn't been able to climb the fence I'd have died there.

Very likely, though, she hadn't thought I'd be able to escape from upstairs. Smoke rises, and you really have very little time to get out of a burning building before the smoke gets you. I know because I watched a documentary about house fires and how fast they spread. By covering my mouth and nose with the wet towel, I'd bought myself a couple of precious minutes. The other wet towel over my head and shoulders had likely kept me from being burned by the sparks and hot ashes. The rest of it, getting out the second-story bedroom window and climbing the fence, had a lot to do with being angry and desperate, plus having good upper-body strength.

You never know when being a former cheerleader will come in handy.

To get a timeline, they coordinated my statement with my call to 911, of which they had a copy — thus every cop in the building got to listen to me tell the 911 operator that the fire department could tell which condo was mine because it was the one with flames coming out the windows. For some reason they all had to hear it more than once, too.

Then I had to watch the video of the crowd at the scene.

I sat in Wyatt's office with him and Detectives Forester and MacInnes watching the video on a small monitor. Wyatt had made the call to videotape even before talking to me, so I got to see myself, looking as horrible as I remembered, weaving in and out of the picture as the camera had slowly panned from left to right and back again. What I didn't see was the blonde wearing the hoodie.

I was so disappointed. I wrote, *I don't see her. She isn't there.*

"Keep watching," said Wyatt. "The crowd was filmed more than once."

So we did, frame by frame. Finally the camera caught *part* of her, because her face was turned away — the hood pulled up, a curl of very blond hair escaping from beneath the jacket to lie across her clavicle, maybe half of her right jawline. She was mostly behind some guy in a red shirt, so there was no way to enhance the film and get a better picture of her.

Mentally reviewing my memories, I analyzed the moment when I'd realized she was my stalker, when she'd stared at me with such open malice. Yes, this same guy had been standing beside her; I remembered his red shirt. This film must have been made just seconds either before or after, probably after, because her face was turned away as if she was leaving. MacInnes said it was likely she'd spotted the camera.

"That guy in the red shirt is a start," Wyatt

said. "He might remember something about her, might even know her."

"We're still canvassing the neighborhood," said Forester. "I'll get this photo out to the guys. Someone will recognize him."

I had been sipping on something hot all morning long, to ease my throat. Wyatt had even scrounged a tea bag from someone and made a cup of hot tea for me; I don't know what the difference is, but tea seems to work better on a sore throat than coffee does. A couple of aspirin also helped the pain, but I still couldn't make a sound. Wyatt mentioned taking me to the ER to get checked out, an idea I vetoed with a *NO!* that took up an entire sheet of paper.

Things seemed to drag on for a while. During a lull, Wyatt talked to both my insurance adjustor and his. He also called Mom, which definitely earned him points in her book, and gave her a report. He talked to his mother, reassured her that I was fine and he was fine.

By lunch, I was very tired of the whole scene. I was tired, period. I needed to go shopping and replenish my wardrobe, but for the first time in my life I couldn't work up any enthusiasm for shopping. I had liked my old clothes; I wanted them back. I wanted my books, my music, my dishes. I wanted my *stuff*. It was just now beginning to sink in that my stuff was truly, irrevocably gone.

Jenni, bless her, had bought me two sets of underwear and two tops; I didn't absolutely *have* to go shopping today; it could wait until tomorrow. Maybe by tomorrow I'd be able to talk again. Today, I just wanted to do normal stuff. I wanted to go to work.

I'd given the police my written statement; I'd watched the video and pointed out the psycho bitch, for all the good it had done. I didn't see any reason why I should hang around any longer.

I wrote Wyatt a note, telling him that I was going to work.

He leaned back in his chair, looking grim and lieutenant-ish. "I don't think that's a good idea."

I wrote another note. *I think it's a great idea. She knows she can find me there.*

"Which is why I'd much rather one of my female officers drives your car around."

Then set it up for tomorrow. I'm tired of this. I want my life back. The only normal thing I can do now is go to work, so I'm going to work.

"Blair." He leaned forward, green eyes intent. "She tried to kill you just a few hours ago. What makes you think she won't do the same thing to Great Bods?"

Oh, God, I hadn't thought of that. Great Bods was at risk, anyway, though it's possible she thought I just worked there, not that I was the owner. I mean, I don't answer the phone with "Hi, I'm Blair, and I own Great Bods." It's likely most of the members didn't know I owned the place, because it just isn't info that's advertised all over the place. I could as easily be the manager, which of course was the job I did.

The only thing that set me apart from the other employees was that I drove a Mercedes, but even that wasn't a complete oddity because Keir, one of my fitness instructors, drove a Porsche.

I pinched the bridge of my nose, thinking. Maybe I wasn't thinking clearly — gee, wonder why that was — but it seemed to me I couldn't leave Lynn in the lurch again. She had a life outside of Great Bods, and though she'd been great about covering for me, I couldn't take advantage of her or I'd end up losing a top-notch assistant.

I wrote all of that down, explaining it to Wyatt as best I could. I was getting tired of all that damn writing.

To my surprise, he read my explanation, then simply studied my face for a while. I don't know what he saw there, maybe that I really needed to go to work, or maybe on re-

314

flection he agreed with me that the risk to Great Bods might not be that high. "All right," he finally said. "But I'm going to put someone with you at all times. Sit here, and I'll go clear it with Chief Gray."

He could have pulled a fast one on me, he's done it before, but I sat there. When he came back, he got his suit jacket from the hook on the back of the door and said, "Let's go."

I got my tote and stood, my expression asking the question for me.

"I'm your bodyguard for the rest of the day," he explained.

I was happy enough with that.

CHAPTER TWENTY-THREE

Lynn was mightily relieved when I showed up for work not only on time, but a little bit early. Wyatt hadn't mentioned my lack of a voice when he'd called her that morning, and she was concerned enough that I couldn't even whisper that when she left work she went to a health-food store and brought back a selection of teas that were supposed to help soothe an inflamed throat. She even offered to stay late and help me, but I sent her on her way. Wyatt was there if I needed anyone to talk for me.

All in all, it was a nice, normal day at Great Bods. No white Malibus parked across the street; no blond psychos pitched firebombs through the front door. It was my kind of day, just the buffer I needed to help me get my feet back under me. Still, I felt as if I were balanced on the edge of despair, and I kept giving myself pep talks, pulling myself back. Yes, my home had burned, but no one had been killed. Yes, I'd lost all my personal possessions, but, hey, my hair hadn't caught on fire. Yes, the viciousness of my unknown stalker and would-be killer was frightening, but now I knew what she looked like and I was *majorly* pissed at her, so when I saw her again I intended to go for her — unless Wyatt had me locked in some stinky squad car again.

I had a hard time letting go of my resentment over that.

He prowled around like the cop he was, constantly checking the street, the parking lot, walking around the building. I commandeered one of my second-shift instructors to answer the phone for me and that turned out to be a godsend, because when I mentioned, via pen and paper, that we were looking for an assistant assistant-manager, she became very excited and asked if she could train for the job.

Well, who knew? She, her name was JoAnn, was actually my least popular instructor, because her attitude was all business. On the other hand, she was also one of my most knowledgeable instructors. She had no office experience at all, but I really liked her manner on the phone. When she didn't know what to do, she sounded as if she did, kind of like a politician. I would definitely talk to Lynn about her.

Whether it was the herbal teas or giving my voice a complete rest, by the end of the day swallowing seemed to be easier. I was so hungry I was nauseated, though, so JoAnn went to a hamburger joint and picked up a burger and fries for Wyatt, and a nice thick milk shake for me — strawberry, my favorite. The cold felt just as good on my poor throat as the hot tea had.

It was Thursday, almost one week to the hour since my first run-in with the wacko on wheels. I was supposed to have gotten the stitches out of my hairline today, I remembered. I reached up under my wing of hair and felt them. They felt stiff and dry, and the skin surrounding them was prickly with the new growth of hair.

How hard could it be to remove stitches? I'd had them removed before and it didn't hurt, at the most stinging a little, so it couldn't be any big deal. I had manicure scissors in my office, and tweezers in the first-aid kit. I needed those stitches out. I needed to put that episode behind me. Yes, I'd gotten a great new haircut out of the deal, but overall it had been a bummer.

I took my supplies into the ladies' room with me, only to discover my hair wouldn't stay back out of the way; it wanted to swing forward in that great curve Shay had shaped it into. I didn't have any hair clips but I did have a couple of scrunchies in my office. I zipped out of the ladies' room into my office, grabbed a scrunchie, and zipped right back out. Wyatt saw me and called out "Hey!" but I waved at him and kept on going. He probably thought I had an urgent need for the ladies'.

Except he walked in while I was snipping through the third stitch.

"Holy hell!"

I jumped, which is not a good thing when you have sharp little scissors aimed at a newly healed laceration. I scowled at his reflection in the mirror, then tilted my head again so I could see exactly where the next stitch was.

"Oh, fuck," he muttered, coming to stand next to me. "Stop, before you stab yourself with those things. I would ask what you're doing, but I can see what you're doing, I just don't know why. Weren't you supposed to see a doctor for this?"

I nodded, and went for that stitch again.

He closed his hand over mine. "Give those to me. God. I'll do it."

I let him have the scissors, but smirked and shook my head.

"You don't think I can do it?" he asked, challenged.

I shook my head again, absolutely certain he couldn't.

He found out why a second or two later, when he realized there was no way his big fingers would fit into the small holes of the scissor handles. Frustrated, he stared at them, and in triumph I retrieved them and went to work again. Okay, so it was a very small victory. It felt good anyway. I hadn't had many victories lately, and I was feeling deprived.

So I snipped the stitches, and he used the tweezers to gently pull the pieces of thread out. Tiny beads of blood formed here and there, so I opened one of the antiseptic pads from the first-aid kit and blotted them off. They didn't reappear, and that was that. Removing the scrunchie I'd used to hold my hair back, I swung my hair and beamed.

"Whatever it takes," he muttered, then reverted to cop and pushed open the door of each empty stall in turn, until he had inspected all six stalls. He just couldn't help it, I guess.

I closed up right on time at nine, and JoAnn stayed to see what was involved in securing the place for the night. With her help the process went, well, twice as fast — duh

— and we were ready to leave at nine-twenty. Wyatt checked outside before we left.

Once again I took a circuitous route, with Wyatt following me. But I wasn't going home, I thought with a pang. I would never go there again, or at least it would never be home again. I would have to go see it, something in me demanded I do that. I guess it's like viewing the body at a funeral, to build a final memory, a closure. You'd think our brains would understand death and let it go at that, but nope, we need to see that dead person and replace the live memory with the dead memory. Or something like that.

If Wyatt and I got married, his house would be my home from this very day on. If we weren't going to get married, I needed to know pretty damn quick so I could make other arrangements. When I could talk again, we had to have that conversation.

Damn, I had to get things moving! If we did get married, it would be in twenty-two days. Just three weeks! And I hadn't even picked out the fabric for my gown yet! Plus I still had to talk to Monica Stevens, and Sally, and get Jazz and Sally back together, and somehow replace my lost stuff — I didn't have enough days left!

As some friendly advice, I don't ever recommend trying to organize a wedding while dealing with a homicidal stalker. It just gets too complicated.

Wyatt had briefed me on how to shake someone following you, so before we got to a place he'd picked out ahead of time — a service station on a left-hand corner — he turned off and left me alone. My heartbeat picked up speed at my sudden sense of vulnerability, but I didn't see any suspicious vehicles behind me, which means no white Chevrolets. There was traffic behind me, though, so that didn't mean I was in the clear. She could have swapped cars, and be in something entirely different now. MacInnes and Forester were running the registration on white late-model Malibus, but that wasn't exactly an easy thing to do and so far they hadn't come up with anything. In the meantime, she could now be driving a Mazda.

I had to stop at a traffic light, my left blinker on, and wait for oncoming traffic to pass. When I turned left, so did three other vehicles. But I immediately turned left again into the service station parking lot, cut across, and went back into the street from which we'd turned off, except going back the way I'd come. Anyone following me would have to do the same thing or lose me, and, well, that would be noticeable.

No one followed. Breathing easier, I drove to where Wyatt was waiting for me.

We went home — to his house — after that.

The minute I drove into his garage, exhaustion overtook me. I'd had maybe two hours' sleep last night, and I doubted Wyatt had gotten any more than that, plus both of us had burned a lot of adrenaline. I went to the table, scribbled *If you don't mind, call Mom and Dad, bring them up to speed. I'm going to take a shower.*

He nodded, and stood watching me as I stumbled toward the stairs. At the top, automatically I turned toward the master bedroom, where I had slept with him so many times. I was actually in the master bath before I realized my error and reversed my steps down the hall to what I now thought of as "my" bathroom. After taking a quick shower, brushing my teeth, moisturizing — the usual stuff — I pulled on his robe and wrapped it around me, almost literally, before tying the belt as tightly as I could so it would stay snug. Man, I hoped there were sheets on the bed in the guest room, because if there weren't I didn't have the energy to make the bed and I'd just have to sleep on the bedspread.

Except he was waiting for me when I left

the bathroom, patiently leaning against the opposite wall. He wore only a pair of navy blue boxer briefs, and he smelled of soap and water, telling me his shower had been even quicker than mine, but then he didn't moisturize so in a way it wasn't a fair comparison.

I immediately held up my hand, which he simply took and used to pull me into him. Before I knew it, he'd lifted me in his arms and was carrying me to the master bedroom.

"You're not sleeping alone," he said sharply when I thumped his shoulder with my fist and pushed at him. "Not tonight. You'll have a nightmare."

He was probably right about that, but I'm an adult, I can handle a nightmare alone. On the other hand, I believe in making things easy on myself. I stopped thumping and let him put me on the big king bed.

He pulled on one end of the belt and the damn thing came untied. Robes . . . you just can't trust them. I was naked beneath it, which was no big surprise; like I'd have been wearing it if I'd had any pajamas there? He pulled it off me and tossed it aside, then stripped down his shorts and stepped out of them. Despite my conviction that we shouldn't have sex until we had settled all of our issues, despite how tired I was, despite the fact that I was still mad at him about locking me in the squad car — okay, so I wasn't nearly as mad as I had been — naked, he was mouth-wateringly delicious, all broad-shouldered and muscled and nicely hung.

When he slid into bed, it was all I could do to stop myself from instinctively turning into his arms. He yawned, and stretched out one brawny arm to turn off the lamp, plunging the room into darkness. Hurriedly I pulled the covers over me, because he'd followed his usual practice of turning the air-conditioning down low enough to form permafrost on living tissue. Snuggled under the blanket, his body heat already spreading through the bed to warm me, I turned on my side and slept.

He was right about the nightmares. My subconscious always dealt with bad situations for me, which is a handy thing for a subconscious to do. Most of the time I didn't have real nightmares, just vivid, sort of upsetting dreams, but that night it was a real nightmare.

There was no big mystery to figure out, no symbolism, just a straightforward reenactment of my terror. I was caught in a fire, and I couldn't find the way out. I tried to hold my breath but the oily black smoke slid into my nose, my mouth, into my throat and lungs, and its suffocating weight pressed down on me. I couldn't see, couldn't breathe, and the heat kept getting more and more intense until I knew this was it, the flames were about to reach me, and then I would burn —

"Blair, shhh, I have you. It's okay. Wake up."

He did have me, I blearily realized. I was in his arms, cradled against his warm body, the specter of fire fading into unreality. The lamp spilled its mellow light over the bedroom.

I relaxed with a sigh, feeling safe for the first time in days. "I'm okay," I whispered. A second later realization hit, and I blinked at him. "I whispered!"

"So I heard." His mouth curved in a smile. "Quiet time is over, I guess. I'll get you some water; you were coughing a little."

Disentangling from both the covers and me, he went into the bathroom and came back with a glass of water, which I sipped cautiously. Yep, swallowing still hurt some. After a few sips I handed the glass back to him and he drained it to the bottom on his way back to the bathroom.

Then he came back to bed, grasped my hips, and pulled me to the edge of the mattress, onto his out-thrust erection.

CHAPTER TWENTY-FOUR

I gasped, my entire body jolted by the hard intrusion. He pulled me up and reversed our positions, sitting on the edge of the mattress with me astride him, his arms supporting me as I arched back in sheer, overwhelming pleasure.

"Remember that Tantric sex you wanted to try?" he murmured, his voice low and dark. "I checked it out. No moving . . . how long do you think you can go without moving?" He lifted my torso up to meet his mouth, sucking hard at both my nipples, pulling them into erect peaks before moving on, kissing his way up my chest and then clamping his mouth to the side of my neck.

Maybe it was because we hadn't made love in over a week; maybe it was because death had come close to separating us forever. The *why* didn't really matter, not when the sensations of our joined bodies and his mouth on my neck were surging through me. I don't particularly like having my breasts touched; it's either boring, or painful. But something about what he'd just done, that single hard, pulling suction on each nipple, made my whole body tingle. And my neck . . . oh, God, my neck . . . kissing me there always made fireworks go off behind my eyelids.

"Do you think I can make you come by kissing your neck?" he whispered, before taking a small bite just where my neck joined my shoulder, and flicking his tongue rapidly against the captured flesh. My throat was too raw for me to scream but I could moan, almost, the sound not much more than a broken whimper. My body flexed under the surge of intense pleasure, my hips arching inward to take more of his penis inside me.

He released the grip of his teeth on my neck, his breath feathering along the wetness as he said, "Uh uh, no moving. We have to be still."

Was he crazy? My God, how could I possibly be still? But the idea tantalized and tempted. Feeling him like this was incredibly erotic. No thrusting, no rushing headlong into climax, just this . . . his body hard and warm against me, his penis a hard, solid presence pushing up into me, the fluidity of my body around him. I could feel his heartbeat thundering against my breasts, my own pulse beating through me. I wondered if he could feel my pulse from inside me, if his cock was surrounded and stroked by the beat of my blood.

My head drooped on his shoulder and I panted against his warm, damp skin. Instinctively I turned my head and lightly bit the side of his neck, just as he had done to me, and felt the answering throb of his penis. He groaned, a harsh sound in the quiet room.

Thoughts swam through my mind, things I hadn't considered earlier when I'd been listing my immediate needs. My birth control pills had gone up in flames that morning. There was little or no chance of pregnancy right now, I knew that; my body needed to return to my natural cycle first. But the act suddenly seemed fraught with possibilities, with both power and vulnerability. My body felt oddly lush, magically female. I wanted to have his baby, wanted everything our bodies promised.

I dug my nails into his shoulders, lifted my mouth enough to bite his earlobe. "No birth control pills," I whispered into his ear, the words not much more than a breath.

I felt his response deep inside me, a flexing, a seeking. His arms tightened around me and he sank one hand into my hair, cradling my head as he fused our mouths together, his tongue moving, probing, taking. And I took him too, took his mouth, his breath, while deep inside I tightened and flexed muscles that held him, massaged him, drew him groaning to the brink of climax.

He left my mouth and all but attacked my neck, his hand in my hair holding my head arched back so he had complete access. The fierce throb of pleasure that shuddered through me almost took me all the way, almost, so close the first hot flare shot along my nerve endings.

"Don't move," he groaned against my neck. "Don't move."

I wanted to move, I desperately *needed* to move, to rise and fall on his penetrating flesh and end this exquisite torture. I would need only one thrust, just one . . . and yet, because the torture was exquisite, I didn't want it to end. I wanted to quiver here, just on the edge, and feel the shudders rippling through his big body as he struggled with the same need.

"No moving," I whispered back to him, and desperately he grabbed my bottom.

Our bodies were hot, steamy. Where our skin was plastered together we sweated, but the cold air of the air-conditioning washed over my back like the breath of frost. He was kneading my bottom in his big hands, the motion pulling, opening me so that I felt the chill touch damp places that were normally protected. The contrast between hot and cold was disorienting, sending my senses spinning. His fingers slid along my bottom, down, down, until he stroked the tightly stretched skin where he entered me.

I would have screamed, tried to scream, but my throat balked at the effort and refused to work. I tried not to move. I quivered and shook, my head falling to the side while his mouth worked my neck. I clenched him, hard, trying to hold him and take him deeper, and he quivered, too. I loved feeling that, feeling all of his hardness and strength responding to me. I loved the piercing expression in his green eyes, the way he watched me, the complete and utter abandonment of all defenses as we strained together.

And then I broke, shuddering, crying, my entire body in motion as I rocked against him in the most total dissolving of sensation I've ever felt. The spasms were like waves spreading through me. I *felt* him groan, felt the vibration through his whole body, and just as I collapsed bonelessly against him he turned us, pinning me to the mattress beneath him as he broke, too.

We slept like that, without turning off the

lamp, without getting up to wash. And if I dreamed, I didn't know it.

In the morning, we made love in the shower, which, yes, we both needed. We practically had to unglue ourselves with the aid of warm water. As intense as the night's lovemaking had been, the morning's was playful, at least until the last minute or so. I was glowing when I bounced down the stairs.

I always took longer getting ready, of course, so he already had breakfast started. He turned his head and winked at me as I headed for the coffee. "Do you think you can eat real food today?"

I took the first swallow of coffee, considered, then rocked my hand in a "maybe, maybe not" motion.

"Oatmeal it is, then," he said. "Don't try anything that'll make you cough."

I had tried to talk, of course, and could actually make sounds this morning. Unfortunately, the sounds were those of a dying frog. Just being able to whisper, though, was an enormous relief, because I had a busy day ahead of me.

While we were eating he said, frowning, "I can't stay with you today, so your first stop is for a new cell phone. Got it? You can't be out of communication."

I totally agreed with that.

"You gotta tell me what happened to your old one, though."

Just because I could whisper didn't mean I should. The less I used my voice, the faster I'd get it back. So I pantomimed beating the cell phone against the window.

"That's what I thought," he said after a moment, his tone strained.

You'd think no one had ever broken a cell phone before.

"Now. What I want you to do today is stay out of work. Don't go to any of your usual places, places where she could expect to find you. Don't go to your parents' house. Don't go to Siana's. You have a lot of shopping to do, so do it. I'll take you to a car rental agency and you can drive something completely different from that little eye-catcher out there in the garage." He was all cop now, his eyes narrow, his mind working. "I'll have the Mercedes collected, and we'll put one of our blond female officers in it and have her cruise around — to Great Bods, to your bank, to wherever you usually get lunch. This woman may be lying low for a while, a day or so, but eventually she's going to come after you again. But it *won't* be you. There's no negotiation on that."

I reached for the notebook and scribbled, *I*

333

have no problem with that. Yeah, if I'd been able to get to her the night of the fire I was so mad I'd have gone vigilante on her ass, but in the light of day my head was cooler and a big reality was staring me in the face: I needed to get this wedding taken care of, and I couldn't let there be any more delays. Tonight, even if I had to write every word, Wyatt and I would have that conversation I'd been putting off, but I couldn't afford to wait even until then.

Thanks to JoAnn's promising skill behind the desk, she and Lynn could handle things until this nutcase was taken care of. I, in the meantime, would be racing the clock to get my wedding organized. How many days had I already lost because of this woman, assuming she was also the woman who had tried to run me over in the parking lot? She might not be, but hey, she was available to blame, so I blamed her.

I would feel perfectly safe in an anonymous rental car, going to Sticks and Stones to face Monica Stevens in her den, shopping for my fabric, shopping for new clothes — at a different mall, though — going to see Sally. None of that was my usual routine, and I was starting out from a completely different place, a safe place. She didn't know where I was or how to find me, and it felt great.

After breakfast, Wyatt took me to get another cell phone. To my surprise, he didn't take me to my cell service provider, but to his, and added me to his account. I kept my same number, of course, but combining our accounts felt startlingly . . . permanent.

That reminded me of other details I had to attend to, such as canceling my home utilities. I was pretty sure both the phone company and the cable company would continue billing me, even though no home existed there now. And I would need to get an inventory to my insurance company. Man, I'd thought I had my day mapped out, but more and more things were cropping up to eat into my time.

Our next stop was close to the airport, where all the car rental companies were. I got a Taurus — they have nice suspensions — but guess what? It was white. White seemed to be the predominant color for rental cars. I wasn't entirely happy with white, but Wyatt was totally against the apple red. "Too noticeable," he said.

I guess.

Then he kissed me and we parted company for the day.

It was just nine a.m., too early for Sticks and Stones to be open. With time to kill, I went to another fabric store. No luck. That was discouraging, but by the time I'd searched the store over, I'd killed almost an hour, so I drove to Sticks and Stones.

The same stick-thin woman as before came to greet me, her smile chilling a bit as she took in my jeans and lightweight sweater. "Yes, may I help you?"

No way out of it, I had to talk — whisper, rather. "I'm Blair Mallory. I left my card day before yesterday, but Ms. Stevens hasn't called." I saw her expression as she drew back a little, as if I were contagious. "Yes, I have severe laryngitis. No, you can't catch it. My house burned down yesterday morning and this is from smoke inhalation, which means I'm not in a great mood so I'd really like to see Monica. Now, if possible."

That was a lot to say, and even whispering was a strain. I was scowling by the time I finished. I didn't like that woman.

Strangely enough, she brightened at the news that my house had burned down. It took me a moment before I realized she knew a new house and all new furniture meant redecorating. I wondered if she scoured the newspapers looking for news of house fires, the way shady lawyers looked for car accidents.

She led me through the store into the back, where the offices were set up. Back here the feel was completely different; huge books holding swatches of fabric were stacked helter-skelter, different pieces of furniture were jumbled together, framed art leaned against walls. I actually liked this better; this was where work was done. There was energy here, instead of the coldly stylized feel of the front showroom.

The woman knocked on an office door, and at an invitation from within, pushed the door open. "Ms. Stevens, this is Blair Mallory," she said, as if she were introducing me to Queen Elizabeth. "She has laryngitis because her house burned down yesterday — smoke inhalation, you know." With that tantalizing tidbit, she returned to the showroom and left us alone.

I'd never met Monica Stevens before, though I'd heard about her. In a way she was what I expected, but in a way she wasn't. She was fortyish, with sleek black hair in a dramatic, asymmetrical cut — thin, stylish in a studied way, with noisy bangle bracelets on both wrists. I like bangle bracelets only if I'm the one wearing them. Hey, it's different when you're the annoyer instead of the annoyed.

"I'm so sorry about your house," she said, and her voice had a warm tone that made her seem more approachable. What I hadn't expected about her was the friendly expression in her eyes.

"Thank you," I said, whispered, and pulled Jazz's invoices from my tote, placing them in front of her before I sat down.

She looked at the invoices, puzzled, then read the name. "Mr. Arledge," she said in her warm voice. "He was a darling man, so anxious to surprise his wife. I loved working with him."

There hadn't been any working "with" Jazz, who had zero sense of style or decoration. Jazz had given her carte blanche, signed the check, and that was it. "His marriage broke up because of this," I said baldly.

She looked stunned. "But . . . why?"

"His wife loved her bedroom the way it was. She hates the new style and refuses to even sleep in the room. She's so furious at him for getting rid of her antiques, she tried to hit him with her car."

"Oh my God. You're joking. She doesn't like that room? But it's gorgeous!"

She hadn't even blinked an eye at hearing Sally had tried to maim Jazz, but she was honestly disbelieving that anyone could not like her creations.

Wow. I admire alternate reality as much as anyone, but there's such a thing as too much disconnect.

"I'm trying to save this marriage," I said. All of this whispering was really, really beginning to be a strain. "Here's what I want you to do: go pick up that furniture and put it in your consignment shop, or, since it's never been used, sell it again as new. Technically it may not be, but since you never got the final approval on the job I'd say it's still ongoing."

She stiffened. "What do you mean?"

"I mean the client isn't happy with the job."

"I've received complete payment, so I'd say he was." Her cheeks were turning red.

"Jazz Arledge is a babe in the woods when it comes to decorating. He knows nothing about it. You could have nailed skunk hides to the walls and he wouldn't have known to protest. I *don't* think you deliberately took advantage of him, and I *do* think you're a smart enough businesswoman to see the advantage in redoing this bedroom, but this time working with Mrs. Arledge, who is miserably unhappy."

She regarded me thoughtfully. "Explain, please."

I waved my hand toward the showroom. "Your reputation precedes you. People who like the modern avant garde look love your work, but potential customers who go for a more traditional look don't come to you because they think you don't do that kind of work."

"Of course I do," she said automatically. "The look isn't what I prefer, it isn't my signature style, but my ultimate goal is to please my client."

I beamed at her. "That's very good to hear. By the way, I don't believe I've mentioned that my mother is Mrs. Arledge's best friend. She's in real estate, so maybe you've heard of her. Tina Mallory?"

Comprehension crept into her eyes. Mom's a former Miss North Carolina, and she sells a lot of real estate. If Mom started recommending Monica, the business potential could be enormous.

She reached for a sketch pad, and with remarkable memory swiftly sketched out Sally's bedroom. She worked quickly, colored pencils flying across the sheet. "What do you think of this?" she asked, turning the pad around so I could see what she'd done.

The look was richly comfortable, with color in the fabrics, and the furniture warm with wood. "I remember those antiques," she said. "They were wonderful quality; I can't replace them, but I can probably find one or two smaller, really good pieces that will give the same feel."

"Mrs. Arledge would love it," I said. "But I'll warn you up front that Jazz isn't willing to pay another penny. He's very bitter about the whole experience."

"He'll feel differently when I'm finished," she said, smiling. "And I won't lose a penny on this, I promise you."

Having seen the markups on that invoice, I believed her.

Two-thirds of my mission were accomplished. Now for the hardest part: Sally.

CHAPTER TWENTY-FIVE

Even though logically the stalker couldn't know where I was, I still looked around very carefully when I left Sticks and Stones. All clear. I didn't think I'd ever be able to see a white Chevrolet again without feeling an automatic twinge of panic, which, when you think about it, would be a major pain in the ass. As Wyatt had mentioned, there are thousands and thousands of white Chevrolets. I could be in a permanent twinge.

I needed something hot to drink for my throat, and I needed fabric for my gown. And, damn it, I still needed to call the phone and cable companies — no, damn it, I'd probably have to go in person, to prove my identity, since I didn't have the account numbers. I also still had to go shopping for clothes. And my boots! My blue boots! They would be returned as undeliverable, but I wanted them. Unfortunately, I didn't have my order number because all of that had burned up with the condo, so I couldn't even contact Zappos and have them redirected.

I brightened. I could order another pair, though, from Wyatt's computer.

Siana called while I was on the way to my next-favorite mall. "Mom said you couldn't talk at all. Tap the phone once if that's true."

"It was true yesterday," I whispered.

"I heard that! How do you feel?"

"Better." I looked for a McDonald's. A cup of coffee would improve things even more.

"Is there anything I can do to help?"

"Not yet." Right now I was still at the stage where I had to handle it all.

"Do you have any idea who set the fire?"

"I saw her face," I managed to croak, "and she's familiar, but I can't place her."

Logical Siana said, "Well, since all of this started recently, she has to relate somehow to one of the places you've been recently. Start thinking of them, and eventually something will click."

"That's what I thought, but I've gone over and over my routine, and I can't place her anywhere."

"Then it's someplace that isn't part of your normal routine."

I thought about that while I plowed through stores in the mall. This had all started at the other mall, where I had gone into a lot of stores. Was that where I'd seen her? I tried to remember something unusual happening in any of the stores, that would have caused her face to stick in my mind like that. The idea distracted me while I tried on shoes, and that's just not right, because buying shoes is one of the great joys of life. I should have been able to devote my full attention to the ritual.

I didn't try to replace my entire wardrobe in one fell swoop — that would have been impossible — but I did try to cover all possible needs: work clothes, play clothes, dressy clothes. I definitely splurged on new underwear sets, because that's one of my weaknesses, too. Between what had been cut off me in hospitals and what I'd lost in the fire . . .

My breath literally caught in my chest.

The hospital. That was where I'd seen her.

She was the nurse with the bad dye job who had chatted with me for such a long time, while she kept ripping bandages off my scrapes. Then I'd been in so much pain from the concussion that it hadn't really registered at the time, but she'd been unnecessarily rough with those bandages, as if she'd been *trying* to hurt me.

Her hair had been that ugly brown then, and very blond when I'd seen her in the crowd at the fire scene, but it was the same woman. Maybe blond was her normal color, and the bad dye job was because she'd hastily dyed her hair that very morning, as a disguise. A disguise from what? I hadn't known her from Adam's house cat then. But for some reason she hadn't wanted me to see her with blond hair.

In that case, why would she then bleach her hair? Why not leave it the ugly flat brown?

I grabbed my cell phone and checked the service; there was only one bar, so I gathered my purchases and made a beeline for the nearest exit. As soon as I stepped out into the sunshine the number of bars went to three, and a second later to four. I punched in Wyatt's cell number.

"Are you all right?" he barked as a greeting, in the middle of the second ring.

"I remember her," I said as loudly and clearly as I could, because there was a lot of noise around me, with traffic passing by. My voice croaked horribly, breaking in the middle of the words, then losing volume entirely. "She's a *nurse* at the *hospital.*"

"Say again, I couldn't understand you. Did you say hospital?"

I tried again, this time in the loudest whisper I could manage. At least my voice didn't break when I whispered. "She's a nurse at the hospital."

"One of the nurses? You're sure?"

"Yes," I whispered emphatically. "Not in the ER, on the floor. She came into my room, chatted, ripped my bandages off —"

"Blair, where are you?" he interrupted.

"Mall. Different one." Now I had to think the incident at the other mall had been happenstance, because that was before I'd met Nurse Nutcase.

"Come to the station, right now. We need a description, more to go on than we have so far, and I can barely understand you. I'll meet you there."

The Fates were against me. It was absolutely not meant for me to find material for my wedding gown, to get my errands accomplished, or to get Sally and Jazz back together. On the other hand, not getting killed certainly had to be a priority.

In my need to get cell service, I'd gone out the nearest exit instead of the one where I'd entered, so I went back into the mall and walked to the other end. When I entered the parking deck, once again I found myself checking for white Chevrolets. I started to get angry with myself, then realized she was still out there; I couldn't afford to assume there was no way she could find me. There was always a way, if she was determined enough.

I drove to the police department, took the elevator up. Wyatt was in his office, the door open. He was on the phone, but looked up and saw me, waved me in. He also beckoned to Forester, who came in, too, and closed the door behind him. Wyatt got off the phone, then turned that green laser look on me. "Start at the beginning."

I took a deep breath. "I finally placed her. She's a floor nurse at the hospital. She came into my room, was really friendly, chatted for a while, but she kept ripping my bandages off, and she was really rough doing it."

He looked angry, his jaw working a little. "Did anyone else see her?"

"Siana was there."

"Describe her."

"About my age, maybe a little older. It was hard to tell. Very pretty, with greenish hazel eyes. Brown hair, but it was a bad dye job. She must have bleached the dye out afterward, which is really hard to do, and that threw me off when she turned up at the fire scene as a blonde."

"How tall?"

I swallowed to ease my throat. "I don't know. I was lying down, so I don't have a frame of reference. But she was slim, built really well. And she . . ." I started to say she had really long eyelashes but an elusive picture was trying to form in my mind, another face swimming into focus. I gasped. "I saw her in the fabric shop, too, after I got out of the hospital. I thought she looked familiar then. But her hair was different that time, too. It was red, I think, a dark red." She had been following me around, and not just in a Chevrolet. Glancing at Wyatt, I knew from his grim expression that the same thought had occurred to him.

"Wigs," said Forester.

Wyatt nodded. "That's what it sounds like."

"The blond hair could have been a wig," I said. "It was covered with a hood so I couldn't tell. But the brown hair in the hospital wasn't a wig, it was her hair, and it was dyed. Trust me." My whisper was going; I started coughing at the end of that speech. The laryngitis was something else I could lay at her door, and though it was minor in comparison to burning my condo, not being able to talk was a pain in the ass. If I needed to scream or something, I'd be S.O.L. When you think of the situations in which you might need to scream, having a voice suddenly becomes more important.

"I'll contact the hospital," said Forester,

"see if we can get photos of everyone who was working — when?"

"First shift, last Friday," supplied Wyatt. "Fourth floor, neurological wing."

"We might not need a warrant," said Forester, but without much hope. "But this hospital tends to get pissy on privacy issues."

"I get pissy on attempted murder issues," said Wyatt, his tone icy.

I wondered what he could do if the hospital administration balked at providing photos without first being served with a warrant, then remembered that, courtesy of his previous celebrity status, he could pick up the phone and talk to the governor anytime he wanted. Wyatt could affect fundraising, appointments, any number of aspects that were pertinent to a hospital. Way cool.

Forester left to get on the phone with the hospital and Wyatt turned his attention back to me. "Was the first time you saw her while you were in the hospital?"

"So far as I know."

"Can you think of anything you said that might have set her off, anything she said that can give us any idea what's going on here?"

I thought back over the conversation and shook my head. "I mentioned I was getting married in less than a month and didn't have time for a concussion. She said something about when she was planning her own wedding, how crazy the last month was. She asked if I liked your mother, said it must be nice to have a mother-in-law you liked, from which I gathered she doesn't like hers. She thought I'd been in a motorcycle accident, because of the road rash. Just . . . conversation. I said I was hungry and she said she'd have a tray sent up, but she never did. That's it. She was very friendly." I did some more coughing, and looked around for a pad to write on. I'd strained my throat enough. If I kept this up, I'd be right back where I'd started.

"That's all the questions," he said, getting up and coming around the desk to haul me to my feet, his arms closing around me. "Rest your throat. We'll get her now; that's the lead we've been needing."

"It just makes no sense," I whispered. "I don't *know* her."

"Stalkers don't make sense, period. They form illogical obsessions in an instant, and a lot of times the victim has done nothing more than be polite. It isn't your fault, and there's nothing you could have done to prevent it. It's a personality disorder. If she changes her appearance that often, then she's looking for something, and you're probably everything she wants to be and isn't."

That was a pretty neat psychological assessment. I was impressed. "Hey, you're not just another pretty face," I said, looking up at him. "And everyone says football players are dumb."

He laughed and patted my butt, though his hand probably lingered too long for it to qualify as an actual pat. At the quick knock on his door, though, he dropped his hand and stepped away.

Forester popped his head in, a frown knitting his forehead. "I talked to the floor supervisor," he reported. "She said there's no one answering that description on her floor at all."

Wyatt frowned, rubbing his bottom lip as he thought. "Could have been someone from the ER who saw Blair when she was brought in, took a little side trip up to see her. There should be security film of the hallways, almost every hospital has that now."

"I'll get in touch with hospital security and see what I can do."

"How much trouble will that be?" I asked Wyatt when Forester had gone back to his phone.

His smile was thin. "Depends on what kind of day the chief of security is having. Depends on whether hospital rules say he has to clear this with the administrator before letting us see the film. Depends on whether the administrator is having a dick-head day. If he is, then it depends on whether or not we can find a judge to sign a warrant, which can be a little iffy on a Friday afternoon, and especially iffy if the hospital administrator plays golf with a few of the judges."

Good God. And he'd *wanted* to be a cop.

"Do I need to stay?"

"No, you can go do your thing. I know how to get in touch with you. Just be careful."

I nodded my understanding. As I rode down in the elevator I sighed. I was *tired* of looking for white Chevrolets, and anyway, if she were smart, which she appeared to be, why wouldn't she swap up her vehicles? Renting a car wasn't difficult. For all I knew she could be in a *blue* Chevrolet by now.

A chill went down my back.

Or a beige Buick.

Or even a white Taurus.

I'd let myself be blinded by the idea that I'd recognize her by what she was driving. She could be driving anything. She could have been following me all morning, and I wouldn't have known it because I'd been looking for the wrong color car.

She could be anywhere.

CHAPTER TWENTY-SIX

I had a choice. I could bolt for Wyatt's house, using the technique he'd taught me the night before to evade any followers, and hole up there like a scared rabbit, or I could use that same technique to break free and then go about my business. I chose to go about my business.

Why not? I had a wedding to pull off. What else could go wrong? What other complication could be added to my list of things to do? Not only did I have to be ready for a wedding in three weeks — a wedding for which I didn't even have a gown yet! — someone was trying to kill me, my home had been burned to the ground, I couldn't talk, I had to decide whether the man I loved truly loved me in return or if I should call off the wedding I was in the middle of planning, and I somehow had to repair the marriage of two people whose own children couldn't get them to talk to each other. I felt like a crazed bee, unable to stop going from flower to flower despite the hurricane blowing the stems flat and sometimes ripping them entirely from the ground.

To top things off, the stores had put out their Christmas decorations. I needed to start my Christmas shopping in the middle of all this, because the decorations are a signal to all those lunatic early shoppers who descend on stores like locusts and strip them of all the prime gifts, leaving only leftovers behind for the sane people who like to do their Christmas shopping after Thanksgiving — you know, when the Christmas season actually starts. Even if I didn't start my Christmas shopping now, the pressure was on, evidenced by the colored balls and little fiber-optic trees popping up in stores.

I couldn't play it safe and hide out. I had too many things to do. I could even rationalize it and say any on-the-ball nutcase out there would *expect* me to play it safe, therefore I was actually safer by not playing it safe, or something like that.

So I went to see Sally.

She had started working outside the home, at an antiques auction house, when her youngest finished high school. Basically Sally drove around to estate sales, yard sales, junk sales, searching for antiques she could get at low prices, which the auction house then spruced up and sold for profit. The auctions were every Friday night, which meant that on Fridays she could be found at the auction house helping with the stickering, cataloging, and arranging. The other four days of the week, and sometimes on Saturday, too, she was out doing her thing.

There was a mix of cars and pickup trucks, plus a midsize delivery truck backed up to a loading dock, parked outside the auction house, but the door was locked since they weren't open for business yet. I walked around to the loading dock and found a set of steps leading up, and I went in through the open bay door.

A skinny middle-aged guy with bug eyes and Coke-bottle glasses, pushing an empty hand truck, said, "Y'need help, ma'am?"

He was probably twenty-years older than I was, but this was the South, so he "ma'amed" me. It's just good manners.

I held up my hand, signaling he should stop, because no way could he hear me from where he was, and hurried over. "I'm looking for Sally Arledge," I whispered hoarsely.

"Right through there," he said, pointing toward a door at one end of the small dock area. "That's a bad case of laryngitis, if you don't mind me saying so. You need to take some honey and lemon in hot tea for that, and if that don't work, then put some Vicks salve on your throat and wrap it with a hot towel, and take a spoonful of sugar with kerosene dripped on it. Sounds crazy, but that's what my mama always gave us when we were little and had the sore throat, and it worked. Didn't kill us, either," he said, his bug eyes crinkling merrily.

"You actually took kerosene?" I asked. Huh. That sounded like something I needed to ask Grammy. The salve and hot towel remedy actually made sense, but I wasn't about to take kerosene dripped on anything.

"Sure did. Not very much, mind. A bunch would likely kill you doornail dead, or at least make you puke your guts up, but a little tad didn't hurt us."

"I'll keep that in mind," I promised. "Thanks!" I hurried toward the door he'd indicated, trying to envision how that remedy had gotten started. Somewhere, someone had thought, "Boy, my throat hurts! I think I'll get some kerosene and drink it. Bound to help. I'll put it on sugar, though; make it go down better."

The world amazes me.

The first person I saw when I went through the door was Sally, perched on a ladder, wiping down the top of a huge

carved headboard that was leaning again
the wall. It was a gorgeous piece, the wooc
blackened with age, and if it fell on anyone it
would likely kill them. No way would I have
sex with that thing looming over me, though
I guess going out with a bang isn't a bad way
to go.

She didn't look around, so I had to go over
and knock on the headboard to get her attention. "Blair!" Her mobile face expressing
both pleasure and concern, which isn't an
easy thing to do when you think about it,
Sally left her rag draped over the top of the
headboard and climbed down the ladder.
"Tina told me about your condo, and your
throat, and everything. Poor baby, you've
had a rough week." Once on the floor, she
hugged me tightly in sympathy.

Sally was about five-two and weighed
maybe a hundred pounds, a tiny dynamo
who was never still. Her dark red hair was
stylishly shaggy and spiky without being over
the top, and she'd had interesting blond
streaks put in it to frame her face. The broken nose that she sustained when she drove
into the side of the house while trying to hit
Jazz had left a tiny bump on the bridge of her
nose that somehow looked good. She had
worn glasses before, but the glasses were actually what had broken her nose when the air

ag deployed; since then she'd switched to contacts.

I hugged her in return. "Is there somewhere we can talk? I have something to show you."

She looked interested. "Sure. Let's go over here and sit down."

She indicated some folding chairs that were haphazardly grouped in the middle of the auction floor. Later they would be arranged in neat rows for the bidders. We took two of them, then I reached in my tote bag and pulled out the invoices from Sticks and Stones and handed them to her.

Puzzled, she looked at them for a couple of seconds before it registered what they were, then her eyes widened in shock and fury. "Twenty thousand dollars!" she yelped. "He paid . . . he paid *twenty thousand dollars* for that *dreck?*"

"No," I said, "he didn't pay that for the dreck. He paid that for you, because he loves you."

"Did he send you over here?" she demanded furiously.

I shook my head. "I'm interfering all on my own." Well, also because Wyatt had forced me to, but that was between us.

She stared down at the invoice, trying to get her mind around the amount. To her, the furniture and artwork Monica Stevens had used to replace Sally's prized antiques were worth maybe a couple of thousand, tops. To say the two looked at style from the opposite ends of the spectrum was to understate the case.

"He *knew* how much I loved my antique pieces," she said, her voice breaking a little. "And if he didn't, he should have! Why else would I have put so much work into repairing them and refinishing them? It wasn't as if we couldn't have afforded different furniture if I'd wanted it!"

"But he didn't know," I pointed out. "For one thing, you didn't work on the pieces when he was at home. And for another, I have never in my life seen a man more clueless about style and decorating than Jazz Arledge. That orange couch in his office —" I broke off, shuddering.

She blinked, distracted. "You've seen his office? Isn't that place *horrible?*" Then she shook off the disturbing image. "That doesn't matter. If he'd listened to me *at all* during the thirty-five years we've been married, if he paid any attention to the house he lived in, he couldn't possibly have thought —"

"That's just it, he literally has no clue about different decorating styles. He didn't know different styles existed. To him, furniture is furniture is furniture, period. I think he sort of gets the concept now, but only in the vaguest way, like he knows there are different styles but he has no idea what they are or how any of them look. It's a language he doesn't speak, so he doesn't understand what you're saying when you talk about antiques."

"Surely to God he knows that 'antique' means *old.*"

"Maybe," I said doubtfully. "Look, can he tell the difference between navy blue and black?"

She shook her head.

"Most men can't. They don't have the necessary number of color rods in their eyes to tell the difference, so even if you put a navy blue sock beside a black sock they look the same to a man. It's the same principle. It isn't that Jazz isn't interested, that he's ignored what you like, it's that his brain isn't wired to see style. You don't ask a wingless bird to fly, do you?"

Tears glittered brightly in her eyes and she looked down at the invoices in her hand. "You're saying I'm wrong."

"I'm not saying you're wrong to be upset about the furniture. I would have been, too." Understatement, there. "But you were definitely wrong to try to hit him with the car.'

"That's what Tina said."

"She did?" Mom was in my corner! When had that happened?

"When you were in the hospital," Sally said, as if she'd heard my thought. "She said that seeing how much pain you were in even though you hadn't actually been hit by that car changed her mind. She said that hurt feelings were one thing, but physical injuries were way more serious."

I sighed. I'm not one to downplay hurt feelings, but considering everything that had happened the past couple of months I had to agree. "She's right. You didn't catch him in adultery, you know. He bought furniture you don't like."

"So get over it."

I nodded.

"And apologize."

I nodded again.

"Damn, I hate apologizing! It isn't just this. We've said things since this happened that we shouldn't have said . . . "

"So get over it." I could barely even whisper by then. It's amazing how whispering can strain your throat.

"The heck of it is, I didn't intend to hit him at all. We'd been arguing and we were both mad, but I had an appointment and had to leave. He followed me out, still argu-ing. You know Jazz, know how stubborn he is. He had a point he wanted to make, and intended to drive it into the ground. I started backing up and he was still standing there, waving his arms and yelling, and I was so mad I shoved the gear shift into Park so I could get out and yell in his face, except I didn't shove it all the way up, and my foot was on the gas, and, well, right then I wouldn't have minded if I had hit him, but it wasn't deliberate. The next thing I knew the air bag was in my lap, my glasses were bro-ken, and my nose was bleeding." Ruefully she rubbed the tiny bump on her nose. "A broken nose at my age. And now I'll have to live with that dreck."

Smiling, I shook my head. "I talked to Monica. She'll take the furniture back and work with you to redo your bedroom the way you like. She does other styles, too, you know. I think you'll even like her. Plus I told her Mom would spread the word to her real estate clients that Monica isn't a one-note Joanie, that she can do things other than steel and glass."

"If she does, I've never seen it," said Sally doubtfully.

"That's because most of her clients are people who like her signature style. She wants to branch out more, attract other clients. Redoing your bedroom will be good business for her."

"I'm not willing to pay one more cent to her. Twenty thousand dollars!"

"She isn't asking for more money. She isn't the bad guy here. There isn't a bad guy."

"Well, crap."

If I could have laughed, I would have. We looked at each other in perfect understanding.

"I'll call him tonight," she said, and sighed. "I'll apologize. I'm an eagle and he's a penguin. He can't fly. Got it."

"I took him to see a piece Mr. Potts was refinishing, a big armoire. Mr. Potts told him he'd already put in around sixty hours on it. Jazz will never know furniture, but now he has a better appreciation of how much work you put into your bedroom."

"Oh, God, Blair, thank you," she said, grabbing me and hugging me again. "I hope we would have worked it out on our own, eventually, but you've speeded up the process."

"It just needed an outside view," I said modestly.

CHAPTER TWENTY-SEVEN

All that talking had done a number on my whisper, so I stopped at a pharmacy for a jar of Vicks ointment, intending to give it a try. I would smell like a cough drop, but if this stuff would help my throat I didn't care how I smelled. I intended to have the Big Talk with Wyatt that night, so it would help if I could, well, *talk*.

I was on my way to a third fabric store when Wyatt called my cell and told me to come back to the police department. He was in lieutenant mode; his tone of voice made it an order, not a request.

Frustrated, I changed directions. I remembered to watch and see if any of the cars behind me changed direction, too. None did.

I wasn't going to be able to put this wedding together on time. The Fates were against me. I accepted that, now. I wouldn't be able to find the material for a gown, the wedding cake maker wouldn't come through, the caterer would bail out, and all the silk flowers that were supposed to be woven through the arbor would get some mysterious silk rot and fall to pieces. Wyatt hadn't even *started* sanding and repainting the arbor. I might as well save myself the wear and tear on my nerves and give up.

In a pig's eye, I would. The stakes were too high. It was either do it, or find myself in some drive-up wedding chapel in Las Vegas. *If* we got married.

This was driving me nuts.

When I got to the police department, Detective Forester met me in the parking lot. He must have been waiting for me, because he said, "You're going to the hospital with me. We have permission to look at photographs and review film, if it still exists. The hospital chief of security is checking that out as we speak."

The front passenger seat of his car was piled high with notebooks, files, reports, a clipboard, a can of Lysol, and some other official stuff. I wondered why he needed the Lysol, but didn't ask. I picked up the stuff out of his seat, slid in, and held everything on my lap while I buckled up. The files looked interesting, but I didn't have time to read them. Maybe he'd have to stop and get gas or something; I could give them a quick look-see then.

At the hospital he asked for the chief of security by name, and in a few minutes we were met by a short, slender man in his forties, with close-cropped hair and the erect posture of someone who hasn't been out of the military very long.

"I'm Doug Lawless, chief of security," he said, shaking hands with a brisk, firm up-and-down when Forester introduced both himself and me. "Let's go to my office, Ms. Mallory, to review the photographs in question first, then the security tape if necessary."

We followed Lawless to an office that was nicely middle-of-the-road — not so big that it would inspire jealousy, but not so small that he'd get the idea he wasn't appreciated. I've heard hospital politics can be cutthroat.

"I pulled up the files myself," he said, "and pasted the only photographs into a separate file, so no privacy concerns will be compromised. Sit here, please." He indicated his chair in front of an LCD monitor and I sat down. "This is everyone with whom you came in contact the night of your accident," he said. "This includes radiology and nuclear medicine, as well as laboratory personnel. And admitting, of course."

I had come in contact with more people in the hospital than I ever would have guessed. I recognized several faces, including that of Dr. Tewanda Hardy, the physician who had released me. Because hair can be changed I didn't look at hair at all, just faces, and particularly eyes. I remembered that she had very long eyelashes, and even without mascara her eyes would be striking.

She wasn't there. I was positive of it, but went over the faces again at Forester's insistence, then shook my head just as firmly as I had the first time.

"We'll go to the security recordings of the hallways," said Lawless. "I'm sorry this particular floor doesn't have digital surveillance, not yet, but I'm working on it. The ER and critical care areas do, and some of the other floors, but not this one. Still, our tape quality is good."

He closed the blinds in his windows, darkening the room. The tape was already in the VCR, because all he did was punch a button and a color picture swam into focus on a second monitor.

"The tape is on a timer," he said. "Do you remember about what time this nurse entered your room?" With a pen he indicated which room was mine. The proportion of everything seemed off, because the cameras were in the ceiling, but the images were sharp and clear.

I thought back. Siana had arrived about eight-thirty that morning, but even though Mom had had an appointment she hadn't yet left, so . . . "Between eight-thirty and nine a.m.," I whispered.

"Good, that's a relatively narrow window. Let's see what we can see." He fast-forwarded the tape, and people began zipping up and down the hallway and in and out of rooms like Chihuahuas on speed. He stopped the tape twice to check the timer, then overshot a little and had to rewind. "Here we go."

Surveillance tapes are interesting. I watched Siana saunter into my room, and gave both Forester and Lawless a moment to recover from their silent appreciation. "She'll be along any minute now," I whispered. "She was wearing pink scrubs."

And then there she was, at eight forty-seven. "That's her," I said, pointing. My heart started pounding, hard and fast. There was no doubt about it: pink scrubs, tall and slim, no hesitation, walking directly toward my room and entering. That flat brown hair looked unnaturally dark on the film, hanging around her shoulders. She was carrying a clipboard, which I hadn't noticed at the time, but hey, I'd been concussed. The camera angle caught her from the back, so there wasn't a good view of her face at all, just an occasional hint of the angle of her jaw.

Both men were leaning close to the monitor, watching the screen as intently as two cats waiting for a mouse to venture from its hole.

Mom left my room and I heard their quick little intakes of breath. "That's my mom," I said, before either of them could slip and make some kind of guy comment that would require me to take action.

Then, at eight fifty-nine, she left my room, but again the angle on her face wasn't good. Either the clipboard was in the way, or her head was down, or her shoulder was hunched.

"She's aware of the cameras," Lawless said. "She's hiding her face. I don't know every employee in the hospital, of course, but I don't recognize her. I wish you remembered her name, Ms. Mallory —"

"She wasn't wearing a name tag," I whispered. "At least, not one that I saw. I thought maybe it was clipped to one of her pockets, or the waistband of her pants."

"That's against this hospital's regulations," he said immediately. "The identification tags are to be readily visible, photo I.D. required, her clipped or pinned in the upper left chest area. I'll have to investigate further before I can say for certain, but I don't think she's an employee here. For one thing, she didn't knock on your door, she just walked in. Everyone employed here knocks before entering a patient's room."

"You can get another angle on her, can't you?" asked Forester. "She had to get to the fourth floor somehow, she didn't just materialize there."

"Perhaps," said Lawless. "That was a week ago. Some of the records, both digital and tape, have already been recorded over or erased. If nothing happened that requires us to make a permanent file, then we don't. There is also the possibility that she entered the hospital wearing something else entirely, carrying a bag, and changed in one of the public restrooms, so even if we did record her entering or leaving, we wouldn't know it."

She could also have worn her hair twisted up, or had on a baseball cap. My hopes had been up, but now they came crashing down. She was smart, savvy, and she was still one step ahead of us. I had no idea who she was, and this review hadn't provided any answers. I should have realized anyone working at a hospital would be required to have their I.D. tags highly visible, because of security concerns.

"I'm sorry this wasn't more productive," said Lawless. "I'll review what we have from that date, but I'm not optimistic."

"At least I can guess height and weight," said Forester, jotting notes down in one of the little notepads all cops seemed to carry. "That's more description than we've had before. Height . . . five-eight to five-ten. Weight, one twenty-five to one forty."

We thanked Lawless and left the hospital. My thoughts were racing, because it seemed as if the likelihood that she wasn't a hospital employee at all meant something — something other than that she worked somewhere else, of course.

As soon as I was belted into Forester's car, my lap loaded down with his stuff again, I got one of the notebooks, flipped to a blank page, and began writing because I thought it might be a good idea to share my thought about the rental cars with the police, but I wanted to save my voice.

"Throat not any better?" he asked as he buckled himself in.

I nodded and held my left hand up, thumb and first finger about an inch apart.

"A little bit, huh?"

I nodded again, and kept writing. When I

as finished I tore out the page and handed t to him. He read and drove at the same time, frowning at my note, and I don't know why because I used nice clear printing without a single curlicue or a little heart used to dot an *i*. I never did that anyway.

"You think she might be changing up rental cars, huh? What gave you that idea?"

I wrote some more, then gave him that page.

He read what I'd written, his gaze darting back and forth between the street and the sheet of paper. "Hmm," he said.

My hypothesis was that, if she didn't work at the hospital, then logically the only way she could have known I was even *in* a hospital would be if she'd called to see if I'd been admitted. But why would she think to do that, unless she'd been the one to put me there? Therefore, logically, she had to be the driver of the Buick.

I wrote him another note. I distinctly remembered telling her that Wyatt was a cop and that he was reviewing the mall parking lot security tapes, trying to get a tag number of the car that had almost hit me. No, I *hadn't* told her he was a cop, not exactly, but who else would be reviewing security tapes and getting tag numbers, and when she'd said something about it being nice having a

boyfriend who was a cop I hadn't correct
her, so indirectly I'd confirmed it for her.

In any case, Wyatt hadn't been able to pull
any useful information off the tape, but she
hadn't known that. So she'd switched cars,
to a white Chevrolet. And now I hadn't seen
the white Chevrolet in a while, so possibly
she was in something else, which to me
meant she either had access to a used-car lot
or she was using rental cars.

Forester grinned when he was finished
reading my notes. "You think like a cop," he
said approvingly, and I was so proud of the
compliment that I blushed.

When we got back to the police department he insisted I go in, so we rode the elevator up to what I thought of as the cop
floor. I guess technically they were all cop
floors, except for the ones where the cells
were, but that one seemed to be where the
actual cop work was done.

I naturally went to Wyatt's office, while
Forester went to his desk. Wyatt's door was
open and he waved me in. He was on the
phone, pacing in his small office, his suit
jacket off and his sleeves rolled up as usual.
I paused in the door for a moment, admiring
his ass as he paced, because Wyatt had a
mighty fine ass and I appreciate art wherever
I find it. In this case, it was in his pants.

He looked a little sweaty, I thought, as if he hadn't been here in the office all this time. In fact, he looked as if he'd just come back in. It was a nice warm day, warm enough to make a man sweat if he was wearing a suit jacket, so he'd been out on a scene somewhere. That was why Forester had gone with me to the hospital instead of Wyatt; he'd been available, and Wyatt hadn't been. Actually, Forester would normally have gone anyway, but Wyatt took a close interest in my cases.

He noticed that I was still standing in the door and he solved that by tucking the phone against his shoulder, holding it with his head tilted to the side as he pulled me into his office with one hand and closed the door with the other. I could hear some man's voice on the other end of the call, droning on and on. Still holding my arm with his left hand, Wyatt grabbed the phone with his right and held it down against his thigh while he bent his head and kissed me very thoroughly.

He definitely smelled a little sweaty, too, damp heat rising off him, and that was enough to flash me back to our lovemaking the night before, to the hot, sweaty intensity of it. I clutched at his ribs and put a little extra into the kiss — okay, a lot extra, melting against him, automatically checkin the status of Old Faithful. He broke from me, growling a little, his pants tent His fierce green gaze promised, *Later.* The he patted my butt and returned the phone to his ear. After listening a second or two he said, "Yes, Mr. Mayor," as he resumed his seat.

I was sitting decorously on one side of the desk and Wyatt was leaned back in his own chair when Forester knocked on the door a moment later. Well, I didn't know it was Forester until I got up to open the door, but it was. Wyatt waved him into the office, too. Forester's eyes were very bright and full of anticipation.

Finally Wyatt was able to get off the phone and he clicked it into its cradle with a snap, his focus already on Forester. "What did you find?"

"She was on the tape, but not in the employee photos. Because of certain behaviors, plus the lack of photo I.D., Lawless, that's the chief of security, thinks she isn't a hospital employee. So we don't have an I.D., which puts us back at square one — almost." Forester shot a glance at me. "Blair came up with a theory that makes sense to me, though our information is so slim I don't think we have enough to cross-check it." He my notes over the desk to Wyatt.

att swiftly skimmed my notes, shot a ck look at me, and said, "I agree, she was obably driving the Buick, which means nat wasn't a sudden fit of road rage, it was a deliberate attempt at murder. But we can cross-check by the dates. The rental agencies have some overlap in the type of cars they rent out, but not all of them will have Buicks available. Find the ones that do. If she's using rentals, the beige Buick would have been turned in last Friday. She would have gotten the white Chevrolet the same day, but I very much doubt she would have used the same rental agency. I think she would have gone to another agency, but hell, there's a row of them at the airport. If she's that smart, then she would have turned in the white Chevrolet and gotten something else on Wednesday, before she set the fire. Since Blair survived that, too, I'd say she would have turned *that* vehicle in yesterday. So now she's in something else, and we don't have a clue what to be on the lookout for."

Forester was taking notes, writing rapidly, pausing once to scratch his jaw. "I can get the rental agencies to give me the names of all females who rented vehicles on these particular dates. If any of them pop up twice, I'd say we have a person of interest."

Wyatt nodded. "Get on it. We're r.
out of time today, if any of them balk ar
quire a warrant." For routine investiga
stuff like that, most judges wouldn't d.
with signing a warrant on the weekend; 1
would have to wait until Monday.

Forester glanced toward the door, and in it
appeared one of the female detectives, her
eyes big with excitement — and focused on
me.

"Ms. Mallory," she gushed, her voice loud
enough to attract the attention of everyone
on the floor. "I'm so excited to meet you!
Would you autograph this for me, please? I
want to post it in the women's locker room."
She handed over a sheet of paper with
ragged edges, while a crowd gathered behind
her, peering into the office. I could almost
feel the accumulation of glee.

Automatically I took the sheet of paper
and looked down at it, recognizing it immediately. It was one of the notes I'd written
while I was locked in DeMarius Washington's squad car, and stuck to the window
with chewing gum. But what was it doing
here?

In a flash I remembered DeMarius leafing
through the notes and grinning, and
Forester doing the same. One of them must
have filched this particular note, instead of

ing it in my tote with the others.

"Let's see that," Wyatt said with resignation, recognizing a setup when he saw one.

Very helpfully, Forester plucked the note from my hand and placed it on Wyatt's desk, while everyone gathered outside the door burst into raucous laughter.

In very big block letters, which I had gone over several times to make them darker, was what I had meant to be the coup de grâce on all the asshole men who hadn't let me out of that stinky squad car:

SIZE MATTERS

CHAPTER TWENTY-EIGHT

"Size matters, huh?" Wyatt growled, grabbing me around the waist when he entered the house not five minutes behind me late that afternoon. I'd escaped his office amid the howls of laughter and made a beeline for the third fabric store, where — tah-dah — I'd found my fabric. I'd been so happy and relieved I hadn't even questioned the price, which had been steep, but then you don't get quality fabric for a dollar ninety-nine a yard. My booty now rested safely in the trunk of my rental, and I was taking it to Sally's house in the morning. She intended to work on the dress all weekend.

Now I had to deal with Wyatt.

"Well, yeah," I managed to gasp between voracious kisses. What, you expected me to lie?

"Then it's a good thing I have enough to handle you." He'd unsnapped my jeans and was peeling them down.

e did; oh, he did. He knew it, too, and ɔved it once again. At least he got me to ɪe couch that time, instead of simply taking me down to the floor as he'd done on more than one occasion.

And then he lingered, stroking in and out, looking down at my body as he clasped my hips between his strong hands. "It makes a difference," he said roughly. "No birth control. It makes a difference."

It did. Not a physical difference, but a mental one. Since the brain is the most important erogenous zone . . . wow. Everything was heightened, intensified, and sex between us had already been pretty intense.

He lay heavily on me afterward, absently stroking my hip as he often did. Dazed, I became aware that he hadn't undressed at all, though he'd managed to get me out of the bottom half of my clothes. His badge was still clipped to his belt, scraping really close to where I didn't want to be scraped, thank you very much, and that big black automatic was uncomfortable against my inner left thigh.

I wriggled under him. "You're still armed," I complained.

"Yeah, but I unloaded."

I pushed at his shoulders. "Badge — ouch!"

Pausing several times for kisses, he braced his hands on the cushion I was lying on and carefully pulled away from me. Logistically, this hadn't been well planned, and now we had to deal with practicalities. You know what I mean. Thank God the couch was leather.

After we cleaned up we made supper together. Before, he would have eaten out, but since we'd been together I'd stocked his freezer with premade stuff that just had to be heated. That night we chose lasagna, and added a salad. Salad fixings were something else I'd added to his refrigerator. I was teaching him about girl food.

After supper, I bit the bullet. I'd been thinking and evading and thinking some more since Tuesday night, and I couldn't put it off any longer. We were having sex without birth control, for heaven's sake, and even though there was practically no chance I could get pregnant, still . . .

"The things you said," I began as we loaded the dishwasher.

"I was horny. Men will say anything to get sex."

I frowned at him. "Tuesday night. When you were mad."

He straightened, giving me his full attention. "You've thought about it long enough, nuh? Okay, let's have it, so I can apologize again and get it over with."

That wasn't exactly the serious tone I'd wanted. My frown changed to a glare. "This isn't something to apologize for, it's something we need to face, straight up, and make a decision."

He crossed his arms and waited.

I hoped my voice would hold up to the explanation. Giving it a rest that afternoon had returned me to that awful croak, which at least had *sound* to it. I blew out a breath and started.

"You said that I pull dumb-ass tricks, that I expect you to jump through hoops and get pissy with you when you don't, and that I call you for everything that pops into my head and expect you to check it out. You also said I'm high maintenance. Duh. All of that other falls under that category. I'm high maintenance, I've always been high maintenance, and I'll always be high maintenance. That won't change. I won't change."

"I don't want you to change," he began, reaching for me, but I stepped out of reach and waved him to silence.

"Let me finish, because I don't know how long my voice will hold out. I don't consider my tricks dumb-ass, so that's a difference of opinion there. I don't think I expect you to

jump through hoops, but I put you first and
I expect you to put me first — within reason,
of course, and that goes for both of us. If
you're at a murder scene, for instance, I
wouldn't expect you to come jump my car
off if my battery goes dead. That's what I
have AAA for.

"And I *don't* call you to check out every little thing. Honest. But I will definitely expect
you to do things for me, like fix any parking
tickets I happen to get, but I wouldn't ask
you to fix a speeding ticket or falsify a report
or anything like that, so I think that's reasonable. But in the end this is *your* decision,
whether or not to go on with this marriage.
If the high maintenance bothers you that
much, if I'm already not worth the trouble to
you, then you should get out now. We'll
probably stay together for a while, but we
should call off the wedding —"

He put his hand over my mouth. His green
eyes were glittering. "I don't know whether
to laugh, or . . . laugh."

Laugh? My heart had been breaking, I'd finally gotten the courage to lay it all out for
him, and he wanted to *laugh*?

Men can't be the same species as women.
They just can't.

His other hand slid around my waist,
pulling me against him. "Sometimes you

make me so mad I could spit tenpenny nails, but since we've been together there hasn't been a day I haven't woken up smiling. Hell, yeah, you're worth the trouble. The sex alone is worth the trouble, but when you throw in the entertainment value —"

Furiously I tried to pinch him, but he laughed and caught my hands, pulling them up to hold them against his chest. "I love you, Blair Mallory Soon-to-be-Bloodsworth. Everything about you, even the high mainte-nance — even the notes you write, which, by the way, have completely alleviated the re-sentment toward me from the older guys. I don't know how that bastard Forester man-aged to steal that note without me noticing, but I'll find out," he muttered.

"I didn't write it to be funny," I snapped, or tried to snap. "I was making a *point.*"

"Oh, I got the point; we all did. You were mad as hell, at all of us, and after we knew why we had to admit you had the right. But I'd do it again, to keep you safe. I'd do any-thing to keep you safe. Now, how is it macho men are supposed to phrase this? Oh, yeah, I'd take a bullet for you. The wedding is still on. Does that answer your questions?"

I didn't know whether to pout, pinch, or punch. I settled for looking sulky. God, I was so relieved! He knew I wasn't going to

change, and he still wanted to marr
Good enough.

"Clarify something for me, though."

I looked up, questioning, and he took a
vantage, stealing a couple of kisses.

"Why would you want a parking ticket
fixed but not a speeding ticket? A speeding
ticket costs more, counts against your driver's license, and makes your insurance pre-
mium go up."

I couldn't believe he didn't see the difference. "A speeding ticket would be for something I *did*. But a parking ticket? Excuse me!
Who owns city property? The taxpayers,
that's who. Am I the only person who thinks
it doesn't make sense for someone to be
charged for parking on *their own property*,
and then fined if they park too long? That's
un-American. That's downright . . . downright *fascist* —"

He didn't use his hand to shut me up, that
time. He used his mouth.

CHAPTER TWENTY-NINE

The weather turned chilly again overnight, and rain had started by morning. Normally I would be going to work early on Saturday, because it was a busy day, but when I talked to Lynn she said that JoAnn was working out great and she suggested offering the job full-time. I agreed, because otherwise these next three weeks would kill me.

Wyatt slept late, sprawled across the bed, and I entertained myself that morning by writing his list of transgressions. Like I would forget something that important? No way. I sat curled in his big chair with a throw over my feet and legs, perfectly content to laze away the morning. The rain seemed to do away with any sense of urgency. I love listening to rain anyway, and seldom get the chance to because I'm usually too busy. I felt safe and happy, cocooned with Wyatt, letting the detectives do the legwork in tracking down my stalker. They were on the right track with the rental cars, I just knew it.

I could talk. To my delight, I could actually talk. My voice was very raspy, but at at least it worked. I never could have been one of those nuns who took vows of silence. Come to think of it, I couldn't have been a nun, period.

I called Mom and talked to her. She had talked to Sally and was greatly relieved; Sally had already called Jazz and apologized, and they were supposed to meet this morning and talk in person. I wondered if maybe I should wait until tomorrow to take my fabric over, and Mom said yes. I got the picture, having gone through something of a reconciliation with Wyatt.

Then I called Siana and we chatted for a while. After hanging up with her, I took all of my new clothes upstairs and laid them out on the bed in the guest bedroom. I tried on all my new shoes again, walking in them to make certain they didn't rub my toes. By then Wyatt was up; I heard him go downstairs for a cup of coffee, then he came back upstairs and leaned in the doorway while he drank it, watching me with a sleepy sort of half smile on his face.

My shoes perplexed him, for some reason. I'd bought what I considered the basics: athletic shoes for the gym — three pairs — plus high-heeled boots, plus some clogs, plus some black pumps, a pair of black flats, and, well, the list goes on.

"Just how many pairs of black shoes do you need?" he finally asked, staring at them lined up on the floor.

Okay, shoes aren't a laughing matter. I gave him a cool stare. "One pair more than I have."

"Then why didn't you get them?"

"Because I would still need *one pair more than I have.*"

He said, "Hmmm," and wisely let the subject drop.

Over breakfast I told him I thought the Sally/Jazz situation was resolved. He looked a little stunned. "How did you do that? You've been evading a stalker and getting burned out of your home. When did you have time?"

"I made time. Desperation is a great motivator." I was a little stunned myself. He truly had no idea how desperate I'd been.

After breakfast I went back upstairs and puttered with my new clothes, cutting off tags, washing what needed to be washed before I wore it, pressing out stubborn wrinkles, then rearranging Wyatt's closet and hanging my clothes in there. Except it wasn't Wyatt's closet now, it was our closet, which meant three-quarters of it was mine. That was okay for now, with my sparse wardrobe that was just for the fall months, but by the time I bought winter clothes, then spring clothes, then summer clothes — well, there would have to be more rearranging.

The dresser drawers had to be cleaned out and rearranged, too. And the bathroom vanity space. Again he leaned in the doorway and watched me while I emptied all the dresser drawers, piling all the stuff on the bed for now. He kept smiling a little as if the sight of me working my ass off while he just watched was somehow satisfying to him. Why his conscience didn't kill him, I don't know.

"What's so funny?" I finally asked, a little irritably.

"Nothing's *funny.*"

"You're smiling."

"Yeah."

I put my hands on my hips and scowled at him. "So why are you smiling?"

"I'm watching you nest — in *my* house." He gave me a heavy-lidded look as he sipped his coffee. "God knows I've tried long enough to get you here."

"Two months," I said, scoffing. "Big deal."

"Seventy-four days to be exact, since Nicole Goodwin was shot and I thought it was you. Seventy-four long, frustrating days."

Now I *really* scoffed. "There's no way a man who's had as much sex as you've had could be frustrated."

"It wasn't sex. Okay, so part of it was sex. It was still frustrating, for you to be living somewhere else."

"Well, I'm here now. Enjoy. Life as you knew it is over."

Laughing, he went to get more coffee. The phone rang while he was downstairs and he answered, only to come upstairs a few minutes later to get his badge and weapon. "I have to go in," he said. That wasn't unusual, and it didn't have anything to do with me or he'd have told me. This was more about the police department being understaffed than anything else, which was pretty much a chronic situation. "You know the drill. Don't let anyone in."

"How about if I see someone carrying a gas can and sneaking around the foundation?"

"Do you know how to shoot a pistol?" he asked, and he wasn't kidding.

"Nope." I was regretful, but I figured that was something I shouldn't fudge.

"By the time I'm finished with you next week, you will," he said.

Great. Something else to take up in my spare time, assuming I had any. I should have kept my mouth shut. On the other hand, knowing how to use a pistol would be cool.

He kissed me and was out the door. Absently I listened to the rumbling sound of the garage door as it opened, and a moment later closed again, then I returned to my sorting and arranging.

Some of the stuff that had been in the dresser could clearly go somewhere else, like the baseball glove (?!), the shoeshine kit, a stack of books from the police academy, and a shoe box full of photos. As soon as I opened the shoe box and saw the contents, I forgot about the other stuff and sat cross-legged on the floor by the bed, looking through them.

Men don't care much for photographs, which is why these were dumped into a box and forgotten about. Some of them, obviously, his mother had given him: school pictures of both him and his sister, Lisa, at various ages. Six-year-old Wyatt made my heart melt. He'd looked so innocent and *fresh,* nothing at all like the hard-as-nails man I loved, except for those glittering eyes. By the time he'd been sixteen, though, he was already getting that cool, piercing expression.

There were pictures of him in his football uniforms, both high school and college, and then other pictures of him as a pro, and the difference was obvious. By then, football hadn't been a game anymore, it was a job, and a hard one at that.

There was one picture of Wyatt with his dad, who had been dead for quite some time. Wyatt looked about ten, and he still had that innocent look. His dad must have died soon after the picture was taken, because Roberta had told me Wyatt was just ten when it happened. That was when his innocence had begun to go; all of the pictures taken after that showed an awareness that life wasn't always safe and happy.

Then I found the picture of him and his wife.

I saw the writing first, because the picture was upside down. I picked it up. In a pretty feminine handwriting was the inscription: *Wyatt and me, Liam and Kellian Greeson, Sandy Patrick and his latest bimbo.*

I turned the picture over, looking at Wyatt's face. He was laughing into the camera, his arm draped carelessly over the shoulder of a very pretty redhead.

A pang of very natural jealousy shot through me. I didn't want to see him with any other woman, especially one he'd been *married* to. Why couldn't she have been someone either plain or hard-looking, someone obviously unsuited to him, instead of being so pretty and —

— my stalker.

I stared at the photograph, not believing my eyes. The photograph was easily fifteen years old and she looked so young, not much more than a teenager, though I knew she'd been just a couple of years younger than Wyatt. The hair was very different, of course: 1980s big hair, carried forward into the nineties. Too much makeup, not that I was judgmental or anything. And those long, long eyelashes that made her look as if she were wearing artificial ones.

There wasn't any doubt.

I reached for the bedroom phone.

No dial tone.

I waited, because sometimes it takes a few seconds for a cordless unit to get a dial tone. Nothing happened.

Now, there have been more than a few times when I've been unable to get a dial tone and it's no big deal, but when a homicidal stalker is after me and there's no dial tone, yeah, I automatically assume the worst. My God, she was here! Somehow she'd cut the phone lines, which can't be easy.

That's when I noticed how still and quiet

the house was. There was no background hum of the heating unit, electrical lights, refrigerator. Nothing.

I looked at the digital alarm clock. Its face was blank.

The power was off. I hadn't noticed because the bedroom had enough windows to let in sufficient light to see, even on a rainy day, plus I'd been engrossed in the pictures.

The power had been on when Wyatt left, because I'd heard the garage door. He hadn't been gone more than fifteen minutes, so it couldn't have been off long. What did that prove? Anything? That she waited until he was out of the house before she came in? How could she even know where he lived? We'd been very careful, no one had followed us here.

But she knew where he worked. Knowing that, all she had to do was wait there and follow him home, probably even before she started following me. Following him would have *led* her to me.

Silently I got to my feet and retrieved my cell phone from where I'd tossed it on the bed. I'd taken it upstairs with me because so many people call my cell if they want to reach me. The lack of electricity wouldn't affect my cell phone, unless it was an area-wide problem that took out the cell towers, too, but if it was an area-wide problem then I didn't have anything to worry about. It was the localized-to-this-house scenario that scared the crap out of me.

I was shaking as I punched in Wyatt's cell number, my hair lifting from my scalp. No doubt about it, I was spooked. As quietly as I could, I crept into the bathroom and closed the door, to muffle the sound of my voice.

"What's up?" he said in my ear.

"It's Megan," I blurted. "It's Megan. I was looking through your old pictures, and . . . it's her."

"Megan?" he repeated, sounding astounded. "That doesn't make —"

"I don't care what it doesn't make!" I whispered frantically. "It's her! She's the stalker! And the power has gone out. What if she's here, what if she's in the house —"

"I'm coming back," he said after the merest hesitation. "And I'm calling in for the nearest patrol car. If you think she's in the house then *you* get out of it, any way you can. You got that? You've been right too many times, and you've had too many close calls. If you have to go out a window again, do it."

"Okay," I said, but he'd hung up and there was only dead air.

He was coming back. He'd been gone

about fifteen minutes, so it should take him about that to get back here, unless he drove like a bat out of Hell. There might be a patrol car that was closer.

Oddly, his assurance that he trusted my instincts calmed me down. Maybe it was because I didn't feel so alone, because help was on the way.

I set my cell phone on silent mode, and slipped it in my pocket. At least this time I wasn't caught wearing flimsy pajamas and no shoes. A long-sleeved T-shirt and a pair of cargo sweatpants offered much more protection. Well, I still didn't have on shoes, but at least I was wearing socks — and even if I'd had on shoes I would have pulled them off, in the interest of silence.

I was probably letting my nerves get to me, I thought, but the last time I'd reassured myself of something like this, she'd burned down my home. I seemed to have some sixth sense for her that let me know when she was near, and I intended to trust it.

At least I no longer had to wonder why, what I'd done that someone would try to kill me. I knew now. It was Wyatt. Wyatt loved me, and we were getting married. She couldn't stand that.

Roberta had told me how, when Megan filed for divorce, Wyatt had simply walked away. He hadn't cared enough to try to make their marriage work, or enough to rethink his decision to become a cop. She hadn't been important enough to him. How that must have eaten at her through the years, that she hadn't been enough for the man she loved. I knew something of how she'd felt, not that I was sympathetic toward her or anything stupid like that. Please. The psycho bitch had tried to *kill* me.

She'd gotten remarried within the year, Roberta had said. The second marriage must not have worked out either, because how could it, when she was in love with Wyatt? But she'd held on, because Wyatt hadn't married anyone else, and she could cling to the thought that deep down he still loved her and maybe one day they'd get back together — until I came along. Our engagement announcement had been in the newspaper. Had she made a habit of going online and reading the local newspaper, or Googling his name every so often? Maybe someone local knew her, and had told her. How she'd found out didn't matter, but her reaction to the news very much mattered.

I tried to think of any weapons that were available. Knives, of course, down in the kitchen. I'd felt safe going down for a knife while I was in my condo, with the alarm system to tell me if anyone broke in, but Wyatt didn't have an alarm system. He had locks, dead-bolt locks, and triple-pane windows that only someone very determined could get through. Unfortunately, she was very determined.

I had nothing up here to protect myself with, except the big, heavy flashlight on Wyatt's bedside table. I slowly eased out of the bathroom, fully expecting to come face-to-face with an ax-wielding lunatic, but the bedroom was silent and empty. I got the flashlight, gripping it in my right hand. Maybe I'd have the chance to conk her on the head. One good concussion deserved another.

Cautiously I moved into the hallway. It, too, was empty. I stood for a moment listening, but there was no sound within the house. Outside, I heard a car's tires on the wet pavement as it passed by, the sound mundane and comforting, but not as comforting as it would have been if the car had slowed and turned in. Wyatt hadn't had time to get here yet, but a patrol car would be welcome, too.

All of the doors in the hallway were closed, except for the door to the master bedroom, behind me. I couldn't remember if I'd closed the door when I'd come out of the guest room where I'd been trying on shoes. That just isn't something you normally remember. But no one jerked any of those doors open and leaped into the hallway to charge me with an ax, so I eased forward, toward the stairs.

I know, I know. In every horror movie, at least once the dumb-ass blonde goes down the stairs after hearing a noise, or down into the dark basement. Something. Well, you know what? If you're upstairs, you're usually trapped. Not many houses have dual staircases, one on each end of the house. At least if you're on the ground floor there's more than one way out. I'd just been caught on the second floor in a fire, and I didn't want to repeat the experience. I wanted to be on that ground floor.

I took another step. I could see part of the den now, and the doorway to the kitchen. No maniac. One more step. A flash of blue at the bottom of the stairs caught my eye. The blue whatever wasn't moving, it was just *there*. And there hadn't been anything blue down there when I came up these stairs.

It looked familiar, though. Whatever it was, I'd seen it before. But, I swear, it looked like two blue pipes sticking up, with odd designs —

My boots. My blue boots, the ones that

hadn't been delivered before my condo was burned.

She'd gotten them. She had picked up my package. And now she was really here, in this house, it wasn't my imagination any longer.

No way in Hell was I going down those stairs. I was going to take Wyatt's advice and bail out the window —

She stepped out of the kitchen, a pistol held in a steady, two-handed grip, aimed right at me. She was wearing soft-soled shoes that wouldn't make any more noise than my socks. Without letting the aim waver, she tilted her head at the boots. "What were you thinking? That you'd join the rodeo, or something?"

"Hello, Megan," I said.

Surprise flared in her eyes. She hadn't expected that. She'd expected to kill me and walk right out, because who would ever suspect her? She didn't live here, hadn't been here in years and years, hadn't contacted anyone she knew here. No one should ever have been able to connect her to this.

"I've already told Wyatt," I said.

A derisive look crossed her face. "Yeah, right. The power's off. None of these cordless phones will work."

"No, but the cell phone in my pocket does." I indicated the bulge. "There's a shoe box full of pictures up here. I was going through them, and came across this snapshot of you and Wyatt and two other couples. Some guy named Sandy and his latest bimbo." I added that so she'd know I wasn't making it up. Getting away with murder was a big part of her plan, I suspected. Knowing that she wouldn't, no matter what, might make her rethink this whole killing-me thing.

I saw the pain flicker in her expression as she recalled the photograph. "He kept that?"

"I don't know that he kept it so much as he never got around to throwing it away. As soon as I recognized you, I called him." I shrugged. "They were already working the rental car angle anyway. He'd have spotted your name."

"I doubt he even knows my last name," she said bitterly.

"Well, look, that isn't my fault," I pointed out.

"I don't care what is or isn't your fault. This isn't about you. It's about him. It's about him finding out what it's like to love someone so much you hurt, and not be able to have them. It's about living with pain for the rest of your life, a pain you can't walk away from."

"Huh. Sounds like you should put yourself

out of your misery." I just hate whiny people, don't you? Bad things happen to everyone. A busted relationship isn't the same as someone dying, so get over it.

"Shut up!" She moved closer to the foot of the stairs, that two-handed grip still as steady as ever. "You don't know what it's like. When we got married I knew he didn't love me as much as I loved him, but at least I had a chance, I thought. But I never got to build on it. A pro athlete is gone a lot. I had to share him with the team, both before and after the season. I had to share him with his family, because he came down here every chance we got. I even had to share him with Sandy Patrick and his bimbos, because he was Wyatt's best friend. Do you have any idea how many meals we ate where it was just us?"

I shrugged. "Two? That's just a guess. I don't know how long you were married. He doesn't talk about you." No, I didn't like her, didn't feel sorry for her, didn't give a damn about her other than I wanted to keep her talking long enough for Wyatt to get back.

"How would you feel, sharing him with the whole world," she began hotly.

"See, that's the difference between us," I said, leaning on the newel post. "I think the whole concept of sharing is overrated. It's unnatural. I don't like to share. I *don't* share. I *will not* share." Unspoken were the words, *You worm.* Do you think I'd have put up with being ignored for a single minute?

She looked a little rattled, as if she'd expected me to be hysterical by now, crying and begging. Rattled wasn't good. Rattled did stupid things, like pull the trigger. To get her mind off my unnatural behavior, I asked, "How did you get in here, anyway?"

"I've been watching this house. I've watched the two of you back out of the garage a dozen times. Neither of you ever waits to make certain the door is completely down. In fact, you're around the house and out of sight before the door is halfway down. When he left, I just rolled a ball into the garage. The automatic sensor stopped the door and raised it back up. I walked in. How hard was that?"

So she'd been in the house since Wyatt had left. She could have caught me unawares, killed me, and already left, but she'd wanted to play her little game with the boots. She'd *wanted* me terrified.

I said, "Not very, I guess," and shrugged. If I lived through this, a security system was going in *immediately* — the kind that beeps whenever a door is opened. "I guess you threw the master breaker switch, too."

She nodded. "The box is in the garage. Why not?"

"And you were playing musical chairs with the rental cars, right? And wearing wigs? Except for that horrible dye job you had at the hospital."

"I didn't plan as well as I could have. I hadn't even thought about security cameras in the mall parking lot. Thanks for telling me. I thought about the wigs after it took a stylist *hours* to get that shit out of my hair."

"You could have saved yourself the trouble. The tapes were worn out. Wyatt couldn't get any useful details from them."

Now she looked annoyed, because I'm sure she went to a lot of trouble, swapping cars. And she was right: stripping artificial color out of your hair is a long, messy job. I'd have been pissed about that, too.

"You missed with the car in the parking lot, but I can't see that as a very effective way to kill someone."

She shrugged. "Spur of the moment decision. I'd been following you around and all of a sudden there you were, strutting across the parking lot as if you owned it. You were a . . . target of opportunity."

"Strutting? Excuse me. I don't *strut*." Indignant, I straightened from the newel post.

"Prancing, then. I hated you on sight. I'd

404

have smothered you in the hospital if you'd been alone."

"Boy, you aren't good at this killing shit at all, are you?"

"It's my first time. I'm learning as I go. I should have been more straightforward. Walk up to you, put a bullet in you, walk away."

Except she still hadn't learned that lesson.

Fifteen minutes hadn't gone by yet; I was certain of that. I hadn't heard any cars drive up. Would Wyatt drive up? Or would he park down the road and sneak up on the house?

No sooner had that thought crossed my mind than he half stepped out of the kitchen door behind her, keeping part of his body behind cover. His automatic was in his right hand and aimed at her head. "Megan —"

Startled, she whirled. She might have been a good shot, in fact we found out later that she really was, she regularly shot at a target range, but she'd never practiced a real-life situation. She was already pulling the trigger as she whirled, the shots going wild.

Wyatt's didn't.

And neither did her last one.

My heart literally stopped, for a couple of agonizing seconds. I don't remember moving, but I was down those stairs, leaping over her as she lay there moaning. If she hadn't already been lying down, I'd have plowed over her getting to him.

Until the day I die I'll see the expression on his face, see the way the bullet jerked him back, see the red spray of blood from his chest, arcing almost in slow motion. He staggered back, then went down on one knee. He struggled to get up, to get on his feet again, then sort of sprawled sideways. And still he kept trying to get up.

I was screaming his name. I know that. I screamed his name over and over. I slipped in his blood, there was already a pool of blood on the floor, and went down beside him.

He was breathing in shallow, jerky movements. "Shit," he muttered thickly. "This hurts like hell."

"Wyatt, you jackass!" I shrieked, sliding my arm under his head to cradle it. " 'Take a bullet for me' is just an expression. An *expression!* You aren't supposed to really do it!"

"Now you tell me," he said, and closed his eyes.

I'm ashamed of what I did. Almost. I guess I *should* be ashamed.

I ran over to that bitch and kicked her.

CHAPTER THIRTY

Twenty-one days out

I looked out the window of Roberta's wonderful Victorian, watching Wyatt standing in front of the arbor below, in her marvelous flower garden. "He should be sitting down," I said anxiously. "He's been standing too long."

"Here," said Mom, pulling me around and handing my earrings to me. "Put these in."

I turned back to the window as I slipped the posts through the holes in my earlobes and secured them. "He looks pale."

"He's marrying you," Siana murmured. "Of course he's pale."

Roberta and Jenni both started laughing. I gave Siana an indignant look and she burst out laughing, too. For the past three weeks, all I'd heard was jokes about how I'd kick someone when she was down, how bloodthirsty I was, things like that. Even Wyatt had gotten in on it, saying that he'd never felt safer in his life than he did with me guarding him. Dad had told me once, in apparent seriousness, that the NFL had heard about my talents and called wanting to know if I'd try out as a place kicker. Only Mom hadn't made any jokes, but I thought that was probably because she'd have kicked anyone who shot Dad and she knew it.

Wyatt had spent three days in the hospital. I think they should have kept him longer, but insurance companies dictate how long a patient can be hospitalized, and at the end of three days, he went home. The surgeon who had patched him up had told me Wyatt was healing faster than people usually did, but you know, when someone has a hole punched in his chest you just sort of expect him to be hospitalized for, say, at least *four* days. Three was ridiculous. Three was almost *criminal.*

He could barely creep around under his own steam when I took him home. He had to do breathing exercises, huffing and puffing into this pipe thing that measured his lung capacity. He was in a lot of pain, and I knew it because he didn't even argue about taking his pain medication.

A week after he'd been shot, he started refusing the pain medication except at night, so he could sleep. After ten days, he refused it even then. The fourteenth day, he started doing physical conditioning. Exactly three weeks to the day after he was shot, we were getting married.

We didn't make the wedding deadline. We missed it by two days, but it was his fault for getting shot so he had to forfeit.

Megan had been in the hospital longer than Wyatt. Who cared? She hadn't been able to make bail yet, so she'd gone from the hospital to jail, and there she sat. As far as I was concerned, she could rot there. I didn't care about her unhappiness or her ruined life or her personality disorder, or whatever else her attorney might say when the trial started. She had *shot Wyatt,* and I still had very satisfying dreams of tearing her limb from limb and throwing the pieces to a pack of hyenas.

But today, none of that mattered. It was a gorgeous October day, the temperature was perfect, hovering right around seventy, and we were getting married. Our wedding cake, awaiting us in Roberta's dining room, was a work of art. The food . . . well, the food wasn't what we'd planned, because the caterer did fall through, but all the men seemed relieved. Evidently the testosterone crowd liked chicken fingers better than it did delicately seasoned spinach wraps. The flowers were breathtaking; Roberta had outdone herself with them.

And my gown . . . ah, my gown. It was just what I'd envisioned. The heavy silk flowed around me like water, but didn't cling. The creamy white held just a touch of champagne richness in the color, so you couldn't decide if the color was off-white or the palest gold. Without it being vulgar in any way, I thought it was just about the sexiest gown I'd ever seen. I just didn't know if Wyatt was in any shape to properly appreciate it. We hadn't made love since he'd been shot, to his great annoyance, because I didn't want to put too much strain on his healing body and maybe cause a setback. He was more than annoyed. He was downright pissed off about it.

I hoped this gown shot him straight into lust-induced insanity. And I hoped he didn't collapse under the strain.

My beautiful shoes hurt only a little bit. So long as I kept my broken toe immobilized, I could walk mostly pain-free. I was determined not to limp, though. The bandage was clear, and the shoe straps happened to fall almost exactly on the edges so unless you got down on your knees and stared at my foot you wouldn't even see the bandage.

The guest list was a tad bigger than I'd intended. Just about every off-duty cop — and his or her spouse or significant other — was in the garden below. So were Sally and Jazz, holding hands, and their kids and spouses, except for Luke who had refused to bring a girlfriend to a wedding just on general principle. Wyatt's sister, Lisa, her husband, and their two children were there. Great Bods was closed for the day, because all of my employees were there. Siana and Jenni had both elected not to bring dates because they said they'd be too busy to fool with them. There wasn't a bride's side and a groom's side, there was just a great gathering of friends who could sit wherever they wanted.

"The music's started," said Mom. She was looking out the window, too. "And Wyatt just checked his watch for the second time."

Before he blew his impatience gasket, we all trooped down to the foyer, with Siana and Jenni behind me helping me hold up the short train on the gown so I wouldn't trip on it and fall down the stairs. My latest batch of bruises and scrapes had just healed; we didn't want to start another bunch.

Then they kissed me, the four of them — my mom, my almost-mother-in-law, and my sisters — and walked out into the garden to take their seats. No one was escorting me down the aisle. No one was giving me away. Dad had already done his duty once, and that was enough for any man. I was going to Wyatt under my own steam, walking alone. And he was waiting for me, alone.

The music swelled, turned joyful, and I walked out. The gown flowed around me, showing the shape of my leg here, the curve of my hip there, for a fleeting instant before all was hidden again. The bodice clung to my breasts like the candy coating to an M&M. I did *not* limp. Not at all. Truth to tell, I completely forgot about my broken toe, because Wyatt had turned to watch me walking toward him and his green eyes blazed with fire and light.

After the ceremony, when we were standing holding hands. Mom came up to hug and kiss both of us. Wyatt caught her right hand and carried it to his lips. "If it's true that in thirty years a bride will be just like her mother . . . I can't wait."

He's a smart man, my husband, maybe too smart. With that one sentence, he put my mother firmly in his corner for the rest of her life.

I wanted her in mine.

Thirty-four days out

"I can't believe you did this!" Wyatt barked into my ear.

412

"Can't believe I did what?" I asked inn cently. He was at work, and so was I. Mar ried life had been rocking along just great, thank you, except for a few little details.

"It's *notarized!*"

I waited, but he didn't add anything. "And?" I finally prompted.

"And only legal documents are supposed to be notarized! This is a *list!*"

"But you weren't paying any attention to it." When his list of transgressions had been lying ignored on the table for over a week, just what was I supposed to do?

Have it notarized and sent to him registered mail, that's what.

BLAIR'S KRISPY KREME DOUGHNUT BREAD PUDDING

There's, like, a hundred different versions of this recipe. I only make it for special occasions or when I want to suck up to somebody, because it's so sweet it makes your teeth hurt. And I don't put raisins in my bread pudding; raisins are a Yankee thing. I think they look like bugs.

To begin with, use a 13 x 9-inch glass pan. The glass is so the pudding won't stick. If you want to use a disposable aluminum pan, then I guess it doesn't matter if the pudding sticks.

Anyway, preheat the oven to 350. That's Fahrenheit. I don't do Kelvin or Celsius because they're just weird.

Here's what you need:

2 dozen Krispy Kreme glazed doughnuts, torn into little chunks. Actually, I like the crullers better than the glazed doughnuts, because the texture seems more bread-

pudding-like, but go with your favorite. Put the chunks in a large bowl.

3 eggs, beaten. You may like yours merely subdued, but I want mine beaten. Don't add them to the doughnuts yet.

1 can sweetened condensed milk. Add to eggs. Beat together.

Vanilla flavoring to taste. Add to milk and egg mixture. Use 1 teaspoon if you don't like a strong vanilla taste, add more if you do. The whole point of this is to make the bread pudding the way you like it.

½ stick melted butter

Cinnamon to taste. It takes way more cinnamon than you probably expect, but start out with a little and keep adding until it tastes right.

Pour all this into the bowl of doughnut chunks, and stir. It'll be too dry, because now you have to make a choice. You can either put in a can of fruit cocktail, with the juice, which gives the pudding enough moisture — and in a weird way the fruit cocktail cuts down on the sweetness — or, if the idea of fruit cocktail in a bread pudding gives you the heebie-jeebies, just start adding milk, a little at a time, and stirring it in, until the texture seems right to you, not so juicy that it's soup but moist enough that it's kind of like a lumpy cake batter.

Now you have another choice to make: chopped pecans, or no chopped pecans. I love it with the pecans. If you decide to use them, add 1 cup to the mixture and stir well.

You can also add a little nutmeg, about 1 teaspoon, if you like. I usually don't.

Pour into pan and bake for 30 minutes. Check with a toothpick to see if it's done. If it isn't, let it cook for another five minutes and check it again. Ovens are weird; what's 350 on mine might be 342 on someone else's. And I don't get the altitude thing at all.

Take it out and let it cool. Add a glaze if you like, then dig in. If you don't want to fool with a glaze but the pudding looks naked with nothing on top, then buy some cans of ready-made frosting and put it on. Talk about sugar overload. Whoa, Mama. If you want to make a glaze, here are two recipes:

SIMPLE SUGAR GLAZE

2 cups confectioners' sugar
3 to 4 tablespoons milk or water

Mix together, and beat until it becomes smooth and pourable. Drizzle over the bread pudding. If this isn't enough, make more.

BUTTERMILK GLAZE

¼ cup buttermilk
½ cup sugar
¼ teaspoon soda
1½ teaspoons cornstarch
¼ cup margarine
1½ teaspoons vanilla extract

Combine first five ingredients in a saucepan, bring to a boil, remove from heat. Cool slightly, then stir in the vanilla. Pour over the pudding.

That's it. Have fun! — Blair

ACKNOWLEDGMENTS

Blair Mallory couldn't have been written without the unwitting help of some of my friends and family, whom I have used shamelessly in her creation. Yes, a lot of what Blair thought and said came out of their mouths first. Scary, huh?

This is to express my love and appreciation for, in no particular order: Brandy Wiemann, Beverly Barton, Linda Winstead Jones, Joyce Farley, Catherine Coulter, and Kelley St. John. Your minds are strange and wondrous places.

And to the Children — Andrea, Danniele, Kim, Kira, and Marilyn. You guys rock.

We hope you have enjoyed this Large ⌐
book. Other Thorndike, Wheeler, and Chiv
Press Large Print books are available at yo
library or directly from the publishers.

For information about current and upcoming
titles, please call or write, without obligation,
to:

Publisher
Thorndike Press
295 Kennedy Memorial Drive
Waterville, ME 04901
Tel. (800) 223-1244

or visit our Web site at:

www.gale.com/thorndike
www.gale.com/wheeler

OR

Chivers Large Print
published by BBC Audiobooks Ltd
St. James House, The Square
Lower Bristol Road
Bath BA2 3SB
England
Tel. +44(0) 800 136919
email: bbcaudiobooksbbc.co.uk
www.bbcaudiobooks.co.uk

All our Large Print titles are designed for easy
reading, and all our books are made to last.